TRUSTED INSTINCT

CERBERUS TACTICAL K9 TEAM CHARLIE
BOOK 4

FIONA QUINN

THE WORLD OF INIQUUS

Ubicumque, Quoties. Quidquid

Iniquus - /i'ni/kwus/ our strength is unequalled, our tactics unfair – we stretch the law to its breaking point. We do whatever is necessary to bring the enemy down.

THE LYNX SERIES

Weakest Lynx

Missing Lynx

Chain Lynx

Cuff Lynx

Gulf Lynx

Hyper Lynx

Marriage Lynx

Strike Force

In Too DEEP

JACK Be Quick

InstiGATOR

Fear The REAPER

Striker

Uncommon Enemies

Wasp

Relic

Deadlock

Thorn

FBI Joint Task Force

Open Secret

Cold Red

Even Odds

Kate Hamilton Mysteries

Mine

Yours

Ours

Cerberus Tactical K9 Team Alpha

Survival Instinct

Protective Instinct

Defender's Instinct

DELTA FORCE ECHO

Danger Signs

Danger Zone

Danger Close

CERBERUS TACTICAL K9 TEAM BRAVO

Warrior's Instinct

Rescue Instinct

Hero's Instinct

CERBERUS TACTICAL K9 TEAM CHARLIE

Guardian's Instinct

Sheltering Instinct

Shielding Instinct

Trusted Instinct

Acting on Instinct

CERTIFIED CERBERUS TACTICAL K9

Beowolf

Radar

Tank

CIA COLOR CODE

Red Line

This list was created in 2025. For an up-to-date list, please visit www.FionaQuinnBooks.com

If you prefer to read the Iniquus World in chronological order you will find a full list at the end of this book.

TRUSTED INSTINCT

Cerberus Tactical K9

TEAM CHARLIE
BOOK FOUR

FIONA QUINN

THE PLAYERS

Washington News-Herald and World Reports

Auralia Rochambeau – journalist
Doli Nez (Navajo) – videographer
Kamar Brown, *International Associated Press*

Team Charlie

Honoré (Creed) Duchamp, K9 Rougarou, best sniffer on
either side of the Mississippi

Strike Force

Jean-Michel (Gator Aid) Rochambeau – Auralia's
brother, Strike Force operator
Striker Rheas – Strike Force Commander
Jack
Deep
Blaze
Randy

PROLOGUE

ONE

Auralia planted her feet in the spot her videographer, Doli, had scoped out for today's field report for the Washington News-Herald and World Reports.

Here, the lighting would be good for both a close-up of Auralia as well as a clear view of the stage. The best outdoor lighting angle for Doli's shots typically forced Auralia to look in the direction of the sun. Trying to maintain a neutral expression while the story unfolded was miserable, especially in settings like this one, where a diffuser was a no-go.

Since Auralia and Doli were a hot spot reporting team, diffusers were rarely a usable tool.

Standing where Doli directed, Auralia was grateful to find a slight shadow cast by an enormous black box speaker that shielded her eyes from the glare. Doli had her back. "Thanks, Doll."

The gentle breeze blew strands of long blonde hair free from the bun that Auralia had coiled at the nape of her neck that morning, and she pressed the escaped wisps behind her ear to look neat and professional. "Am I okay for the shot?" she asked, smoothing the blue boatneck shirt so it wouldn't bunch over her breasts and tucking it into her neatly tailored slacks.

Since no one would see her feet, Auralia had opted for the comfort of tennis shoes when she dressed that morning—her first mistake.

"Turn slightly at the waist," Doli waved her hand to indicate the direction. "Better. Listen, I'll get tape of you saying. 'Let's go live to the event.' And then, when you ask your question, you'll be on the hand mic, but my focus will be over your shoulder to grab their reactions."

"I like that plan."

"Serious girl, I hope you put a lifeboat in the back of your car. We may need it if we capsize from all the waves you're about to make."

"Funny." Auralia reached into her pocket and pulled out a Sharpie. She pushed the cotton sleeve up her arm to expose a neatly penned 1-800 number. "Speaking of capsizing, this is Washington News-Herald's lawyer's office. They're on standby just in case things get nuts."

"What do they think's going to happen?" Doli asked, setting her camera down to push up her left sleeve.

"I don't know. Liu told me to do it. Since he's the editor in chief, I assume he had some reason tickling the back of his mind. It's like going to the store and thinking 'I need mayonnaise' and then you talk yourself out of buying a jar because you never eat it and surely there's some in the back of your fridge."

"Always buy the mayonnaise," Doli said as she read the number off Auralia's arm and wrote it neatly on her own. She handed back the pen and waited for Auralia to replace the cap and slide it into the pocket of her rucksack. "What else have you got packed in there?" Doli asked, looking down at the bag resting at Auralia's feet.

"A whole lot of water so we can flush our eyes if things get spicy. We can't drive away if we can't see."

"That sounds like a Remi Taleb truism." Doli cast her gaze toward the back of the grassy dell in the direction of the parking area.

Remi was a war correspondent with their news org who had honed her survival skills by reporting under the world's most dire conditions. When Remi took Auralia under her wing, Auralia became a sponge, soaking up every drop of professional wisdom and life-preserving practice that her mentor counseled.

"First aid kit." Auralia tapped it with her toe, then added, "Stuff."

"Stuff," Doli deadpanned. "Awesome. Stuff is usually helpful. What stuff? Give me two examples of stuff."

"A bottle of pain relievers and a multitool knife."

Doli scowled. "Security let you through with a knife?"

"Security," Auralia pronounced slowly. "I plopped the bag on the table, and they pushed the water bottle aside and leaned in its general direction. Do you feel that was protection or performance?"

Doli looked down at the phone number on her arm, then over to Auralia. "That tells us we need to be extra aware of our surroundings. These are Representative Lambton's peeps. They would call us the outsiders since we're usually on national and international beats."

"This is of national interest," Auralia countered.

"But they're used to local reporters." Doli reached for her camera handle and put the lens cap in place. "Nobody likes strangers showing up in their backyard to rip their worldview apart and toss it in the wind."

"My plan here is simple. I ask my questions on camera—and while I doubt we'll get answers, you get those reactions you mentioned—and then we leave. And I mean leave fast. Also,"

Auralia pulled two waterproof phone bags on lanyards from the side pocket of the pack. "My brother, Gator, uses these on his team. He handed me a couple." Auralia passed one to Doli, then opened the second to slide her cell inside. "The Iniquus operators aren't allowed to be more than an arm's length from their phones, so they wear these when they're swimming."

"Gator Aid Rochambeau," Doli let the name tumble and swirl around her mouth like she'd taken a first decadent bite from a chocolate dessert. With a double pop of her brows, Doli let a slow, lascivious smile warm her features. "Now that is one fine specimen of a man." She clamped her video camera between her thighs while she moved her cell to the plastic bag. "If only he were single."

"If only," Auralia rolled her eyes. "You missed your opportunity." Auralia folded the top over, pressed the clamps into place, and dragged the cord over her head. "I'm going to run my cell phone video the whole time." She adjusted the length of the lanyard so her phone dangled just under her breast line. "Maybe you should do that, too. If, as Gator says, 'things go kinetic,' we might get some action footage for social media."

Doli scowled as she put her camera between her thighs to free up her hands. "Why would they?"

"No clue. But the takeaway I got from Remi, when she was telling us about getting mobbed in the London crowd, was the importance of being prepared for an unwarranted attack. Granted, she also said to be careful because the lanyard could be used as a garrote to choke us out."

"Dying for one's art?" Doli slid the lanyard over her head. "I don't know if I'm down with that."

Doli was the kind of videographer who stood in the middle of the street to get a clear view of the bomb blasting and building disintegration that happened close enough to leave first-degree burns on her skin, so Auralia heard her comment as sarcasm. "It has a quick release, so chances are low your tombstone will read dead because of her cell phone."

Doli retrieved her camera that she'd held clamped between her thighs. "How much action are we talking about here?"

"Considerably less than when we were in Sudan last week." Auralia swiveled her head to take in the atmosphere. "Sleepy, bucolic Northwest Virginia, what could happen here other than us finding a diner and sitting down to a tall glass of sweet tea and a generous slice of pecan pie when we're done?"

Doli furrowed her brow. "Pick-ahn is how you say it?"

"Yes, why? How do you say it?"

"Pee-kahn." One-handed, Doli pulled her stick-straight black hair, reaching behind her head to lift the length of her braid over the loop of the lanyard, and Auralia reached out to help. "But here, I've heard people say pee-can."

Auralia laughed. "Like, 'The toilet isn't working, use the pee can'?"

"Don't turn your nose up like you don't know how valuable a pee-can can be." Doli lifted her brows for emphasis. "I bring you back to last month in Sudan."

"I love a good pee-can," Auralia said. "Very grateful in bad circumstances that conditions don't get even worse for lack of pee-can. But I don't know if I can eat the pie anymore. You've ruined it for me. The pie and finding relief during the Sudan bombings are now tied in my imagination evermore." Auralia wrinkled her nose. "Thanks for that."

"Such a butterfly girl. Don't let your wings bruise so easily." Doli lifted her video camera to her eye. "Let's record a few intros. The clouds keep moving around, and I need to compensate for the shadows."

Despite being in their mid-twenties, Auralia and Doli had been teamed up on journalistic assignments that had sent them to locations where only seasoned report teams were traditionally assigned—into the lawless places where humanity was exploitative and indifferent to suffering.

The two had borne witness to atrocities so that the world would know what was happening.

If the world knew, Auralia told herself, maybe actions would be taken to protect the vulnerable.

Everyone, she reasoned, had their way of helping. For some, it was making a pot of soup for a sick neighbor. For some, like her uncles, it was a night of toe-tapping zydeco that lifted spirits. For her brother, Gator, it meant carrying a weapon into the fray alongside his fellow Marine Raiders.

For Auralia, it was her work credo: Don't look away.

It was easy to look away. To shut the door. To turn on something booming and distracting that drowned out thought.

She had to be louder in her efforts to protect the innocent.

And that was what she and Doli were up to today.

Today was absolutely about exploitative atrocities, just not the kind wreaked by the swing of a machete or the pull of a trigger. This came from an evil person who abused humans' best impulses.

And Auralia meant to stop it.

Auralia grew up in the Bayou, ankle-deep in the ancient magic that infused the land. And she knew that light was defined by its juxtaposition with dark; that sinners and saints breathed the same air.

Some said that the good angel sat on one shoulder and the devil sat on the other, both whispering into the same person's ear.

Who would they listen to?

Sadly, they had listened to one Wesley Price. And Wesley Price and his golden forked tongue had been doing the devil's work.

Today, Auralia's reporting would expose the fact that compassionate citizens had been bamboozled. And she couldn't help but think her big reveal would leave kindhearted people feeling cynical and jaded.

It might have devastating implications for many charities that did a world of good.

There was a lot to be said for the ethical training she got at university. But theory was a hard way to professionally conduct oneself when things weren't black and white, when good people were going to be hurt, when her actions, based on honorable intentions, produced unintended consequences.

Who said there were only fifty shades of gray?

PROLOGUE

TWO

Auralia lifted her chin to direct Doli's attention to what was going on over by the parking lot. "They've opened the gates. Here they come. Our guy is supposed to accept his award first, then allow a few questions as they pass the hat, then they go on to the main speech with Representative Lambton."

"You think they'll go on to the main speech?" Doli asked.

"Absolutely. They'll need to try to stomp on the sparks of controversy and put it out before it has a chance to roar into life and spread."

"Poetic." Doli deadpanned.

"But I don't think we'll be here to listen," Auralia continued as if she hadn't heard Doli teasing. "I already talked to Kamar and his crew." Auralia tipped her ear toward another set of journalists setting up. "They said if we let them ask the first question, they'll share footage with us so we can spread out and cover more angles. I figured, let them get things warmed up, we know they're going for Lambton's throat, and he's not our priority today."

"Yup," Doli said, pointing her camera toward the swarm of

people moving through the gates after their bags had been checked. "Worth it. Did you tell Kamar what you're up to?"

"I didn't tell anyone anything. It's you and me. And them." Auralia's gaze took in the mass of people at the bottom of the field, making their way toward the stage. "All of them." She bladed a hand against her brow as a visor over her eyes. "Were we expecting this many? My research said maybe a hundred. That group moving through security looks like more."

"From my days on the ranch counting cattle," Doli said. "I'm guessing five times projections. It's because they announced they're having the pork pull. Everyone wants a free lunch. I'd like a free lunch. Damned journalistic ethics."

Auralia went ahead and put her backpack on her shoulders. Did it mess up her professional crispness? Yes. Under the circumstances, she thought it wise. "I have snacks in my bag if you need something."

"Nah, I'm good for now," Doli replied.

Seeing the number of people who showed up, Auralia recalled the morning when she had chosen her outfit and decided on her sneakers in case she had to run. But her mentor, Remi, always told Auralia that when she was going to be working in a crowd, she needed to wear steel-toed boots. Remi only ever wore steel-toed footwear. She even wore them to bed, which might seem extreme unless she told you some of her horror stories. Remi said that while sneakers seemed faster, that was only true if you didn't have broken toes.

Yup, Auralia made a mistake with the tennis shoes.

And as she moved her car keys to her front pocket with the fob dangling out, ready for a quick press, she thought her second mistake was that she had pulled nose-in, and that was a major Remi Taleb no-no. Park by the exit, nose out. Even if the vehicle is farther away than the action, it's faster to run to the front exit than to sit in a scrum.

"Good decision on the boots," she told Doli.

Doli looked down at her feet, then over to Auralia. "Sucks to be you. Hey, if we start to get rolled, I'll lead the way and protect your tootsies." There was just the right amount of joviality, the right amount of teasing that masked what both women knew: What they were about to do was to take on an icon. They were here to break things. And people didn't like that.

In Auralia's experience, when people were duped—especially for long times and with an outlay of money—they preferred to suffer the con unwittingly rather than admit they were swindled. Instead of going after the scammer, they targeted the whistleblower or truth-teller.

Egos were fragile, delicate things.

Auralia turned toward the stage, mic in hand. Yes, there was a designated question mic, but in Auralia's experience, the organizers tended to place hefty brutes around it to scowl and flex. Their intimidation was meant to shut down anyone who wanted to take things sideways.

Doli lifted her chin, and Auralia turned to see Representative Lambton and Sergeant Wesley Price, just visible to the side of the stage, bottles of water in hand, offering a jovial pat on the back and the rise of male laughter.

"Enjoy it while you can, gentlemen," Auralia muttered.

People pressed in. They saw the credentials and the camera and left a polite circle around Doli and Auralia. Might have been courteous. It might have been them trying to keep their distance so they weren't caught up in anything, whether it was a frame of film or the vitriol often spat in journalists' directions.

It was good either way. Gator had taught Auralia to always keep reaction space around her. And in her job as a global hot spot reporter, that advice had served her well.

Now, the stream of participants had slowed to a trickle.

People settled onto their hips with their feet spread wide to endure the speeches while standing. It looked like poor planning not to have chairs set up, but Auralia assumed it was purposeful. Lambton had been in the hot seat lately and likely didn't want people to settle in. Instead, they should eat the pork sandwich, feel indebted, and leave.

The two men, Representative Lambton and Wesley Price, with arms lifted and waving over their heads to greet the crowds, strode energetically onto the stage.

Doli signaled Auralia.

"Top of the hour. Here we go." Auralia was taking deeper breaths and relaxing her rib cage so she could speak from the chest instead of being squeezed by anxiety. She began her report: "We are here in beautiful rural northwestern Virginia to hear from Representative Lambton and hear what constituents have to say about their experiences with the newest closure of the rural health clinic, adding a thirty-minute drive to find medical help in an emergency."

Doli signaled the end of the take.

This crowd size was intimidating simply because of the dell shape of the land, which lent well to viewing a stage but also made it feel like folks were clumped together.

Lambton's greeting was brief, all the perfunctory things. The hellos and the "So glad to see y'all out here on a beautiful day," were followed with an awe-shucks good ol' boy, "Hope you came with your appetites."

After pausing for the polite applause, he invited an initial question from the audience.

Lambton hadn't introduced Price. Auralia thought this was strategic, too. And that would be his out if he found himself in a tight corner, she'd lay money on it.

"Kamar Brown, International Associated Press," Auralia's colleague said from his personal mic.

"Mr. Brown," Lambton tried to ease his braced posture, but

it made him look like a wooden puppet manipulated with strings.

"Representative Lambton," Kamar said. "Your opponent in this year's elections has accused you of stolen valor. In your stump speech, you repeat that you were wounded in battle. Records and firsthand accounts indicate that you were wounded when a file cabinet tipped over on you. Do you believe that your office at the base was a battlefield? And if yes, could you explain your thinking on the matter?"

Lambert and his stiff-lipped smile were so saccharin that it made Auralia's teeth itch. "I've said time and again," he said with his old-boy, glad-hand tone of voice, "I was wounded in theater. I was in Iraq when I sustained my injuries that led to my receiving a Purple Heart, an award that is deeply meaningful to me." He placed both hands over his heart and closed his eyes for a momentary pause. "I am proud to have made sacrifices for this great nation."

"I'm quoting you here, Representative," Kamar persisted, "'I know the evils of war; I've seen it with my own eyes. I served in Iraq—"

"All true," Lambton shot out.

"I'll continue the quote, 'and I was grievously wounded on the battlefield. I received a Purple Heart and a Bronze Star.' Sir," Kamar said, "There is a record of the Purple Heart, but not of the Bronze Star." Would you please elaborate on your claims?"

"Yes, thank you," Lambton said with a hard stare. "You seem to be a bit hard of hearing. As I said, I was wounded in service of my country, and I will always be proud of my scars and my sacrifices."

"The Bronze Star, sir?" Kamar pressed.

"Yes, speaking of Bronze Stars," he looked down at Kamar, "and thank you for bringing it up," he reached behind him and grabbed Price's elbow, "I want to introduce you to a Marine who was highly decorated, including a Bronze Star."

"Slick," Doli muttered. "Get ready."

"Yes, yes," Lambton grinned at Price. "I want to introduce you to my old and very dear friend Sergeant Wesely Price, a hero to Marine veterans." Lambton drew Price forward to stand slightly ahead of himself. "How many of you here are from Quantico? Any Marines?"

The ranks echoed with cheers.

"Wesley, here," Lambton continued, swiping away any attention to himself and placing it wherever he could find a resting spot in his P.R. sleight of hand, "was awarded a Bronze Star for heroic achievement in a combat zone. And when he returned to the States and saw that his fellow Marines were struggling, he continued his service by creating the HONOR Charitable Fund."

Auralia had particular disdain for the name of this quack charity.

Auralia's boyfriend was named Honoré on his birth certificate. His parents had sensed his essence from the very beginning. Even joining the Marines, they, too, understood that Honoré Duchamp lived his ethos, and they only changed his name enough that they could pronounce it. He was rechristened Creed at boot camp.

Honor was precious. And honor was rare.

The personal side of Auralia was pissed as hell that this con man tainted the word.

The journalist side of Auralia wanted to present a set of facts and see where that trail led.

"You all know of his good work," Lambton continued. "I'll let him say howdy and take some of your questions as we pass the bucket. As you reach for your wallets to donate, please remember the sacrifices that these Marines have made for you and your family, then consider what you should add to our collection. Ladies," Lambton said toward the stage wings, "if you could please start those buckets up and down the aisles." He faced the audience once again. "Ladies and gentlemen, the hero for our heroes, please give a warm welcome to Wesley Price."

Auralia felt her heart gallop. She was going to get him. This was it.

"Ah, now thank you all. That's such a kind welcome. I'm a humble man. Not much for speechifying even amongst friends like yourselves. I just like to do my quiet part in caring for my brothers and sisters that I served alongside in the Marines. It is the privilege of a lifetime to be of some service through HONOR, an acronym that many of you know stands for Helping Our Nation's Outstanding Marines Recover. Maybe some of you here in the audience have benefited from our good work. I hope so." He put his hand over his heart. "Now, while you are showing your gratitude to our fine servicemen and women with your generous donations today, I'd be happy to answer some of your questions."

"Auralia Rochambeau, Global Reach News and World Reports," Auralia spoke clearly into her mic.

"Yes, ma'am, what do you have on your mind this fine evening?" Price sent her an aw-shucks grin.

"I have a few related questions that I'd like to pose and gain clarity around the implementation of the HONOR charities."

"Happy to oblige."

"My research indicates HONOR is a 501(c)(19) veterans charitable organization. But you are a one-man band when it comes to the HONOR charity." She said it brightly, so he felt flattered by her noticing how streamlined they were able to work.

"Yes, ma'am, we're a small organization." He smiled at her broadly, rocking back on his heels, exuding a humbleness that politicians mentioned when introducing Price—salt of the earth, the best of us, and other drivel. "HONOR keeps our overhead to a minimum, but there's no way I could do this all on my own."

"It's you and the call center that you contract with." She'd been waiting for this for a long time, and now Auralia had to fight to keep the words from tumbling from her mouth. She needed each phrase to be crisp, clear, and well-understood. "That call center takes an eighty-five percent cut off the top of all donations they bring in, leaving you with fifteen percent."

Price shifted on his feet. His lips moved like they wanted to say something, but no words came out.

"The fifteen percent that you take in still represents millions of dollars in donations each year. Of those millions, I was able to track down only six distinct contributions made to Marines over the entire span of time that HONOR has been a registered charity. All six contributions, when totaled, equal less than a hundred thousand dollars. However, I was able to trace a little over eight hundred thousand dollars to political donations. Donations offered equally on both sides of the political aisle. The donations to Representative Lambton, standing beside you, for example, amount to approximately twenty-five thousand dollars over the years. Is it true that you exchange political contributions for the opportunity to stand next to politicians of all political persuasions on stage?"

"Now, why in the world would someone do that?" Representative Lambton blustered out, then looked like he immediately regretted his interjection.

"Would you agree, Representative Lambton, that for a donation, Sergeant Price gets to stand beside politicians like you, people who have the public's confidence?" Auralia didn't want to shift away from Price, but she was going with the flow. It would be odd not to take advantage of Lambton's question. "Would you agree that it lends Sergeant Price legitimacy when you shake his hand in front of a crowd and smile together for photographs?" Auralia pivoted her attention back to Price. "Because Sergeant Price uses those photos on his website and his outreach materials. Those photos give a sense of legitimacy to the HONOR charity and make people feel comfortable making their donations."

While Auralia was talking, Lambton slid sideways to stand in a shadow, disappearing from the public's view.

That meant Auralia found a pressure point, and Lambton believed her questioning was accurate.

He knew. That bastard knew all along.

Price froze with his lower jaw dropped. Auralia knew that meant his brain was in shock at his sudden exposure, a cockroach caught in the middle of the kitchen floor when someone flicked the lights on.

If Auralia wanted a useful comment, she needed to keep filling space with words until Price recovered enough to close his mouth. "This gave you a vestige of credibility," Auralia reiterated. "One assumed that these politicians vetted you and your charity. Those pictures served as your social proof as you went out asking for more donations; that's why you contributed more to politicians on both sides of the aisle than to Marines in actual need. In fact, the donations that came through the telemarketers went directly into your pocket without any meaningful or helpful distribution. It was like a faucet of ill-gotten gains that flowed in."

Price was trying. His mouth kind of chomped at the air as if he were making words.

Let's put another nail in the coffin, Auralia thought. Nah, let's hammer it all the way home.

"On top of that," Auralia said loudly and clearly into her mic, "your name isn't even Sergeant Wesley Price, Marines, retired. It's Eugene Morrison. You're not from aw-shucks Arkansas. You were born and raised in urban Tampa, Florida. And you never received any military decorations or awards because you never served in the military. Not in any branch. Not in any context. With that background, my question to you, Mr. Morrison, is why shouldn't you be in prison right now for defrauding the American people?"

The field stilled.

Perfect silence.

Not a bird, not a rustle, not even a breeze to cool her face.

Price's face turned shades of pink, then red, and finally purple. "You," he pointed his finger, "are an evil, lying Jezebel, hellbent on destroying the good works of these good Samaritans here today. They lift up our dear Marines and you! You! You!" he jabbed and spat. "How dare you call these good people corrupt. How dare you disparage their golden hearts?"

Wow! That's quite a twist, Auralia thought.

And then, as anticipated, as had happened so many times in the past when she exposed a crime, the people who had taken out their wallets and enriched a con man, turned their anger not on the crook but on her for exposing the criminal. They hated the feeling of being tricked in front of friends and family. Hated feeling stupid and manipulated.

So they would sink their claws into the scheme and hold onto it tightly.

Auralia and Doli, as journalists, like whistleblowers and other truth-tellers, suddenly became the bull's-eye.

Feeling small against the wave, Auralia felt the growing tide of their wrath.

"That's a wrap," Doli called out, and both women swung toward the exit.

PROLOGUE
THREE

Red-faced sneers painted their faces. Their fists bunched and lifted high. As a whole, the crowd compressed to encircle the Washington News-Herald team.

Auralia had been in similar situations before, and time was of the essence.

"Go." Auralia grabbed at Doli's sleeve to spin her around toward the unmanned security stand. "Go. Go. Go." Auralia put her right fist onto her left shoulder and ducked her chin, as Remi taught her. This technique should help keep her visual field clear while protecting her face from most strikes. As a bonus, it gave her a sharp point to plow through the outrage.

Auralia had expected the yelling and curses, and maybe some spitting and shoving, but what she hadn't expected was what happened next.

Someone grabbed at Doli's camera.

Auralia heard Remi's good counsel in her head, dropped her pack off her shoulders, and pulled it around to wear it on her front so that people couldn't grab her as easily from behind.

She spun in place to help her camerawoman.

Shuffling a foot forward, Auralia managed to reach around

Doli and wrap her fingers under the vulnerable pinky finger of the guy trying to steal their camera. The weakest finger on the hand, one that caused disproportionate pain, Auralia bent the man's digit back toward his wrist, producing a howl and a release. Auralia gave the finger a little extra thrust to dissuade the guy from reaching out again.

As he violently shook his arm up and down, flicking his hand to relieve the pain, Auralia put her hands on Doli's shoulder, a kind of buttress that gave them stability and hopefully kept them together as she pushed Doli forward.

Auralia's elbows were bent enough to make them stabby and to prevent someone who knew how to fight from shoving a palm fist into the sides of her arm and snapping her like a chicken's wishbone.

They were making headway.

Not fast enough.

A water bottle clipped Auralia's clavicle and bounced away, and another bounced off the side of her head.

Kamar and his camera crew were there to her right, rolling tape and narrating the scene. That was his professional role here: observe, don't intervene. He would do nothing to help. And he was right to make those decisions.

But the debris landing on their heads was getting larger and more bruising.

And now, the crowd had had enough of the hands-off approach. From behind, Auralia felt the tug of someone wrapping their fingers into her hair bun.

Auralia released Doli's shoulders to reach back over her head and grab hold of the man's wrist. With a quick bend to the right, she twisted under his arm, wrenching his wrist into a position that forced him to release her hair as she pressed his elbow straight, capturing the guy in an armbar—a point of stability for her next move.

From there, she swung her shin up between his legs. His

wide stance allowed her to aim for the hair on his head. As Gator always told her, if you aim for the crotch, the power stops there; aim higher so the impact is crippling. Auralia's kick put the shithead in a fetal position where he couldn't teach folks that grabbing was okay.

Doli pressed her back against Auralia's.

How many times had this happened? How many times had they "had each other's backs" as they fought their way through mobs around the world?

There were so many furious faces—men and women—oily and sweaty with bulging angry eyes and spit flying from words that Auralia couldn't make out.

She felt Doli go down behind her, so she spun around to drag her friend up, but someone grabbed Auralia's shirt and bra band, jerking her so that she had to fling her arms and scramble to keep herself upright.

Auralia needed to get Doli off the ground. Down was dangerous, even deadly.

To free herself, Auralia did the same bend and spin. It pulled the strap tight around her ribs, abrading her skin with elastic. She couldn't make it far enough around to twist free. In fact, she probably trapped the woman's fist in the shirt fabric.

Auralia reached up and grabbed the woman's elbows as support while she lifted her knee and scraped the edge of her tennis shoe along the woman's shin, then stomped hard on her insole.

Now Auralia brought her hands together at her navel, as if in prayer, driving them up through the opening made when the woman's grasp encircled her. Hands overhead, Auralia made fists and drove her elbows down, forcing the woman to release.

The shock on her face.

Did this person think Auralia would just allow herself to be beaten?

This was nuts. Nuts!

Auralia's arm twisted to block the blow aimed at her nose, vaguely clocking that this was probably the woman's husband since she was clinging to his shoulder, hopping on one foot as she cried.

And then there was a man with a high and tight haircut who stepped between Auralia and the attacking couple, looking cool and efficient.

A woman with a bun just like Auralia's put her hand on Auralia's shoulder. "We've got you."

Another jarhead lifted Doli to her feet.

Send in the Marines! Auralia's inner voice sang as their group surrounded Doli and Auralia.

"Moving." The guy in front of Doli barked.

"Moving," their rescue group repeated.

They took a small step forward. Then another. Playing at being salmon swimming upstream, they shifted slowly toward the parking area.

Finally bursting through the last of the crowd and out through the security gates. There, the women dove into their rental SUV.

Doli shoved the gear into drive and took off as Auralia breathlessly called their gratitude to the Marines from the lowered window.

"Oorah!" they called in return, looking like that was the most fun ever.

Yeah, good times.

And to be fair, Auralia thought, if that had been Gator and Creed with their Marine buddies, they would have had the same looks on their faces.

Silently, Doli rattled and bucked down the unpaved road toward the rural highway at breakneck speed as Auralia texted their editor what had happened and that he should digitally run the story she'd already developed.

When her phone pinged in return, Auralia glanced at it. "I

got a thumbs up on the story. Hey, Doli, when we get somewhere safe, we should probably pull over so I can type this up and you can edit the film. Did you have your phone video rolling?"

"If I do, will we be able to see anything other than punching and kicking?" Doli reached down and held up the phone case dangling from its lanyard. "Yup, rolling." She tapped the phone to stop recording. "You?"

"Same. Yeah, maybe we can find a hotel or something and work on this. I'd like to record a segment where I narrate the clips that you choose. And also, we should probably give ourselves a once-over. You and I both know that adrenaline can mask some nasty wounds."

Doli flung their vehicle onto the highway. "Go ahead and pull something up on the maps app and make the reservations."

As Auralia scrolled, the cab suddenly filled with Doli's booming laughter. It was infectious and cleansing, and Auralia was grateful for the release.

"Girlfriend, it is never boring getting assigned to you." Doli reached for her water bottle and took a long, hard drag from the straw. "How is it that you keep landing these scoops?"

"When I look at a person, I get a sense of who they are, a taste in my mouth. And I don't know if it's because of how I'm made or where I'm from—maybe a bit of both, but between you and me, when there's evil swirling around, I see my metaphorical pen as the sword getting dragged from its sheath."

"So I take it that my aura is crystal clear since you keep asking for me to be on the stories with you."

"Crystal clear might be a stretch. I ask for you because you're good company in the lulls, and in the red zones, you're a goddamned badass bitch. I need someone to protect my toes when I'm stupid enough to wear tennis shoes to a throwdown."

The phone rang, and Auralia answered, "Hey, Kamar, you're on speaker phone."

"Holy shit, woman. Holy shit! My photographer is driving, and I'm reviewing his footage. He got close-ups when you dropped the bomb on Lambton and Price. Priceless." He laughed at his own joke. When he sobered, he said, "I guess I need to call him Morrison now. Here I was pissed that I got sent to this lukewarm-glass-of-water event. And I was there for *the* event. Yeah, wow. I should have known better when I saw you and Doli setting up. You two okay? Were you hurt any?

"Meh. You know, it could have been worse. We're grateful to the Quantico folks. They're the ones exchanging blows."

"Speaking of blow, this is blowing up all over social media. Not surprising. Did you know that we have a nickname for you at IAP? *RochamBlow'emUp*." He chuckled, then heaved a sigh. "Hey, listen, this time, serious, you'd better be damned sure you've got your ducks in a row. I'm going to send this clip to your phone because you need to be ready. As the Marines were getting you out of the rabble, Price-Morrison said from the stage, he's going to sue the shit out of Global, and then you personally for libel. He says he's coming for you. And there are a lot of politicians whose names are tied to his. They'll either lie low and let this storm pass, or—probably more realistic—they'll use their power to make your life hell."

1

___

Auralia

One Year Later

Auralia stood in the bed and breakfast's Victorian-styled bathroom, heavy on the shelf-tchotchkes and made dim by the flocked velvet wallpaper in bordello maroon and limited lighting.

She pressed a final hairpin into her bun, muttering possible interview questions into the mirror so her lips and tongue could coordinate under stress.

Morrison was going to be back on the stage in the dell.

Released on bail to mount his case, judgment day inching closer, Auralia was itching to hear how he'd spin things today. She'd been on top of this case from her research to the reveal, through the grand jury, to the indictment and the choice of hearing dates.

Up until now, Morrison had squirreled himself away. And this was the first time that he was going to publicly stand in the sun and face the public. Possibly to put out some spin that helped win him public approval, and perhaps sympathy, before they started to seat the jury.

Surely, he had some shit to sell.

Was anyone going to buy it?

"Auralia, when you can, we need to talk." Creed's voice was warm and gruff and mmm just the right kind of masculine. It was a come-hither rumbled with morning grogginess. Typically, on days when he had work, he sprang from the bed like a jackrabbit leaping away from a fox's mouth. But on Sundays, he was slow and luxuriant.

It was the kind of work-life balance that Auralia could enjoy.

This morning, he wasn't calling her to his arms so he could wrap her tight and ask about all the things. He wouldn't be encouraging her to share her stresses, and he wouldn't be rejoicing with her about her successes, both big and small. No gossip from home. No news from friends. No plans for the day.

Because, despite the tone in his voice, they'd both be working—her as a reporter along with Doli, him as a K9 handler and operator for Iniquus's Cerberus K9 Tactical Team Charlie. He'd be working alongside Gator and his team, Strike Force.

And how did she know Gator would be there? Certainly not because Creed talked to her about anything mission-oriented. No, it was because, very strangely, Gator had sent over two bullet-resistant vests last night, one for her and one for Doli.

Auralia stepped into her black lace panties.

Auralia had already worked through the whole conversation in her head. This morning, Creed would surely want to review a safety plan with her and remind her that he was on the clock for work. If things turned really bad, he'd drop everything to get to her side. Then she'd protest that she didn't need him to be her knight in shining armor and remind him that her job was to go into the turbulent parts of the world to report. He would say something about how proud he was of the work she felt chosen to do, but still be careful with his heart. He'd look deeply and sincerely into her eyes as he accepted her promise that she wouldn't take unnecessary chances.

It was a dell in rural Virginia, for goodness' sake. She didn't have any new truth bombs; what could possibly go wrong?

And if something were to go sideways, there might even be some Marines around.

Auralia picked up the matching bra, with the tiny pink ribbon that would rest between her breasts, and leaned over to pull all of the straps and bands into place. She adjusted her breasts into the cups, then came upright.

Tease?

Sure, well, she would need Creed to be a bit distracted because the next subject he'd want to tackle was that today was *the* day.

Today.

She had been low-key stressing about this since Gator's wedding, when there was a seismic shift, and she saw Creed anew.

Creed was a constant in Auralia's life. While Creed was too young at the time to remember when Auralia was born, he had been Gator's first friend and constant companion, so he'd been around when she'd made her debut. Creed and Gator had signed up for the Marines together, had gone to boot camp together, decided to become Marine Raiders together, and had each other's backs through the horrible wars.

Gator had decided to leave and take a gig with Iniquus, while Creed had stayed in the service up until a few months ago, when Cerberus Tactical mounted a new K9 team, Team Charlie. It was a coveted position there—they were few and far between, and applicants had to have at least one Iniquus operator vouch for them as a whole package, from capability to ethics. Gator and Deep, Creed's fellow Marine Raiders, had put his name forward. And after Iniquus had rigorously vetted him, Creed was offered a place.

Career-wise, it was a good move for Creed. And had made Auralia's relationship with him easier now that he lived in Northern Virginia, where Auralia had her home base.

They had been a secret *them* for a while now.

Yup, it was a dance at the Gator and D-Day's wedding that turned into a moonlit kiss that changed everything.

A year and a half wasn't a long time for a couple that had just met, but Auralia had always known Creed. And there was never a time when she hadn't loved him.

It was just the kind of love they felt for each other that had undergone a seismic shift.

A private. Quiet. Not to be shared seismic shift.

Until today.

Auralia took a deep breath and blew out a puff of air.

She might as well go in and get it over with.

They both knew that their time in the cocoon had come to an end.

Auralia rounded out of the bathroom into the slightly overstuffed Victorian-themed suite.

Rou, Creed's black lab, scampered over and dropped her bottom down, her little pink tongue stuck out in anticipation, and her tail swished over the hardwood floor with a pretty-please tilt of her head.

"I know, Rourou, it's time for your run."

"She's okay for the time being," Creed called from the canopy bed.

At that moment, Creed looked ridiculously like the cover of a historical romance novel. With his hands laced behind his head and his toned chest muscles on full display, the sheets draped around his hips, his goody trail pointing its way to the treasure below.

The delicate femininity of rose-covered fabrics pieced together into a wedding-knot quilt juxtaposed with Creed's lascivious grin and the crook of his finger; yes, Auralia could see doing a little role-playing in a setting like this. The Duke of New Orleans ravishing the ingénue might be fun.

His grin widened. "Whatever it was you were just thinking about, the answer is yes."

"What if I were to tell you that you reminded me of the story of Little Red Riding Hood?"

He quirked a brow.

"The quilt across your lap, the lace canopy overhead. The wolfish grin."

"And in this case, you would be coming with your goodies to see me?"

Auralia struck a sexy pose.

"Come here, Little Red Riding Hood," He leaned forward and snatched her wrist, "so I can eat you."

Auralia laughed as she let him gently tug her onto the bed. She crawled forward and knelt across his lap.

For them, it was feast and famine. Not by design, just the way things shook out.

Sadly, this last visit was coming to an end; she had to book her flight to Ukraine before she got her fill. Was it possible to get her fill? Probably not.

With a hand resting on his pec, Auralia bent for a kiss, "I like it when I'm dessert."

Creed chuckled as he dropped his hands to her hips, curling them into her flesh as he dragged her forward, tucking her against him so his hard-on was in the perfect place.

"We need to talk," Auralia said as her blood thrummed.

"Listening." Creed leaned forward and traced soft kisses up her clavicle until Auralia pushed him back.

"Seriously. Talk."

Creed sat up, and the heat in his eyes cooled. "End of the line?"

"You're heading out with Strike Force today. You'll be there, working. I'll be there, working."

Rou, not to be left out of the plans, dashed over to the bed and jumped up to be with them.

"Rourou's going to be there."

Creed's gaze searched around the room with a bemused smile, tweaking the corners of his mouth.

Victorian wasn't their style. With few choices, she took what was available. And that shouldn't be meaningful, but somehow it was. She wanted to be completely authentic in this conversation, and yet, it felt like a movie scene, like play-acting.

This was just too darned important for anything but candor.

"Gator is Bayou blessed. Part of me thinks he already knows about us. But when we're in the same general space, his sixth sense is going to light up like the fireflies at dusk. If we don't tell him first—well, it's just a complexity that I don't want in my life."

"We agreed," Creed said.

"Look, if I had my druthers of falling in love with a stranger or my brother's childhood bestie, I'd take the stranger every time. You know this. You also know I've always enjoyed being around you. I have always thought you were a good person. And you have never let me down. And that was all good enough. If only you hadn't asked me for that dance at Gator's wedding. I'm blaming you for this turn of events and all the complications that come with it."

"Best thing I've ever done. Are you regretting not telling everyone about us from the start?"

"Now, how would that have gone down? Gator, I'm screwing around with Creed."

"Is that what you were doing?"

Auralia didn't answer. He knew better than that. This discussion had been the merry-go-round she'd been on since Gator and D-Day's wedding.

Creed traced a circle on her thigh. "I told you what I want."

"Okay. Well. Yeah." Auralia looked down. This wasn't the direction she'd meant for this conversation to go. "I'm twenty-five. And here is probably the only place where our age difference makes a difference. I'm not convinced that I'll ever get married. It's not something I've aspired to do. I can call you my fiancé in my head and in private to show that I am dedicated to a life of loving you. That doesn't translate to me making governmentally official vows. I just don't think that fits with who I am."

"Auralia," Creed reached up and cupped her cheeks in his palms, "no one's dragging you down the aisle. That doesn't mean we can't tell our friends and families that we're going to give it our best go at a solid, supportive relationship."

"And if it doesn't turn out well, we'll just be damned uncomfortable at the family gathering from now until forever."

"That sounds like what you said last year. I'd have hoped you would have evolved past 'if it doesn't turn out well.' Since then, what I've heard you say is that this relationship hits the sweet spots. That if you were to design a relationship and describe it to the Heavens, then this was the one you wanted most, which is music to my ears—to my heart."

"It's true. It's good. A little salt, a little sweet, meaty conversations."

"You must be hungry," Cree laughed.

Auralia tried on a coquettish curl at the corners of her lips. "Always around you."

Creed didn't take the bait. "I have faith in you when you're far from me. And I have joy in you when you're with me. I like that you're headstrong and free-spirited. I like that you go after what you believe is good and right. I think you've put those qualities to work in making us an 'us'. I think loving you is one of the great miracles of my lifetime."

Auralia leaned forward until they were forehead to forehead and rested there, breathing deeply into her lungs and holding it as long as she could, as if releasing the breath would blow out the magic that she wanted to keep lit.

"Imagine for a moment all of our different family members who have gotten married. They love each other for the season they're supposed to love, then their lives take a turn, and they divorce. When they married, it was always a possibility that they would disappoint their families. Same with us. You and I both know that all they'd ever want is for us to have a—"

Auralia frowned. "Happily ever after."

"We can't promise each other that, and we can't promise our families that."

"So we take a page from D-Day and Gator's love story," Auralia said, feeling some of the tension ease, and she sat up to find his gaze on her, "and we simply love for now. Just for today."

Creed put his hands on her thighs. "Today, Auralia Rochambeau, I will love you the whole day through."

"Thank you, and today, Honoré Duchamp, I will love you the same."

"Here's the plan: Before work revs up, we grab hold of Gator, take him aside, tell him that we connected in a new way at his wedding."

Auralia nodded. "Blame it on him for casting enchantments."

Creed cocked his head to the side. "Does someone need to take the blame for us?"

"No." Auralia could see how that would have sounded hurtful. She sighed. "I'm nervous. I don't want Gator to feel betrayed."

"By us having a relationship or by our keeping it to ourselves."

"The second one. But I'll tell him why, explain that we needed time to see how things went without any hopes or expectations."

Creed chuckled low and deep. "Your mamma."

"Oh, Lord, Mamma. She is going to be beside herself with joy." Auralia lifted a finger. "I can't hurt my mamma. I won't. So you dammed well better live up to my expectations."

Creed kissed her long and slow, then tipped her head to look deeply into Auralia's eyes. "The only way you could hurt your mamma is to do something you didn't want to do or do it with a person you didn't want to do it with. Poor in pocket is fine as long as you're—"

"Rich in heart." Auralia lifted herself, swinging her leg back around, dismounting from Creed's lap. "You're right."

"But just so you know," Creed tugged her down until they were chest to chest and her head tucked into the crook of his neck. "I plan to exceed your expectations for the rest of my life," Creed said with a seriousness that wasn't part of his sunny nature.

Rou came to nestle with them.

"What if I prefer you go away?" She laced her fingers with his. "Maybe I'll be done with you?"

"Since you're precious to me, I'd just have to go away and lick my wounds." He chuckled as he dropped a kiss into her hair. "I mean, our families are tight, so I'd be at the same places when we're gathering for celebrations and times of grief. But that doesn't mean I don't have the fortitude to keep my distance." He laced their fingers and brought the back of her hand to his lips. "I'm safe. You're safe around me. Listen, Auralia," He shifted until she tipped her chin up to look at him.

"I know that relationships past have been casting shadows over us, from your side and mine. But I will never put your safety second. If we're together or we're not, you're safe. I live up to my word. It's how I got my name from the jump. It's who I am, who I've been, who I plan to be. Our telling Gator this morning doesn't change anything about us. I will stand beside you until you say things aren't what you want. You are one of my life's greatest gifts," he reiterated the sentiment, "and I will treat you as precious always."

"What if I'm broken like a china plate?" she pouted as she batted her eyes at him, so Creed would know she was teasing—mostly teasing.

"Depends. Is it me you want to help glue you back together, or would you rather I step away and let someone else handle it? I swear to you, you're safe." His dark brown eyes had a palpable intensity.

"Not if you're the one who dropped me in the first place," she whispered.

"Never, Auralia. Lean on me. Trust me. I will never willingly harm you. That's my oath. I swear it on my life. I'd die before I hurt you or allowed you to be hurt."

Those were actual tears in his eyes. *Shit.*

This was so real, so huge, that the emotions filling her body pressed outward. These were vows deeper than anything said on an altar. These weren't performative. They were rooted in his soul.

His words were home. The warm humidity bathed over her skin. She closed her eyes and breathed them in, felt them enter her bloodstream and circulate through her body.

Creed didn't ask what he'd get in return. He never asked her for anything other than to give him a chance to love her.

A frown tugged at the corners of her mouth, and the playfulness fell away.

She slipped lower into his arms, letting her head rest on his chest, where she could hear the steady thrum of his heart.

Auralia would always think of this bed as the altar where they exchanged their true vows. "It feels like we just jumped over the broom," she whispered.

Creed lifted her chin, and she found his face lit with joy, but the kiss that followed felt like they were tempting fate.

$$2$$

Creed

ROUGAROU WAS A RAGDOLL OF A DOG. FLOPPY AND GANGLY AT eighteen months, she was about as tall as she was going to get; she simply hadn't caught up yet with muscles and coordination.

Petite for a lab, Creed took her size as a bonus, because Rou had passed the assessment for urban search and rescue with flying colors, the type of rescue needed in disaster situations where buildings collapsed, potentially with people inside.

For this, being small and limber was a bonus.

It was a fact that the biggest thing about Rou was her heart.

At Cerberus, Rou had a doggy mentor, Truffles, who was part of Team Bravo. A butterscotch-colored lab, Truffles, wasn't comfortable in wide open spaces. She got anxious in the woods and fields. Truffles was a burrowing dog who liked tight, dark puzzles; the more complex the maze, the more eager she was to solve them. Showing no fear in collapsed buildings and natural disaster piles, Truffles climbed and wriggled her way through her job of finding people trapped in the crush.

Truffles became nationally famous when a U.S. senator, a member of her security team, and Remi Taleb, Auralia's mentor, had found themselves trapped in a Lebanese blast.

In that rescue, on the other side of the world, Creed had one degree of separation with almost every single American player: Auralia had just taken up a new place in his heart, he knew Cerberus Bravo and their K9s from a cookout he'd attended with Gator and fellow Marine Raider Deep Del Toro, and Creed had been on assignment the month before with Delta Force Echo, the same team that had been safeguarding the senator during that disaster.

Those kinds of connections made Creed sit up and pay attention.

Folks say it's a small world, but the truth of it? The world, in every measurable way, was expansive. What was small was the magnetic energy source that pulled certain folks together into the same sphere.

Creed remembered reading the news article, seeing the players involved, and leaning down to lift the skirt on his sofa to look under where Rou liked to hide. "Rourou, I bet you'd be a good fit for a job like the one Truffles does. What do you think? Should we talk to Gator and see if there's a place for us over on Cerberus?"

Rou responded by wagging her tail so hard her whole body jiggled.

Of course, Rou had just been weaned from her mom, so Creed took her puppy enthusiasm with a grain of salt. Not every K9 had the right constitution to be a working dog.

It took Creed a while to assess Rou and decide she'd be happiest with a job to perform, rather than simply being a beloved family member who goofed off in the backyard and went on hiking adventures.

Sweet little princess that she was, her soft, concerned eyes stared at a person with compassion—was that the right word? Yeah, there was a nurturing quality about Rou. Like when Auralia had her monthly cramps, Rou would always jump onto the bed or couch and, landing lightly, she'd use soft paws as she moved up to curl up against Auralia's stomach. Warm and kind, lying there very still, Auralia could nap comfortably.

Rou had the same presence that Creed felt around his mémère, his mother's mother. Mémère had a deep caring for her loved ones, but made no attempt to fix a mood—witness a mood, hold space for a mood, sure. But it was a rare man or beast who had the fortitude to sit with someone's discomfort as a buttress instead of a remedy.

When Creed had his days made dark with remembrances, he liked Rou's quiet company.

Yes, Rou had a sixth sense, going where needed and doing what was required.

And while she was a softy, she was as brave as the tactical Malinois and German shepherds on the team, training alongside them. Her K9 teammates - massive war dogs - treated her as one of them. But at eighteen months, the Cerberus K9s clearly saw Rou as the puppy she was, and they took on an important role in guiding and training her.

Of course, Rou's task list didn't include tactical takedowns; she was purely a sniffer dog—explosives, human live find, and human remains.

Like the German shepherd and Malinois, did Rou train to jump out of helicopters and dangle from a harness on Creed's backpack? Absolutely. Team Charlie's job was to go into areas devastated by natural disasters and man-made events like the explosion in Lebanon that trapped Remi. Under those circumstances, with blocked roads and hazardous terrain, often the only way in was by air.

Did Rou love parachuting?

She put up with it.

What she didn't like was the sound of helicopters.

So Cerberus fitted her with doggy noise-canceling head-phones. Problem solved.

Rou loved to wear her badass tactical gear. When she was dressed out, Rou would swagger about, even if it was just a working dog vest like the one Creed was pulling from his day pack.

Creed crouched beside Rou as he snapped her vest into place, adjusting it so that the Iniquus patch and "Working K9 Do Not Touch or Distract" patch were properly in place. This tactical vest would protect against most stab strikes, but would do nothing about gunshots.

Of course, there was no reason to expect that today, other than a delivery of bullet-resistant vests to Auralia at the bed and breakfast last night.

Though Creed still wanted to check in with Gator about the why of that gift, it made some sense that it was a joke referencing the brouhaha that happened in this very dell after Auralia opened the Price-Morrison can of worms. Once the Marines had escorted Auralia and Doli to safety, there were a few skirmishes in the dell that had landed folks in the hospital.

This property was part of a retreat owned by a corporation that rented the outdoor amphitheater space for local events. Concerned that Morrison was expected on the stage today, the corporation that owned the property reached out to Iniquus.

That corporation had an ongoing Iniquus security contract. However, since no part of that contract included crowd control, Iniquus was asked to be a presence that day but was instructed to remain hands-off with the people.

The Strike Force team was basically at the event to convey a sense of decorum.

They were window dressing.

Easy day.

Responsibility for the attendees, along with newly elected Representative Braxton and the long-standing Mayor Early, both of whom were slated to speak, landed squarely on the shoulders of the sheriff's department.

It didn't look like the sheriff felt there was a significant threat, because she only sent two deputies to an event that was anticipated to have a three-hundred-headcount.

Creed observed that both attending deputies seemed to have reached the point in their careers where they didn't really give a crap—not about their own bodies and health, and not about their public duties. Right now, they could be found lounging against the oak tree, gabbing it up. But what did Creed know? Maybe they'd been here for hours, readying the site and making their plans, and this was their coffee break before the flocks landed.

Or maybe they'd decided they could lean on both the tree and on the team from Iniquus.

Rou was here to practice working in a crowd and building her attention span as she sniffed the eventgoers as they passed by the sheriff's deputies checking bags.

There was a big sign out front that told folks to leave their weapons locked in their cars; this was a weapons-free site.

Rou stuck out her pink tongue as she watched Auralia walking toward them. The closer she got, the more Rou wriggled and squirmed.

Creed reached out and rubbed Rou's ear between his thumb and fingers the way she liked.

She was velvety soft on her ears, and the action slowed Creed's breathing and quieted the blood thrumming through his veins.

Today was the day Auralia had decided to tell Gator about *them.*

He couldn't imagine this going wrong. "What do you think,

Rou?" Creed asked as he sent Auralia an "are we doing this now?" lift of the brow and tilt of the head.

She sent him back a grimace, clenching her fists and drawing them to her chest as if she were terrified.

Auralia was afraid of nada.

The only reason she'd made the decision was that their families were going to be over the moon, and Auralia never wanted to cause pain to her loved ones.

She was right, sometimes chemistry came and went, but shoot, Auralia knew him like the back of her own hand. If there were any red flags, any reason to self-preserve and run for the hills, she already knew.

Did their families need to be managed with kid gloves?

Nope.

Both came from a bloodline of strength and resilience.

But expectations from their loved ones might influence their way of growing their relationship, so they kept it preciously, selfishly to themselves. And as of today, that would no longer be the case.

From the magnetic comms Creed had dropped into his ear canal at the beginning of the day, he heard. "Striker for Creed."

Creed depressed the mic taped to his sternum. "Go for Creed."

"We have a situation. A mother was playing with her toddler on their picnic blanket while her seven-year-old ran in the field. She saw him disappearing into the woods. We need Rou on it. Over."

"Copy." Creed held up a hand to stop Auralia's progress in his direction.

"Operations has programmed your shirt to meet the mother at her spot. She has a scent source and a PLS. Over." Striker used the acronym 'PLS' to indicate the point at which the child was last seen.

"Creed, moving. Out."

Sitting at Creed's feet, Rou wriggled with anticipation. They say a handler can send a thought down the leash to his dog. That was why it was so important for the handler to stay calm and in control when they had a K9 on lead.

Though she wouldn't have been able to hear Striker's command from his magnetic comms—they'd been designed so that even with a parabolic listening device and computer amplification, those communications were private—Rou knew she had been called up for a job.

"That's right, Rou. We just need to follow my shirt and find the mom."

Today, as required on missions where there was a crowd, and team members would be separated without a clear line of sight, they wore upgraded tactical compression shirts.

Because of Iniquus's close relationship with DARPA, the R&D branch of the US military's preparedness, they got to try out a lot of cool new toys in the field. They then conferred with the scientists who had imagined them, so that adjustments could be made.

And these tactical shirts were the bomb.

From Iniquus Headquarters, Logistics could program coordinates into the shirt. The shirt would determine the best route to direct the wearer. So, for example, as he jogged forward, if he saw something that needed a brother on the spot immediately, Creed could simply tell Logistics, "Send Striker here stat." Logistics would plug the information into its computer, and Striker would simply follow the shirt's directions. Veer right, the right sleeve would inflate a bit. Turn left, and the left sleeve would inflate with more air.

It took a bit of practice. The brain had to release some of its visual control. Creed had to build in some trust. He had been in the woods under a cloud-covered, dark moon sky with nearly zero ambient light. And though he'd been slow as Christmas molasses at the beginning, working hard to follow the instructions sent to his sleeves to follow a trail.

In his youth, Creed, along with his brothers and sisters, helped put food on the table. Since his mamma wouldn't let him have so much as a BB gun, he'd learned to stalk small game with his slingshot, so he could bring home a rabbit for a stew. Creed had let his muscle memory from his youth resurface as he focused on his sleeves. Step by step, he learned to trust the system. Soon he sped up to a normal walking pace, and then a soft jog.

The exercise helped him to trust the technology and the idea that Iniquus had his back. The shirt could either work him out of his labyrinth or help his team find him.

Not to say there weren't drawbacks.

The system worked by connecting GPS satellites. Tree canopies, foul weather, and cell-tower-free spots meant that the shirt often couldn't optimally work in environments where Iniquus took assignments. Sometimes the system stuttered when intermittent information got through.

So in locations like this one, with its sketchy cell reception, Creed wouldn't lean too heavily into shirt directions.

As he jogged past Auralia, he said, "Missing kid."

And as he would expect, she said, "Yup. Go! Go now. Bring that baby back to their mama."

Auralia pivoted to go back to her videographer, Doli, probably to report this as a possible story.

But there was a noticeable air of relief that changed her posture.

Maybe she wasn't ready for this revelation to Gator. And despite what they'd shared on the canopy bed that morning, maybe she wasn't fully convinced about *them*.

3

—————

Creed

On Cerberus Team Charlie search and rescue missions, each team member performed a specific job.

There was the team leader who called the shots in the field, which would be Striker in this case. The leader pointed a finger and said, "Go there. Do this."

The K9 search teams were assigned an area to search. Typically, they entered that grid area as a group of three: the K9 and its handler, followed by a walker. The reason they went out in groups of three was that the K9 followed the scent, the handler kept the K9 safe, and usually handled the land navigation. The walker had their head up, looking 360 degrees to keep the K9 team safe and time-oriented.

In this case, Rou and he were on their own, with his high-tech shirt serving as a land navigation aid, freeing Creed to keep his eye on the surroundings.

This made sense for now.

If the kid had gone missing a short time ago and they had a good scent source from the mom—a shirt, a shoe—then Creed and Rou could probably overtake the kid. The winds were picking up, but not so much that they would have blown the scent cone all over kingdom come.

The part of the search team that Creed wished was on-site was the manager—the one who did the intake and asked the vital questions. And more importantly, who was able to extract the necessary information from an emotionally distraught family member.

There was no doubt in Creed's mind that he'd found the right woman because she was wide-eyed and pale-faced, staring out toward the wood while she crushed her toddler in her arms and rocked to soothe the little one as he fought to be free of his mother's crushing anxiety.

Creed moved forward and took a knee within her view, but not directly in front of where she was staring, so if she was holding on to a sighting, she could maintain the connection.

"Ma'am, Creed Duchamp, Cerberus Search and Rescue Team, my dog, Rougarou. I understand a child wandered off."

The child in the mom's arms turned his snot-covered, tear-streaked face toward him with a look that pleaded for help.

Creed gently reached out and pulled the mom's arms to loosen them.

It seemed to bring her back into her body. She looked down, startled to see what had happened to her kid. "Sorry, Cabell. Mommy's sorry, kiddo." She sat him on the blanket and reached for a baby wipe and a juice box. The baby wipe swiped over the kid's face, then she flipped it to the clean side of the wipe and swiped again before she thrust the juice box in his direction.

The kid pulled the plastic straw from the side and held it out to his mom, who was back to staring into the woods and not paying attention to the child beside her.

Creed unwrapped the straw and pressed it into the hole, "Here you go."

The mom's chest was heaving and her hands shaking; she looked like she was about to burst into tears, and that would help no one.

Creed, after almost a decade and a half in war and explosives training, had hearing loss. If this woman were speaking through sobs, Creed simply wouldn't be able to make out the words he needed to understand in order to act.

"Ma'am. I need your attention, so I can get after your child. Can you tell me about your child? Is it a boy or a girl?"

"Boy."

"Good. And how old?"

"Seven."

"Do you have a picture of him?" he asked, picking up the woman's cell phone and handing it to her. "Maybe a picture from today, so I know what he's wearing? Maybe one standing up?"

She swiped the phone open, held it up to her face to unlock it, flipped through the photos, and then handed the phone to Creed. "That was right when we got here."

Creed took the phone from her and laid it on his knee, then took a picture of the picture, sending it on to Iniquus Logistics to have on record. He pulled a field notebook from his pocket, along with an all-weather pencil, and handed it to the mom. "Can you write down your name and this cell phone number. As soon as I locate him, I can get in touch and let you know what's happening."

Her hand was shaking too hard for the writing to be legible, so Creed reached for it. "I can write it for you."

"Ginny," she said, then reeled out her number.

Creed took a picture of the information, sent that on, then slid the notebook back into the thigh pocket on his Iniquus gray camo tactical pants. "What's the boy's name, the name he would come to if I called it out?"

"Jeb."

"Jeb," Creed repeated. "And when did you see him last?" He handed the phone back.

She accepted it and looked at the time. "Fifteen minutes ago, I saw him going into the woods. I told him he could run around a bit, but to stay on the grass. But when I looked up, I saw him going in over there." She pointed out toward the place she'd been staring. "Then I shouted at the big guy with the red hair and the security uniform, and he said he'd get the dog team. You. He got you." The woman's gaze bore into him almost accusatorily as if wondering why he was over here lollygagging around.

"Yes, ma'am, two more things, and I'll be out looking for Jeb. From the picture, I couldn't see what kind of shoes he was wearing. If you could remember that, it would be helpful, and if you had something he was wearing for a while, I can give that to Rou so she can help me track him down."

"You're it? There's not a whole team?"

"We're going to see what Rou and I can come up with." He pulled a bag from the side pocket of Rou's vest. "If it looks like we need to get more people involved, I'll call it in, and they'll gather the State emergency services to mount a full search."

"Jeb's wearing tennis shoes. They have paw prints on the bottoms." The mom opened her backpack and began digging through it. After a moment, she pulled out a dirty sock and spread it on her thigh.

Creed thought she was checking the size to make sure she got the right child's scent, then held it out to Creed, who opened the bag for her to drop it in. "Does Jeb have any disabilities? Is he on any medications? Is there anything I need to know about in advance?"

"No." Her breathing started to hitch, and Creed needed her to hold off just a bit more.

Creed put his hand on hers to keep her focused on the exchange of information, rather than her feelings. Her feelings had a place, just not now. "When I call Jeb, what was he taught? Will he hide from a stranger?"

That seemed to startle the mother. She looked down at the ground and stared hard.

"Is there a family code? A word that you use to tell Jeb that this is a safe person that his parents sent?"

"Yes." She blinked back the tears and shifted to stare at the sky.

Creed took a chance to look up too. The storm wasn't supposed to be here until after fifteen hundred hours. Everyone should be good and gone by then. He brought his gaze back to hers, so she would look at him.

"Yo-ho-ho," she whispered.

"Yo-ho-ho?" Creed asked.

"No, well, 'Yo-ho-ho, Jeb. There you are, matey. I have a message from your mum, I do.'" Her voice warbled as she put on a pirate's accent.

Creed pulled out his phone. "I'm recording. Say it to Jeb and tell him what you want him to do. When I find him, I can play the video for him. I want him to feel safe."

Creed watched the mother's face being molded into calm as if by hands on clay; the terror lifted from her eyes. She pulled in a breath, then tapped the red record dot. "Jebadiah, I saw you wander into the woods, and I couldn't chase after you. I found this good guy to go get you. He has his dog with him. When you see this, you should know," her voice took on the same pirating lilt as earlier. "Yo-ho-ho, Jeb. There you are, matey. Follow the man back to your mum and Cabell." After she finished talking, she tapped the button and pressed the phone back toward Creed. The desperation was back in her eyes.

That effort looked like it had physically cost her.

"Nothing else I need to know?" Creed asked gently. "Anything that will be an issue out there?" he verified.

"He's naughty by nature—impulsive. But that's evident, right?"

Creed bladed his hand and pointed to a dark space between two tall trees where she'd been staring.

"Yes, right through there," she whispered.

"But he started off by speaking with you here on this blanket?"

"Yes," she whispered and reached for Cabell, pulling the toddler back into her arms.

A tree was a tree was a tree. In the woods—or in this case, looking at the woods—someone can get turned around. If Creed started Rou at that gap in the trees and it was the wrong one, they could lose precious time outside of the scent cone.

Creed stood and made a call to Iniquus Logistics to apprise them of his search task.

"Copy, Creed, we have you and Rou up on the board. We're tracking your progress."

Creed programmed his shirt to track Rou's GPS collar, then pulled on his wrap-around clear plastic glasses to protect his eyes from the foliage and his leather gloves to deal with briars.

Rou knew exactly what it meant when Creed dressed out like that, and her tail got to thumping.

Creed walked Rou a few steps from the blanket, putting her in a sit-stay in front of him. "Rourou, we're going on a search." He bent and removed her leash.

Rou's tail thumped faster, her mouth opened, and her pink tongue hung out; her eyes were bright with anticipation.

Holding the evidence bag with the child's sock under Rou's nose, Creed commanded, "Rougarou, scent. Scent."

Rou ducked her chin, thrusting her nose into the bag where she chuffed, pulling the scent into her olfactory system. Once she was locked in and memorized the scent, her head popped back out, and she focused on Creed.

"Rougarou, search." Creed folded the top of the bag and

moved it to the cargo pocket on his left thigh to pull out if Rou needed a refresher.

Rou's nose went up in the air, her nostrils working, then she tipped her nose down to skirt the ground. She circled the family's picnic blanket then took off running, nose hovering just above the grass, so close that Creed thought she could trip over her velvety ears. She ran this way and that, making big circles and small ones.

People everywhere saw her in her bright orange working-dog vest with no one in close proximity, and they chuckled at her antics. Creed knew what she was doing; she was right on track, following the trail for the entirety of the boy's time running around the field.

A woman saw Rou stop and sniff a particular spot and reached out to grab her collar.

She thought she was being a good Samaritan, helping to capture a loose dog.

Creed cupped his hands around his mouth and called out. "Working dog, please release her collar, ma'am."

The woman startled and jerked her hand back, grimacing at Rou, who had been thrown off her task and sat staring at the woman. As Creed jogged over, he made a mental note that they would need to teach Rou what to do if such a thing were to happen on future searches.

"I'm so sorry," the woman said as Creed pulled out the scent source bag. "I thought I was helping."

"It came from a good place, I'm sure. Misunderstanding is all," Creed said as he got Rou back on task.

Soon, Rou was in the woods, and Creed had high confidence they were on target.

Creed predicted that there he wouldn't find a footprint with paw prints or otherwise. This debris was dry throughout its entire thickness, down to the clay below. On the way in, Creed noticed that a fire hazard warning sign had the needle pressed to the far extreme of red. Tracking behind Rou, Creed could see the dangers that a nonchalantly flicked cigarette could pose.

Where that impacted his ability to find prints, there were places where the leaf litter was disturbed, and the stride seemed short enough to be a child's track. And there, it looked like someone had dragged a stick.

This property was situated on a bowl-shaped peninsula with two rivers ribboning around it. That bowl formed the dell, which was a natural place to set up a permanent stage. Folks could sit on the slope and see clearly. The acoustics were good.

Following that slope away from the water and up the hill, there was an opulent mansion from back at the turn of the nineteenth century, when coal lined pockets with enormous wealth. The company used it as a retreat center for their national conventions. The boy might catch a glimpse of that and go to investigate.

If the boy continued in this direction, the rivers would act as a natural barricade. The child couldn't wander but so far before he was stopped on three sides by the water.

One of the risks of searching for children who were about seven years old was that they knew enough to think they might be able to get themselves out of their mess. They'd try to back-track, and usually that's how they got themselves lost.

A tree was a tree was a tree.

If you thought you could find your way because you recognized a tree, you were lost for sure.

Right now, Rou was a red dot on Creed's map app. She was running faster than a human could catch up, and she wasn't holding back for anything. She had her scent. She felt the call of her genes to do the job she loved. And off she went.

Of course, she was wearing her collar with the camera and two-way communications. Creed could recall her if necessary.

Right now, Creed was peeking at his phone app because he was still learning to trust his shirt.

Mind-boggling that he could just run along and know where to go because of smart clothes.

Seeing that his shirt had him in line with the phone—again, mindboggling—Creed slid his cell phone into the zippered pocket on his right hip and paid attention to the pressure on his arms.

Did the shirt understand that sometimes Rou went in a straight line and sometimes she had to zigzag to pick up the scent again? Apparently not.

The right sleeve would inflate, then the left.

Creed would have to discuss the extra steps and pivots the shirt wanted him to take with the software engineers. There should be a way to put the data in a straight line from his position to Rou's.

The engineers wouldn't know how things went down in the field unless it was explained to them, so Creed made a mental note to bring it up.

By this point, Jeb had been in the woods for almost forty minutes, and Creed would admit, he was starting to worry that Jeb had made his way to the bank of the river and might get swept in.

A major storm was raging in the mountains. There, the waters were already high from a previous downpour that hadn't made its way down to this parched patch of land at the base of the Blue Ridge. Coming over the bridge this morning, they'd seen how the water was running fast and muddy.

A foot of muddy water could carry off a truck. Six inches could take an adult.

It didn't take much to sweep a child.

If Jeb had stepped in to retrieve a cool-looking rock, he could have been pulled into the current without much hope of keeping his head above water.

Creed stopped and stilled.

He strained to hear past his own heartbeat thrumming in his ears.

From a distance, Creed thought he could hear Rou barking.

This was highly unusual. If Rou found someone, she'd come back and signal Creed to follow her. But in this instance, it was so apparent that Rou wanted him to be with her *now*.

Creed pulled up the video feed that linked to Rou's collar.

On Cerberus Team Alpha, there was a German shepherd officially named Valor, but she was known as Little Mama because she would never leave a child in distress.

As a matter of fact, it was because of Valor's resistance to leaving a child—or anyone who had a serious injury—that Cerberus's search K9s were outfitted with two-way comms and video. The dogs could remain with the subject, and if the person was communicative, the subject could be assured that help was on the way. And sometimes, even if they weren't communicative, the team could use the video feed to assess the situation to get the right equipment heading their way.

Right now, all Creed could see from Rou's angle was that she was among the trees and stationary. But the ambient audio was that of a screaming child.

Creed raced through the woods, running at breakneck speed.

From his time growing up as a feral child in nature, he knew from his own experiences and those of his siblings and friends just how badly things could go, and just how fast.

Up ahead, Rou stood using her whole body to amplify her barks. But louder still was the screaming child. The boy was clearly Jeb. He stood next to a tree, his hands gripping his throat, screeching. Eyes squinted tightly, tears bubbled from the corners of his lashes and ran down his cheeks.

This wasn't the sound of fear. It was pain.

Rou stopped barking and lay down, looking both relieved

that Creed had shown up and hyper-alert, waiting for her next command.

"Good girl, Rourou, good girl." Normally, Creed would take out a tug toy and reward her. Rou looked like a better reward would be to make the small human stop screaming.

"Here! I'm here," Creed called. "I've come to help." He pulled out his phone to show the child the video his mom had recorded.

But as he spoke and as the video played, nothing changed about Jeb's posture or behavior.

Breathing heavily from his sprint, Creed pressed his sternal comms to open a connection to Striker to let him know that the child had been located, was in distress, and Creed needed backup.

"Copy," the response came through the magnetic comms. "Gator was securing the area behind the stage. He's not that far out. I'll head him your way. He's on your trail. Out."

Having the shirt navigate Gator meant he'd be here much faster than holding out a phone app and lining up with a red line that didn't account for trees and the ubiquitous sweet briar and rhododendrons that blocked a beeline.

Slowing his gait, Creed approached, "Jeb. Hey, there, buddy, your mom sent me out to find you."

The boy sucked in a breath, peeked through his eyes, then was right back to it.

"Jeb, my name is Creed. And this good girl is Rou. Can you tell me what's hurting you?"

The boy faced him, opened his mouth wide, and a screech came out that made the hairs on Creed's arms stand up.

Creed took a moment to sweep the area, looking for any clues.

March, in Creed's experience, just wasn't as dangerous a month as others.

Animals were still mostly sleeping through the cold.

"I'm going to check you over, buddy. I see you have your hands around your throat. Can you tell me why?" Creed asked as he knelt beside Jeb, scanning the child's front and back for blood. He saw nothing. Creed thought that he'd been screaming loud enough and hard enough that he was sounding hoarse and his throat would probably hurt for a few days from that.

Pulling his first aid kit from his day pack, Creed unzipped the MOLLE system and pulled out a penlight.

From the way the boy was squinting his eyes tight, Creed thought that he might have been running into a branch and gotten a flick in the face.

Eye injuries on searches weren't uncommon, and Iniquus required eye protective gear in the woods.

There were no welts or other signs of trauma on either side of the child's face, no scratches or scrapes.

At a loss, Creed went with a methodical approach.

He started by examining the boy's hair, head, and neck. Next, he felt along his limbs for signs of abnormalities. He found nothing that suggested dislocation, break, or even a sprain. There was no blood. He didn't see a sting, swelling, or bruising.

Just screaming.

Screaming that was unabated by time or attention.

Gator raced up the hill, and the men caught each other's gaze.

Creed gave a shake of the head as he lifted the pen light to look in the boy's mouth.

Saliva pooled under the boy's tongue and drooled out the sides of his lips. The flesh looked red and irritated.

"Did you eat something that made your mouth hurt, buddy?" When Creed asked that, Gator seemed to realize they were dealing with more than a frightened child.

Creed looked at the child's hands and saw no tell-tale stains or residue. When he released the boy's hands, Jeb moved them straight back to his throat.

"Check his pockets," Gator suggested.

Creed slid his fingers into each pocket to see if there was anything in there, then looked over his shoulder and shook his head.

Not knowing the cause of the distress meant they were unable to counteract it.

Gator pressed his sternal mic and called in a possible poisoning to Striker, who got an ambulance headed their way.

The problem was that the closest fire station with a paramedic on duty was a good thirty minutes up the road, even if they went heavy on the pedal, running lights and sirens. A rescue squad was even farther away. Better to get them in motion, imagining the worst, and turn them back around if this were a false alarm.

"Are you allergic to anything, buddy?" Creed asked, lifting the light to find what clues he could in his assessment. It couldn't be a sting; the damaged tissue was all over Jeb's mouth. His throat was red, but at that moment, it looked angry, not swollen. Jeb wasn't wheezing. He didn't have a high-pitched sound on the inhale. Creed wasn't immediately afraid of anaphylaxis. "Hey, Jeb, are you itchy anywhere?"

The boy shook his head.

That first piece of communication was a step forward. "What about your tummy? Do you feel sick to your stomach? Have a tummy ache?"

Jeb shook his head.

Creed rested his fingers on the boy's wrist and checked his pulse. His heart rate was elevated; the kid was obviously in distress, so that was expected.

Gator pointed to scuffs in the pine needles that were heading toward their present position. At one point, Jeb had been farther down the trail.

Creed turned to Gator. "Take Rou and see if there isn't something where he's come from."

Gator brought Rou over to the boy and tapped his leg. "Rou, scent. Scent."

It didn't take many chuffs for Rou to resurface the odor in her memory.

"Track back," Gator commanded.

"Track back" was a useful skill that took a bit for the dogs to understand. If this was their scent they were asked to find, why would their handler ask them to go away from their scent source?

There were several reasons why that skill was helpful, not the least of which was that if someone sustained an injury in the woods and their friend left them to get help, the person coming out of the woods might not remember how to get back to the injured subject. If a K9 could follow the trail back, it was golden.

Off they went, Rou, looking determined, leading Gator.

And Creed was left to search for clues and try to coax the boy into communicating. Finally, after long minutes of gentle questioning, Creed asked, "Did you feel okay when you went into the woods?"

Jeb nodded.

The kid had to be exhausted from his adventure and the sheer physicality of his distress.

Creed timed his next question to land as the child took a breath between screams. "Something happened to you in the woods?"

Jeb nodded.

"Can you point to where the bad thing happened?"

Jeb turned and pointed behind him as Gator rounded the tree with a piece of paper folded into a cup that he held gingerly in his hand. Gator crouched by Jeb, lowering the cup so the boy could see inside. "Jeb, did you eat some berries you found?" Gator asked.

Jeb pointed at the cup, and his screams turned to sobs.

Creed pressed his sternal comms, "Creed here. Possible Virginia creeper berry poisoning. Gator's calling Logistics. Over."

"Striker. Copy. Follow the medical instructions. The ambulance and paramedics are en route. Out."

Gator waggled his phone. "Logistics is patching us through to Medical."

"Dr. Jefferson, here. I have the picture of the berries and the plant. Our system confirms that the specimen is Virginia Creeper. Package the berries and send them with the boy to the hospital. You're on the trail? How far are you out?"

Pressing the button that filtered out ambient noise so Dr. Jefferson would be able to hear Gator despite Jeb's wails, Gator said, "Sprinting? Twenty minutes."

"The berries have calcium oxalate, which are small, sharp crystals that can embed into the tissues in the mouth and throat and can be very painful. Any signs of anaphylaxis?" the doctor asked.

"I'm seeing redness and irritation," Creed lifted his voice. "The boy is in obvious distress."

"It's not pleasant. Tiny cactus-like needle sensation is how I've interpreted the information. Let's see if we can't get him more comfortable. With a cloth, try to wipe his mouth out. Then, rinse and spit out the water to remove as much of the plant material as possible. See if he won't drink some water to wash the crystals out of his throat and into his stomach. Ice chips would help."

"They have ice back at the event site," Creed said. "We can hook him up there."

"You've put an ambulance en route?" Dr. Jefferson asked.

"Affirmative."

"It's up to the parents, of course, but I'd send him on to the hospital for an assessment, especially if you don't know the quantity he's eaten. We need him in medical care if he were to develop worsening symptoms. I'll stand by while you implement the care plan."

Creed wiped his hands with an alcohol cloth, then pulled on a pair of Neoprene gloves. He opened a package of gauze and wrapped it around his index and middle fingers. "Hey, Jeb, sounds like you have plant needles in your mouth. I'm going to swipe them out for you. I just need you to hold your mouth open for me."

Creed looked at Gator. "Sounds worse than the rose hip seeds we used to torment the girls with when we were little. That just made us itch. You think wet or dry with this gauze?"

"Split the difference. Go with moist."

Creed held out his fingers, and Gator drizzled a stream of water onto the gauze.

The first swipe went fine.

Creed set that gauze aside and opened a second packet, so he didn't risk re-embedding any crystals he'd wiped out.

This second time, Jeb clamped down hard on Creed's finger, growling at him, with the wide-eyed fierceness of a kid that didn't give a shit; he just wanted the pain to stop.

If someone did this on the battlefield, Creed would have punched the guy lights out and called it a day. Here, though, he tensed his muscles so he wouldn't flinch and kept his eyes soft as he asked in a soothing tone if Jeb would please open his mouth.

Jeb was seven. This was probably the most intense, scary pain of his little life, and his developing survival brain was glitching. It happened. Creed could stay soft. Speak to the boy kindly and wait for Gator to intervene.

Gator reached around Creed to press gently into the boy's temporomandibular joint, easing the bite enough for Creed to extract his hand. The gauze, catching on Jeb's teeth, was left behind, and Gator snatched it.

As soon as Creed's finger was free, the kid was back screeching.

"Brother, check that Jeb didn't bite through your glove and that he didn't draw blood. Did you know that a human bite is one of the most deadly bites there are?"

"Not Komodo dragons'?" Creed asked, removing the glove and inspecting the deep dents the boy had left in his fingers.

"Yeah, well, that's more a case of venom. I'm talking bacteria here. And I paraphrase Dr. Jefferson the last time I had a call patched through, 'the pathogens are diverse and aggressive, the bites tend to lead to infection, and those infections are treatment resistant, keep people's mouths off your body, please.'"

"Good counsel," Creed said as he gave his hand a vigorous shake to stop the throbbing. "Hey, Jeb, I'm taking you back to your mom. It's your decision: Do you want me to try to remove the berry needles from your mouth, and then we go? Or do we just go?"

The boy pointed—it was in the wrong direction, but that was probably how they'd ended up on the search in the first place. It was the easiest thing in the world to get turned around in the woods.

Creed caught Gator's eyes so he could weigh in. There was no way they could force their help on the boy.

"Speed of extraction," Gator said.

Creed opted for a quick text to the mother because a call might get involved. Gator gathered the equipment and put the berries into a bag, marking the date, time, and probable plant source.

Then Gator took over Creed's backpack. "Do you want me to put you on my back like a piggyback, or do you want me to put you on my shoulders?"

The kid held out his arms.

Gator lifted the boy onto Creed's back, and Jeb immediately wrapped his arms tightly around Creed's neck, cutting off his airflow.

"Hold your elbows like this. See? Nice, safe, and much more comfortable. You can put your head on my shoulder if you'd like."

Jeb squirmed around, and Creed was afraid he'd want to get down. It would be a long damned trail; the child was too invested in screaming to make progress walking on his own two feet. Then Creed realized that Jeb was looking for Rou.

Rou was the one who found him and stuck by him, lending her sharp bark, which traveled the furthest, so Creed could locate the sound.

"She's here. Rou's going to lead us out."

Rou looked up at Creed when she heard her name. And because it was the easiest way to make this work and keep Rou out front where Jeb could see her and feel comforted, Creed held out his leg and commanded, "Scent. Scent."

Rou booped him with her nose.

"Track back," Creed said, so she'd follow his trail to the dell.

The boy only stopped his screaming for the brief moment that he was clamped down on Creed's finger.

With the screeches in his ear, and little Rou racing by his side. It was a hell of a twenty-minute run.

Striker liked to repeat the seal phrase, "The only easy day was yesterday."

But who could have predicted that in the grand scope of the day, Jeb's Virginia creeper, scream-filled rescue was the easiest part of their mission?

4

———

Auralia

"Hey, Deep," Auralia called out. "Do you know where Gator is?"

"Yeah, he's in the woods. Creed was on a search for a missing child."

"Still missing?" Her body tightened.

"They found him, but Creed needed backup. They're coming out now. I'll tell Gator you're looking for him."

"Thank you," Auralia waved.

"Gator's here then?" Doli asked as she pretended to focus on adjusting her lens.

"Married."

"I know." Doli looked up with a smile. "But damned, he's nice to look at. I can still look, can't I?"

"Depends. I mean, the man can probably read every thought in your head, so if you can keep things clean and rated G, I guess you're okay. Move a step over that, and I'd say it's probably inappropriate to drool over another woman's husband."

Doli bent to unzip the camera bag and pulled the sides

wide. "Fine, I'll stay away. Because there's no way that I can keep things from turning salty in my imagination."

"That's my brother, I'll remind you. I don't want anything to do with your salty thoughts in his regard, thank you."

Squatting beside her bag, Doli fished out a lens cloth. "Okay, here's a non-sexy question: Why does Gator call you Seren?"

"*Nom du jour*." Auralia spread a towel on the ground and sat. "I'm going to have to take you on a bit of a longer story to explain it."

"I have time." Doli rubbed the cloth over her lens, then lifted the camera to her eye.

"He got his military name back when his unit was training for swamp survival. Some damned alligator attacked him. A beast, fifteen feet. After that incident, his fellow Marines christened him Gator."

"It fits somehow, like when I look at him, I always think *gladiator*, but then there's that boy-like quality, like everything's fun."

"Yeah, I hear that a lot." Auralia pulled her knees to her chest and wrapped her arms around them. "So anyway, another time out, there was a group of Rangers pinned down in a firefight. Gator saw it through his binoculars and went in and bare-handed crawled from tango to tango, taking them out."

Doli hugged her camera to her chest. "Surely, they would have known he was coming and shot at him."

"Nope. Remember my daddy died when I was still little, and my mamma worked hard, but teachers aren't paid much, not enough for a family of five kids. The only fresh meat we got was what we could hunt or pull from the water. Silence was the only way to put food on the table. On the night Gator was rescuing the Rangers, it was zero dark thirty, and he had night vision goggles. No one knew he was there, or, you're right, he would have been killed." Auralia's mouth went dry; she hated it when the memory of that story came up.

"Horrible and heroic," Doli whispered.

"Since he came to their aid, that group slapped on the second part of his name. After that, he was either Gator or Gator Aid."

"Still not following why that would make you Seren as a *nom du jour. Du jour?* What else does he call you?"

"Depends on his mood. See, he tells folks that's his name, Gator Aid, making out like Aid is his family name."

"Easier to spell than Rochambeau."

"Very true. Ask kindergarten me how well that went. Anyway, then Gator says that his mamma has a wicked sense of humor—which, in fact, she does—and gave her children names that go along with that surname. So, for example, he usually says my oldest sister Genevieve is named 'First' cause she came first. That would make her First Aid."

Doli grinned.

"And he says he was named Gator because when he was born, he already had two teeth, and he bit Mamma straight away—that part is true. Sometimes he calls me 'Lemon' because he says I'm in a sour mood. If he's calling me 'Seren,' it's because he's feeling nostalgic."

"Serenade, aww." Doli pulled out a ball cap and looked much more comfortable without the sun glaring in her eyes. "And the twins?"

"'Medic and Legal' or 'Deck and Marmal,' really anything that pops into his head. Genevieve thinks it's clever. The boys hate it."

"And you?"

Auralia beat. "I find it endearing and inclusive. You know, like there's no part of his life that he doesn't want to scoop me into and make me feel welcome, including his time in the military. And it's so funny how he tells people his siblings' names with such pride and sincerity, and everyone around him gets all awkward as they put the names together."

"Not everyone can do that—I don't mean put the names together like First Aid and Marmal Aid. Marmal Aid," Doli snort laughed, "that's terrible—I mean that many of our soldiers would rather keep their families out of their military careers when they get out, they want to leave those years behind."

"You're right. I'm not saying we get the blow-by-blow of his work, but we get stories."

"Storytelling runs in your blood," Doli said as she spread her own towel and dropped from her squat into a more relaxed posture. "Your job as a journalist makes a thousand percent sense. But I can't imagine Gator likes where you're working."

"He's supportive. He never said boo to me about it. Now, I will say that after I landed my job, Gator started sharing a whole bunch more stories with me. But they were heavy on the technical aspects of how to escape. What to do *if* kinds of things. But one of the most poignant things he's ever said to me was that I have the same fierce blood in my veins that our many-greats-grandfather did when he came to America to command the French forces at Yorktown alongside George Washington. As Gator likes to say, 'He done good that day.' I call on my ancestors in times of need, and the Comte and I have had our fair share of visits where I asked for courage and strategy. I feel him in my bones." She shrugged her shoulders up, then dropped them. "As our friend Lynx likes to say, 'It's good juju.'"

"We do that in my family, seek advice and the courage of right action from our ancestors. Yeah, it feels good to know that they're at my back." Doli stared off into the distance.

"Since Gator's his military name, what's the one on his birth certificate?"

"Jean-Marie, that's what Mamma named him."

"Jean-Marie," Doli let that play on her tongue. "He should only use that for special occasions. He is a Jean-Marie, too. But Creed and Gator work better, I think. I never asked about Creed's name because it fits him like a glove."

"He was born Honoré," Auralia's tone softened. Today was the day of the grand reveal.

"Honoré. Yeah, same thing only, it's best kept for when he wears his dress uniform."

"He won't do that anymore," Auralia said.

"Oh? It's been a while since I was on assignment with you, but not that long. A few months? November? What does it mean by "not any more"?

"Creed retired. He didn't feel like the Marine Corps was a good fit moving forward. When his contract was up for renewal, he let the deadline pass. He's with Iniquus now, which is nice because I can see him a lot more."

"He's on Gator's team?"

"No, he's a K9 handler, so he joined their Cerberus Team Charlie. He's been obsessed with training his black lab Rougarou."

"Ragout?" Doli asked. "Like French stew?"

"Roo-ga-roo. That's what he decided to name her. It's like naming a King Charles spaniel 'Killer' or a Pomeranian 'Thor', it's supposed to be ironic. It's just stupid if you ask me."

"Because Rougarou means what then?"

"Like a swamp werewolf from Cajun folklore. It's a huge shaggy-headed dog-like monster with glowing red eyes. Mamma brought us up on stories of the Rougarou to keep us from getting up and wandering off in the night. You'd better believe she scared me to death with her stories. The only thing Rou and a Rougarou have in common is the black fur. Rou's job is actually a counter purpose to a Rougarou. Where a Rougarou gets blamed for missing livestock, it's Rou's job to find people on search and rescue missions. She's a sniffer only.

She doesn't bite. Labs typically have soft mouths anyway, and, in a takedown, you want chomping pressure."

"Like now with the missing kid in the woods kind of stuff? There aren't many people going missing in this area, and my understanding is that there's a fairly strong volunteer search and rescue team in Virginia. Why would Iniquus hire Creed to do that? I mean, I've taken pictures at plenty of events where Cerberus is doing security. I've seen their dogs—they're magnificent beasts."

"And you're saying Rou isn't?" Auralia was offended on Rou's behalf.

"I've never seen her. Just asking questions and wondering which Cerberus guys might be around today."

"Just Creed and Rou, so you can put your tongue back in your mouth. I guess I did Rou a disservice when I told you that she's just search and rescue. She's got an amazing nose for all kinds of searches. Mostly, they want her to go into collapsed buildings when the team gets called out to extract clients from whatever mess they found themselves in."

"Like that Bravo K9 that found Senator Blankenship over in the Lebanon explosion?"

"She's the one, Truffles. Truffles is Rou's doggy mentor. Her handler's name is Bear, but it would be so much funnier if his name were Pig or Hog."

"Nah, then it would be the handler finding the dog and not the dog finding the treasure." Doli squinted toward the woods. "Speaking of Rougarou, I think they're coming through the trees now."

Auralia turned to look over her shoulder. Rou was out in front, Creed had the kid on his back, and Gator was taking up the rear. Auralia squeezed Doli's arm. "I think we have a few minutes until the speakers step up to the mic. Creed and I need to talk to Gator for a minute. I'll be right back."

Standing, Auralia brushed her hands over her clothes, then

adjusted her shoulders back and down. She waited off to the side, giving the team time to make their way to a picnic blanket, where a distraught mother dangled a baby on her hip with a stormy face.

Creed handed off the screaming boy to the first responder, and Gator fished a bag from his tactical pants and then handed it over.

Off they went—mother, toddler, rescued child, and first responders.

Gator looked bemused.

Creed looked like he could use a drink. He bent down and scrubbed a hand over Rou's fur, then clipped her lead into place.

Things were already riled up. Better head on into the fray and take advantage of the agitation.

5

Auralia

AURALIA CAUGHT CREED'S EYE AND HELD IT UNBLINKING AS SHE made her way over to the men.

Once there, she closed the circle, standing between the two, trapping Rou in the center.

"Nervous?" Creed asked.

Auralia lifted her brows high. "About?"

Gator posted his hands on his hips and turned to face Creed. "Are you asking for her hand in marriage 'cause that's Mamma's role."

"You know already." Auralia painted her tone with exacerbation.

Gator swung back with that same bemused look on his face that he'd come out of the woods wearing. "Of course I know. I saw the dance at my wedding."

Auralia frowned. "I thought you only had eyes for D-Day that day."

"For my baby *sourette*, I have eyes all the way around my head. And my antennae up, always."

She gave Gator a shove, which was ridiculous because he was a boulder of solid muscle.

"You mad right now?" Gator asked.

"Yeah, I am. That was just damned anti-climactic. Days of hives and not even a *soupçon* of surprise on your part. Don't you know how to feign surprise or excitement?"

"Auralia, I saw how you looked at each other at my wedding. I knew something had shifted. Creed wouldn't be my lifelong friend if I didn't know he was a good man. He came preapproved."

"That's a damned sexist thing to say," she grumped. "I don't need your approval."

"You don't, that's for certain. It's Creed that needs to go through me." Gator stretched out a fist and tap-punched Creed's shoulder.

She wrinkled her nose. "Still sexist, patriarchal bullshit."

"Now, come on, Auralia," Gator crossed his arms, rocking back on his heels, "that isn't true. You want to play tit for tat with me? Remember back before I brought D-Day around? Remember Amy?"

Auralia wrinkled her nose. "How could I forget Amy?"

"She told me you had a set down with her and you told her point blank that she weren't near good enough for me."

"And what happened?" Auralia lifted her brows and jutted her chin forward, ready to defend her right to safeguard her brother.

"I let her vent, then I told Amy that you have Bayou blood, and you knew what you knew. Then I thanked her for sharing the conversation, thanked her for our time together, and I told her we were done."

"As simple as that?" Auralia was stunned by this revelation. "I thought you told me it was because your teammate Lynx was kidnapped, and Amy didn't like that you spent all your time trying to save her."

"There was definitely that, for sure. I could put up with Amy's grousing. She could move on if she wanted, but I weren't walking her to the door." He pointed a finger at Auralia. "You're a journalist by nature. If she got your blood to boiling enough that you stepped out of that role in defense of me and my future, you had my full attention. And you didn't tell me what you thought of her behind her back. You told her what you thought of her to her face. That's conviction, not—" Gator held up a finger as his face stilled, obviously listening to someone in his ear. Gator pressed his fingers against his sternum. "Gator. Copy. Out." When he let his hand drop, he focused back on Auralia. "Seren, Creed, and me are on the clock here, and they're telling me in my ear that the mayor just pulled around back. We need to get a move on. Listen, are you and Doli wearing the bullet-resistant vests I sent over?"

"You didn't say why," Auralia wanted the scoop both professionally and personally.

Gator tapped her back where he could feel the plates beneath Auralia's jacket, "I appreciate you doing that. Doli, too?" He looked over at his commander, Striker, and called out, "We're on the way!" He turned to Creed and sent a silent message that fixed their features in what Auralia called a battle-ready state. She'd seen it all over the world and in all manner of cultures. Something dangerous was in the wind.

Gator turned his gaze to Auralia. "Make sure, Doli, too. Y'all be good now. Safe. Today isn't going to be a walk in the park. Antennae up and ready to get off your X and get gone."

"Okay, oh Harbinger of Doom." She grinned, but Auralia felt trepidation congeal in her stomach.

Since Creed was on duty, Auralia didn't kiss him but squeezed his arm in parting and headed back to the spot where Doli was camped out.

As Auralia approached, Doli tipped her chin up and

squinted her eyes. "You look a strange combination of bemused and, yeah, I don't know, miffed comes to mind."

Auralia thought that through, and Doli was off, but not that far off. Unsatisfied maybe?

If Gator knew since his wedding, then Mamma knew, too. Hell, everyone in the family probably knew, and they were quiet about it so "the young'uns could tell us in their own time."

Yeah, she'd admit it. Auralia felt like this whole thing was high schoolish. She hadn't meant it to be. She simply wanted to give Creed and herself the space and time without expectations from the family; no snide "and now, when are you and Creed going to tie the knot" pressures would mean that she was exploring her feelings and their relationship without the sideline cheer squad.

They'd made a good decision. But the banality of their coming clean with the air of "We all know" was as irritating as getting rose hip seeds down the throat.

"Gator wants me to make sure you have the vest on," Auralia said. "Don't ask me why. I don't think that even Gator knows."

"Despite the attack on journalism from last time, what could go wrong today? Do you have any new crimes to accuse the guy of doing?"

"I've got nothing but curiosity. Morrison wasn't originally slated to speak, but his name was suddenly added to the roster. Color me suspicious. That's why we're here. This is my story, and I don't want anyone to scoop me." Auralia lifted her chin so that Doli would turn and see that Kamar Brown, along with his photojournalist from the International Associated Press, had arrived.

"Good to see you," Auralia called out. "It feels like *deja vu*."

"We figured you'd be here to listen to the Morrison lament and that you might have some pointed questions. The last mob action garnered us a lot of exposure. We thought this might be the ticket to another good ride."

His wording seemed unfortunate, and the way Auralia received the words made Kamar stop and rethink, but he obviously didn't see how exploiting a woman's work and calling it a "good ride" might not be a good look.

"I see you're not wearing combat helmets," the videographer called over. "You're brave as hell."

Doli opened her jacket to reveal her bullet-resistant vest.

"Shit." Kamar strode across the short gap between the crews to whisper, "Do you think it's going to turn to live rounds?"

Auralia grinned. "I think I have a protective big brother who's here on work detail."

"Iniquus? I saw they have a team out here. Who are they protecting?" Kamar asked, turning as the videographer joined them.

"Mohammed," the guy said, moving his camera from right to left hand to free himself to shake hands with Doli and Auralia. "Glad to meet you. Heroes, both. Big fan of your work."

"Thanks," Auralia said. "Iniquus isn't protecting anyone. They're here to provide oversight on the property, is all."

"That's what your brother told you?"

"Nope. My brother doesn't share Iniquus information with me. But I can guess. Creed Duchamp has his K9 here, and her job is nose only. If they thought they'd need to take down people brandishing guns, they'd have brought along a tactical K9 who would be overjoyed for the opportunity to bite a bad guy."

"No tactical dogs?" Mohammed looked relieved.

"Not this time," Auralia pointed, "just that little black puppy heading toward the security gate. Looks like the crowd is starting to come in."

"All right. Well, I'm setting up just over there." Kamar

pointed. "I don't mean to crowd you. But you two were the money shot last time."

Again, Doli and Auralia's scowls at his word choice seemed to leave him perplexed.

"I need to be close enough just in case there's a repeat performance," he finished lamely.

As they walked away, Auralia pulled her buzzing phone from her pocket and opened her messages.

Creed: **Gator and I both feel a buzz in the air. You?**

Creed: **I need you to be safe. Look at the topo. We're in a bowl. Make a plan.**

Creed: **Get Doli on board. If you were after a story that would make a difference in protecting innocent lives, I'd never say this to you, but this is Asswipe Morrison. Figure out now what will signal you to get off the X.**

Creed: **Be prepared to lose the close-up on the story, but get something different from high ground.**

Creed: **You can't report the story if you are the story.**

"Who the hell is pinging you like that?" Doli asked.

Auralia handed Doli her phone as she lifted her voice to call out, "Hey, Kamar," then flagged the other team back over because it felt like the ethical thing to do.

6

Auralia

KAMAR AND MOHAMMED LEFT THEIR BAGS AT THEIR CHOSEN spot and came over to sit with the women.

Auralia accepted her phone back from Doli and said, "I'm going to show you something." She paused, looked over to Doli, who had her phone out with her fingers tapping, and then turned back to Kamar. "This is a personal text string from a Marine friend."

Kamar accepted Auralia's phone and read over Creed's texts. "Creed's your friend with the dog, and Gator's your brother, right?" Kamar let his gaze slide around the dell. "Bunch of combat vets saying they got a prickle on the back of their neck? Shit." He handed her phone back.

"He mentioned the bowl of land. Doli said earlier that there's a rainstorm coming." Auralia pulled up a topo. "They've been having an inundation in the mountains since the early hours last night."

Kamar and Mohammed exuded urban energy, and Auralia

wasn't sure they had rural survival skills under their belt. She held her phone in the flat of her palm, and all four looked down at the map. "This is us here. Can you see how this dips down?"

"The red lines there?" Kamar pointed. "Those mean dip?"

"Right." Auralia wiggled her finger over the blue line. "It would take a lot of water to breach these banks. I looked over the side of the bridge on the way in this morning, and they're pretty steep. But if the water did rise above that, can you see what would happen?"

"This dell would become a swimming pool?" Mohammed asked.

"Worse," Doli said. "There are two sources of water. These rivers join here, and this new section takes it on to the James. If both rivers are flooding to the point that the rivers rise to spill over the banks, all the land in this whole area, this whole property, and everything between the two will turn into one massive raging water source."

"We'd be trapped," Kamar said on the exhale. "I mean, there are the two bridges out, but they're old as sin, and I could see them washing away pretty easily. Being in this dell, that's not survivable. A person couldn't swim out of that." He eyed Mohammed.

Mohammed put his hands on his head. "I don't know how to swim."

"Is this a setup?" Kamar asked. "Are you trying to scare us off, so we don't report?"

Auralia and Doli stared at him.

"Sorry." Kamar placed a hand over his heart. "That was so wrong of me. I'm flustered, I guess. What are you going to do? Does it depend on the rain falling here? We could just leave if it starts to rain?"

"Everyone will leave if it starts to rain," Mohammed pointed out. "We'll be in traffic, trying to get to the bridge."

"Rain here isn't the problem," Doli explained without looking up from scrolling her phone. "Rain that lands here moves on. Rain in the mountains accumulates. I'm trying to pull up a recent report from west of us. They're all on flash flood alerts. Their topography is less worrisome than being in this bowl."

"Your brother's team can't just up and leave," Kamar said. "What would they do?"

"The corporate mansion has a basement, which makes it less likely to float away. It's on high ground and has three stories and the servants' quarters in the attic," Auralia said. "They go up there and move to the highest floor, if not out onto the roof."

"We could do that."

"Not if the hundreds of people expected today panicked and headed in that direction," Auralia countered.

"Iniquus would announce the problem from the stage and talk people through. I've seen their work in hundreds of videos," Kamar said.

"You seem to think I'm suggesting you leave," Auralia said. "I'm not. I know what Doli and I have trained to stay alive in natural disasters. We're both whitewater swimmers. I have support here. I don't know what you know or what skills you have tucked away. I'm simply providing you with this warning because it's the moral thing to do for a fellow journalist."

"Doing this search, there's not much," Doli said. "A guy up in a cabin says it's coming down too hard to see to drive, and while he has connectivity, he's trying to read up on what happened in North Carolina and the mudslides. He's looking for survival techniques."

"I looked at the radar earlier, and it says the band of precipitation is still pretty far west," Auralia said.

"What are the survival techniques for that man in the cabin?" Mohammed asked.

"Pay attention to the warnings and get out in advance," Doli said dryly. "I know this much: If you have time, open the down slope windows. Move upstairs into an interior room or closet. Unlike an earthquake, you want to stay away from heavy furniture unless you're sitting on it to get up higher because it can shift and trap you."

"Jeezis." Mohammed had yet to drop his hands from his head. He gripped his hair in fistfuls.

"And from there, you listen for sounds that might give you a clue what's coming next, things like trees snapping or boulders tumbling."

Doli came from canyon country, and they had flashfloods on the regular. The last time Doli talked about it, she'd told the story of a group of tourists who went hiking and got swept off the cliff wall. Only one survived, and he had all of his clothes and most of his skin abraded away.

"But that's not here," Mohammed said.

Auralia's phone pinged. "Creed sent me this map of river depths," Auralia held the phone out. "So you see the problem."

Kamar looked at the phone, then lifted his gaze to look at his cameraman.

"Naw, man," Mohammed said. "I got nothing."

"Look down." Auralia slid the heel of her boot out to scuff the ground. "Clay."

"I'm from Philly," Kamar said, "this all means zip to me, Blue Bayou."

Did Auralia mind that he called her Blue Bayou? He was probably trying to convey that they were teammates of some kind by giving her a nickname. She needed to remember that Kamar spoke English as a second language and nuance was often difficult. She'd let it slide. There were worse things to be called.

Auralia saw the look on the men's faces that she recognized as the one she often wore when she sat with her mentor and

Remi explained the dangers. It was a lot. "Let's walk through it. Bowls fill with water. That can happen in one of two ways. First, the water from the mountains overflows their banks, flooding the parking lot. But, looking at the river heights Creed sent me, I don't see that happening."

"Okay, good," Kamar said.

Auralia shook her head.

"Something worse?" Mohammed asked. "Aw shit, what?"

"The rainstorm on the radar is heading in our direction. We've been in a drought. The clay is baked and can't absorb moisture. That means the clay turns slick, so no one can get traction as they try to drive up out of the bowl. Imagine all these cars start skidding down the hill and crashing into each other at low speeds. Damage? Some. Not much. People could get trapped, especially if they're unable—for whatever reason— to get out of their windows or moon roofs. Tow trucks couldn't get in and deal with it. Nope, if we get a heavy rain here, this is going to be a big ol' mess. If the rain is coming down hard and we have limited visibility like the guy on his search engine looking for a way to save his life, if I were a betting woman, I would see a slippery hill as the problem."

"Where'd you park?" Mohammed asked.

"Nose out right by the gate at the top of the bowl," Doli said.

"All right, yeah, I saw Auralia's car coming in. We're a bit lower on the slope than you," Kamar said. "So water's coming down, it's heavy, people run for their cars."

"Tires are spinning," Auralia painted the picture. "People are fighting for space to get momentum to get out, they slide like it's ice, it's a pile up."

"Are you positioning to tape and report?"

"Me? In pouring rain?" Doli asked. "No. I plan to be the first car over the bridge."

"But if we get up on our roof," Mohammed said, "I'd have a

great view of it. After the rain stops, we could even live-stream the aftermath and get eyeballs involved."

Auralia wrinkled her nose.

"What?" Mohammed asked.

"Nothing. You do you. I hope it all works out the way you want it to."

"Don't play, Auralia," Kamar scowled, "just say it."

Doli leaned in. "The mud wrestling only happens as a single event to contend with if it were raining heavily here and only here. You seem to be forgetting that it's raining on the mountain. All that water from up here," Doli tightened the map so they could see a bigger surface area, "is flowing somewhere from two separate river systems. And this is a delta of land surrounded by the two."

"Auralia just said that the river heights looked okay," Kamara said.

"That's a picture of now," Auralia was patient with her explanation. If you didn't know how to extrapolate data to possible outcomes, if you'd never been exposed to the possibilities, this was a lot to take in. Auralia got it. She still felt that way in war zones. "It has nothing to do with what we might contend with if the cars are in a mud pit, people are trapped, and hours of water accumulation change that calculus." She flipped back to her maps app. "And I'll add that there are two bridges that can take you to a main highway," Auralia said. "Both bridges were flagged as needing immediate repairs because of their age and decrepitude."

"Decrepitude?" Doli asked. "I like that word, *decrepitude.*" She turned toward the parking area. "What I don't like is that we have to drive on them. They seemed fine to me. But I wasn't dangling over the side assessing the rusted joints."

"One of Cerberus Charlie K9s, Mojo, was over in Namibia, Africa, that was dry as a bone," Auralia said. "Then a squall of some sort came through, and Mojo and his handler were on the roof of a building, sailing down the river, trying to survive. I will tell you here and now that the harrowing stories Levi tells about how he and his dog escaped that mess make me prefer a war zone. It's bad when bombs are dropping, but they're not dropping on every square inch. It's luck of the draw rather than a clean sweep."

"Tell me the truth, are you planning to confront Morrison?" Kamar asked, leaning forward.

"I'm here to hear what he has to say, and then I'll research if that warrants further reporting."

Kamar caught Mohammed's gaze. "I vote we go. I can't afford car repairs, and I don't have the skills to stay safe in what they're describing."

"Good," Mohammed finally released his hair and brought his hands down. "Yes. I vote this, too. We go."

The men heaved themselves back to their feet and moved back to the spot they'd staked out.

"Good job running off the competition." Doli teased.

"Come on." Auralia turned to watch the International Associated Press crew gathering their things. "Sharing is caring. I said that, and it sounded sarcastic, but everything we were saying is accurate. When I strapped this bullet-resistant vest on this morning, I thought—"

"That you'd be dodging bullets?" Doli asked.

"No, that if someone were to try to punch me this time, it would be a huge surprise when they hit my ceramic plates."

"No lie." Doli pressed her hand against the solidity of the vest. "But I was thinking bullets. I always think of bullets when I'm pulling one of these over my head." Doli turned and watched Kamar lifting a bag strap onto his shoulder. He raised a hand at the women, and they saluted him in return. "Yeah, he's local beat. I don't think he'd have a single clue how to get out of a flood, and worse, he'd feel obligated to report on the situation, which takes the attention away from survival. I'm glad they're going."

"As a goodwill gesture, we could send them some footage that we're not using and notes from the speeches."

"Good idea. And speaking of ideas, I really am curious whether Gator said anything about the vests. He's never sent you anything like this before, has he?"

"Do you want my real impression?" Auralia raised her brows. "It might be a little woo-woo."

"I'm up for some goosebumps."

"For the last few days," Auralia whispered. "I've had an earworm."

Doli held up her hand, "Stop. Do not sing some jingle or half-lyric and get that in my head. I do not want."

"It's a phrase. 'Whelp, looks like I dodged a bullet.'"

"Are you serious right now?" Doli held up her hand again. "Don't say 'deadly serious' as your answer. I'm not cool with that, Auralia."

"I …" Auralia shook her head. "What?"

"Nothing. Except I've noticed that when you sing a song over and over or repeat a phrase over and over, it comes true in the days that follow."

"And those are words of wisdom, right?" Auralia asked.

"Oracles of Delphi are how I classify them." She frowned. "'Dodged a bullet.' Are you suggesting that Gator picked up on your thoughts, snatched them from the ether, and decided to act on them? Just like I can't go hanging out near Gator with salty thoughts about what I'd like to do with his—"

"Stop."

"You and Creed do that between you, too."

"Yup."

"I can see how that could lead to a whole lot of misunderstandings and hurt feelings. I can also see how it would be helpful."

"Always has been a double-edged sword. And my mamma was the worst of them; she could snatch your thoughts out of the air before they evolved into a full thought. 'Auralia, don't you even think about sneaking a cookie. I have those made up for the potluck this Sunday.'"

"Bullet-resistant vests, I asked if Gator gave an explanation?"

"Yeah, no, he didn't say anything." Auralia pulled a pin from her bun, put it between her teeth, smoothed her hair, then slipped it back into place. "I got a box at the front desk with a note for us to wear them. He might not be able to tell us. No harm in following through, though. I kind of like the weight."

"Remember when we were here to confront Morrison the first time, and Liu said to put the number of the lawyer on our arms. And you said—"

"It's like going to the store and thinking I need to get mayonnaise. You should never talk yourself out of it."

"You'll always need the mayonnaise."

Auralia turned to see three men in suits making their way toward the backstage area, followed by two women. It was hard to tell from this angle, but Auralia thought that was Morrison's wife and daughter. "What do you think he's up to today?"

"Who? Morrison? I think he's here to try to win back hearts and minds—"

"And pocketbooks."

"And pocketbooks," Doli nodded. "I think we need a plan if things start to go sideways. Unless we have some Marines in from Quantico again, we're on our own this time. Even if Gator and Creed are here, they're on the clock. We're on our own." Doli's face tilted skyward, where she scanned with a frown between her eyes.

"What do you see up there?" Auralia asked.

"Nothing good," Doli said as she turned her head to take a

sweep of the horizon. "When the sky looks like this in the Navajo Nation, we prepare for thunderstorms and flash floods."

Auralia took a moment to consider the people coming down from the parking area into the dell while Doli scrolled through her phone.

"Timetables moved up slightly, and warnings are stronger. The weather forecast said high winds with the possibility of heavy rain early afternoon."

"We should be good and gone by then," Auralia said. "I'm not going to die for the opportunity to stand in a field and ask Eugene Morrison a question. I don't care if I'm mid-question, you put your hand on my shoulder, and we're turning and hightailing it out of here. When you say move, we move."

"All right." Doli laughed. "No pressure."

"Psh. You stand out in the middle of a road as bombs are dropping from drones on the buildings to get your footage. I think you can take the pressure off predicting a good time to dodge a rainstorm."

Doli tipped her head back and sniffed the air. "Do you smell that? That's not good."

Auralia sniffed, and it smelled like East Coast air, like bathwater rising and tickling the inside of the nostrils. It was too cool today; it shouldn't smell that way.

Auralia pulled out her phone and opened her maps app. "If things do turn dangerous, I'm going to head north. I think the south and east will be a mess. We'll need to get back over that bridge fast, though. Look at this." She held out the map for Doli. "Do you agree?"

Doli took the phone, searched the map, and then handed it back. "I say we get up to the next town and grab a hotel room and hunker down."

"Yup." Auralia typed a quick message to let Gator and Creed know, then shoved the phone away.

Auralia imagined, for a moment, that she and Doli were running away. Iniquus would be here doing their best to help everyone.

She pushed the idea of Creed and Gator being in harm's way down, down into her bowels the way she did when they were deployed, because how could she survive thinking they were in danger?

7

Creed

CREED WANTED SOME TIME TO ASK GATOR ABOUT THE BALLISTIC
vests he sent to the bed and breakfast for Auralia and Doli.

"Not his place to meddle" didn't mean Creed didn't want to.
'Cause he sure as hell did.

Not because he lacked respect, not because he questioned
the women's capabilities, just the thought of someone or something
touching a hair on Auralia's head in a way that might
cause her harm meant Creed had to restrain the beast that
wanted to roar, then to sprint forward, to drag and thrash and
lay waste to anyone or anything that would come against her.

"See that Rougarou?" Creed looked down to catch Rou's
gaze. "If things were right in this world, you and I would
change names, and I'd bear the name of the feared beast 'cause,
honestly, that's sometimes how I feel."

These sensations were new to him, but they felt older than
time, like they'd been handed down through his ancestors.

It was a man's sense of protection that Creed was learning
to manage now that he loved so deeply.

Thinking of Auralia today, a tremor rumbled down Creed's bones until it crowded his toes in his boots. His ears filled with the sound of a hummingbird directly overhead—like a tongue trill that moved air from the lungs to the atmosphere.

It vibrated him. It made his gut clench.

What did Gator know? Why had he sent the ballistic vests? Why hadn't he told Creed what was going on?

Then, of course, Creed realized the spot he'd put Gator in.

How could Gator have spoken up and warned Creed that Auralia was in danger? After all, they hadn't said out loud that they were a couple.

That left Gator to do what he could, while honoring Creed and Auralia's decision to keep their relationship a secret.

Gator was a good man, the best.

They'd been friends since their mammas found out they were pregnant at the same time. The Rochambeau family lived on the other side of a creek that ran clear and fast between their houses.

Crawdads liked to build their chimneys there in the soft mud. The boys could lie on their bellies talking about their dreams—both those they'd woken up remembering, and those they formed for their futures—as they slid their arms into the holes all the way up to their pits to grab at the crawdads and fill the baskets with protein for dinner.

One of the dreams the boys had shared was to join the military, just like their dads had done, and like their granddaddies before them.

As for Gator, he could trace his ancestry clear back to the Comte de Rochambeau, who fought alongside George Washington at Yorktown.

For Creed, his many-greats-grandfather went to Mexico under the orders of Napoleon III. Rather than head back to France, Hugo Duchamp took a job escorting a lady of French Creole descent, whose ancestry traced back to the Caribbean, as she returned home to her family's plantation in Louisiana. On the trip, they fell in love. Once she got her family's approval, the two married and farmed a field of native pecan trees. Every generation of the Hugo Duchamp family line joined the military and lent their talents to what they believed was the greater good.

Creed's dad had served as a Marine, sustaining disabling injuries bad enough that he retreated to the Bayou to live alongside family support. He married and settled.

That's how Creed ended up living in a little hut on the shores where the great Mississippi reached for the Gulf. There, the smell of salt and damp wood filled his nostrils. He was steeped in the ancient magic that sank into the soil and swirled in the foggy nights.

Incantations were called by the tree frogs and echoed in the music.

Creed remembered one day they were playing Hansel and Gretel. But Gator and he played the roles of the witches who were also the heroes. The witches had been minding their own business, performing rituals and making salves, when Hansel and Gretel (Gator's twin brothers) showed up, playing the role of bratty kids, disturbing their carefully laid spell. The twins started picking up all the goodies that Creed and Gator had gathered and ate them without asking permission, and without knowing their uses and powers.

Yeah, that was the way Gator's mamma told the story, casting the witch as the righteous one and the children as naughty pillagers.

In Creed's house, they saw priestesses and witches as wise women.

Creed's own Mémère had taught Creed about the powers of plants even from the youngest age. She knew just what kind of poultices to put on his chest and just what kind of oil to rub into his back to make him feel better when he got sick.

In their game, Gator and Creed had grabbed up the naughty twins and sat them on a rock. Then the Duchamp and Rochambeau sisters created a circle of salt on the ground and placed rocks to form different shapes.

As the children played, an elder, stooped and leathery, walked along the shore, wearing men's clothing that hung loosely on her tiny frame. She was collecting things in her basket. Seeing their game, she walked, looked down at what they'd done, and asked, "Who taught you this here?"

"We're just playing," Gator had said.

She'd looked him dead in the eye. "You can see, can't you?"

Creed had thought that was an odd question because Gator —Jean Marie back then—had two eyes and was looking right at her. Then she pointed at Auralia and then him, "Your visions are hazy; his are clearer." She swung a gnarled finger around to point out the rest of their siblings, "The rest of you all didn't come natural to the gift—a pity and a blessing as everything is like a coin, it has two sides." They were all kind of spooked. She told the twins to get out of the circle. Then she picked through her basket, found three stones, and added them to the design.

When she finished, the wind picked up, the leaves turned to show their undersides, and dark clouds moved in from the Gulf. "We need the rain." She turned to Gator, "Leave your work in place until after the storm passes, then give the elements back to the water. And be careful playing at things you don't understand."

Then, she walked away.

All eight kids tore back to the Rochambeau cabin like they were on fire and dove under the covers on the kids' bed. And that's how Mamma Rochambeau found them when the rain started, and she came in from the garden.

They told her the tale and described the woman.

"That was PittyPat Brown. You described her very well."

Creed had never heard of PittyPat Brown, but he tucked her name away.

Mamma Rochambeau looked hard at Gator, "She said you could see clearly? Creed and Auralia could see hazy? But she said the rest of you couldn't see?"

"Yes, ma'am," Auralia said. "But I see fine. Creed says he sees fine, too. And then she said the twins and Genevieve couldn't see at all. That seems mean, doesn't it, Mamma? I mean, of course, they can see."

The storm was raging, and Mama Rochambeau opened the windows so she could pull the shutters closed and latch them. "Miss PittyPat has her own way of speaking. She's old."

That night, Creed asked his Mémère if she had any idea who Miss PittyPat was. He thought he knew everyone within walking distance.

"Where'd you hear that name, Honoré?"

"Mamma Rochambeau said it." And he told her his story.

"Well, Miss PittyPat is long from this world. She died before any of you were born. She was a healer in these parts. And she was my midwife when I gave birth to your mamma."

"Dead then?" Creed asked. And it felt very true and not at all strange that a ghost would walk down the beach and offer them her insights.

In their little neck of the woods, he never again saw the woman with the gathering basket. And that tale was just one of many such tales that filled Creed's childhood.

But that one stuck out to him because it was so very true.

Creed and Auralia had astigmatic psychic vision, but Gator could sometimes sense things as clear as day.

How was it that he and Auralia could believe that Gator wouldn't sense that they were a couple and had fallen in love?

It had to have been a love spell that kept them convinced that they could choose when they'd tell the world about their feelings.

Gator's response today was not how Creed had seen things playing out.

But looking back?

Yeah.

Stupidly, willfully blind to think that they had space and time, and a choice.

Watching Deep jog across the field, Creed remembered the day when that might have changed everything about Deep's life span.

Creed, Gator, and Deep were heading outside the wire when the Raiders were moving out on a mission. Creed and Gator often compared notes before they left the base, leaning heavily on things that they read in the ether alongside data they could gather from conventional sources.

That morning, Gator had seemed off his game. He kept staring over at Deep with conflict in his eyes. Since back when Creed and Gator hunted the swamps together, they'd learned to have whole conversations with a glance. Creed took advantage of that skill, shooting a thought to Gator, "Deep deserves to know." Know what? Creed had no clue beyond a sense that Deep's life was about to change.

Gator nodded and turned to Deep. "Hey, man, I'm not trying to jinx you nor nothin'. But today, I need you to listen to your gut. If you hear a whisper, you feel an inclination, act on it without thought nor hesitation."

And sure enough, Deep later told them the story of how he'd felt someone grab hold of his chin and turn his head in time for him to see a grenade lying at his feet. He threw his hands over his head and dove out the door.

Not soon enough to stay whole.

But the reflex bought him enough distance that the doctors could piece Deep back together. Over time, he regained his tactical capacity to the point where he could function on Strike Force.

Deep brought Gator onto his team.

And this year, Gator and Deep both stood up for Creed when he threw his name in the ring to get one of the coveted spots on Cerberus Team Charlie.

What did Gator know about that day that made him send the vests to the women?

Creed made his way over to Gator, framing their conversation as a fact-finding mission. He simply wanted to know how Gator saw today's events spinning out, rather than an intrusion into Auralia's capabilities as a reporter. "Hey," he lifted his chin to catch Gator's attention. "I wanted to talk to you about your gifts for Auralia and Doli. You picking up something different from me?"

"What have you got?" Gator asked.

Creed looked off at the distant sky that looked like it might be juicing up for a fight. There was a storm on the radar up in the mountains, and it was supposed to reach the dell well after today's event.

"I woke up smelling smoke," Creed recalled. "Last night, my dreams were about a whole lot of banging around, metal on metal – more like pots and pans and less about ammunition."

"Tell me about the smoke. Do you remember the smell? Was it gun smoke?" Gator asked.

"Acrid. I'd say that in my half-sleep, I was thinking about a big old bonfire back home." Creed looked over Gator's shoulder and scanned the tree line. He had Gator's six; it was a habit of war that he didn't feel a need to change. "The vests?"

"Hard to say. I feel like Auralia and Doli need something protective around them, like I want to wrap a big ol' mattress around them, but that don't make no darn sense. I wanted to ask my friend Lynx, but she weren't around. I may try and reach out to her again if we get a lull."

Creed had heard tales of Lynx since back when Gator first got going with Strike Force. She had started out under their protection after an attack that left her as the only survivor of a serial killer. She'd seen the man, and since she was the only witness, the FBI had gone the extra mile to keep her safe.

Then other stories sifted into their conversations, about how she could snatch ideas from the ether and solve crimes and mysteries, grabbing the answers as if out of thin air.

But the tale that Gator told Creed one dark night camping in the back woods, just the two of them like old times, was the tale of how he met his now-wife D-Day and how Lynx had saved them from half a world away because she could link up to Gator and wear him like a coat.

Now, the linking-up thing, Creed had only heard about when the veil between the worlds was thin—Halloween and new moons, when hoodoo magic was incanted and floated like incense through the air.

Creed believed in psychic connections. His mamma seemed like she'd had some part of herself tethered to her children and knew what they were up to even when she had to leave the house to go to the laundromat or run errands.

And Creed seemed to have some kind of connection with Auralia, like when he reached for his phone to call her, and it rang with her on the line. Or when Auralia was thinking about pizza all day, and he got a craving and decided to pick one up. It was the "I love you, we're on the same wavelength" kind of connection.

Did he want more?

Maybe. Sometimes. Much of the time, it would be problematic. They both had hazardous jobs; living in someone else's emotional sensory space could be distracting and dangerous.

Creed would take what he could get, especially when it came to keeping loved ones safe from harm.

He was, for sure, picking up something now, a low hum just over the horizon.

With the ether, at times, he knew as clearly as Rougarou did when someone had come strapped.

And sometimes it was as muddy as the Mississippi, where the crawdads burrowed deep.

Creed looked down and told Rou, "All I know is that you and me need to be ready for damned near anything to happen today."

8

_____

Auralia

THE CROWD WAS POURING IN.

Mountain Smokey Pig was set up to feed the masses, and a bluegrass band had people's toes tapping as they found their spots and spread their blankets.

In these parts, entertainment could be hard to come by outside of church on Sunday.

And people liked their free food.

Auralia wondered if it was Morrison who was footing the bill, pulling people in to hear his plea, perhaps to garner some good press and build civic support as he headed into jury selection the following week.

Mayor Early, with his belt encircling his rounded belly like an equator line and his pink cheeks brightened by a cheerful smile, didn't mention Morrison at all. He simply talked about the beautiful day, the fine music —"Thank you to the Green Horn Boys" — and mentioned the concerning weather. "Folks, just so you're aware, we're cutting things short here today. I'm sure it won't be a hardship that the speeches were cut in half.

But we wanted to give you all plenty of time to grab a plate—have you all tried a fried pickle?"

The crowd cheered.

"You can expect that when you line up for your box. Let's all be good citizens and make sure all the trash is disposed of properly. I believe we have some scouts here today who will be roving around with trash bags. Let's give our young folks a round of applause, as they learn how to be helpful citizens of our fair county."

He waited for that cheer to die down.

"As I was saying, we want you to enjoy your food and the music, have some fellowship, and let the kids run off some energy, but know that we're keeping an eye on the weather. My understanding is that we have a second system that has popped up, and we don't want any injuries as we head home. Better early and safe than later with problems." Mayor Early leaned to the side, "How's that?" he cupped his hand to his ear. He nodded. Then faced the crowd again. "Yes, too much good food to waste, and that storm coming on up. I'm sure you folks can feel the wind shifting. So here's what we're going to do. I want everyone to sit tight. The scouts have been gathered. We've borrowed some wagons from the moms and dads, and they've been loaded up with meal boxes. Let's talk to our neighbors and listen to the music from your picnic spot. The young'uns are gonna come round with your food and a choice of soda." He lifted a piece of paper. "You've got bottles of water and sweet tea, then we've got cans of cola and diet cola. It'll speed things up if you know what you want before they come around."

"I want a Mountain Smokey Pig fried pickle." Doli grumped.

"Oh, hush now, ethics are ethics, please enjoy your sad sandwich." Auralia turned to pull her lunch bag from her day pack. "What did you bring?"

"Peanut butter and chocolate chip."

"That sounds good," she emptied her paper bag of food items and spread them out to serve as a plate. "I didn't have a kitchen, so I just have a tuna kit and a can of Mandarin oranges." Auralia pulled out her water bottle, then a plastic box. "Oh, hey, I have pickle-flavored potato chips if you'd like." She set them down by Doli.

"Thanks, but that goes with your food, and the fried pickle goes with BBQ, a glass of milk goes with mine."

"We'll go out for BBQ tonight." Auralia popped the lid off her fruit cup.

"Yup, sounds like a plan," Doli's words were sticky with peanut butter. "I don't love that a new front has shown up, and the organizers are figuring out how to boot everyone quickly." She reached for her napkin. "I bet Kamar and Mohammed are off somewhere, wondering if we were pulling a gag."

"Free will." Auralia tore open the mayonnaise packet to mix with the tuna fish. "We did our part. The consequences of their decisions belong to them."

"Wow, that didn't sound like you."

Auralia paused with a cracker in one hand and a plastic spoon in the other. "I've got an itchy feeling, Doli. I don't know what it's about, but it started when I got the ballistic vests from Gator."

Doli held up a hand to speak past the bite she'd just taken. "It's fair to say that bullet-resistant vests are the kind of gift that might make any normal human a bit anxious."

"True." Auralia popped the cracker into her mouth and reached for the potato chip box. Once she'd swallowed, she added, "Not necessarily true in this case. Last night, though, I was dreaming about smoke and clatter and something about that got my adrenaline flowing."

"Smoke and clatter, like me trying to cook?" Doli asked before biting into her sandwich.

"The clatter? Yeah. Metal on metal, I guess it could sound like pots and pans. But I'm remembering a dream."

"Gunfire smoke?"

"More like a bonfire." Auralia grabbed a handful of chips, feeling the acidic saltiness on her fingertips.

Auralia had meant to talk all this over with Creed and Gator, but this morning in the bed and breakfast was a special cocoon of time. She and Creed had driven here separately. Then was the big reveal that was more sputter than sparklers, so she'd forgotten, and now the men were at work.

Everything was flowing.

For the next half-hour, people did as they were told.

They waited patiently, gave their drink orders efficiently, and spoke kindly.

The scouts were coming around with the black leaf bags to collect trash.

And there were Mayor Early and Representative Braxton back on the stage.

Auralia and Doli gathered their things, cleaned their area, and went over toward the others who had chosen to stand. The team didn't want their taping to block people's view. Doli had her camera up and ready to roll. Auralia clenched a mic in her hand to do intros and outros.

Mayor Early threw a hand overhead and called out, "Round of applause, everyone, for Mountain Smokey Pig and our efficient volunteers."

That was met with whistles and cheers. But when Early signaled Morrison up, things fell silent.

Doli was rolling tape.

"Good afternoon, neighbors. I'm happy to be victoriously back on the stage with you. Why, just last year, a terrible person, *terrible*, got up here, pointed a finger, made wild accusations, and caused me and my good charity a world of disruption. I am happy to say that I will soon be vindicated." His voice sounded like a preacher wanting a hallelujah to rise and punctuate his assertions.

It didn't get even a whisper. The field was tense.

"I'm about to introduce you to–maybe reintroduce you to your new representative, who swept into his seat in the last special election to replace our beloved Representative Lambton after he resigned. Representative Braxton is a mighty good man. But before I bring him up, I was offered an opportunity to have a word with you about another scurrilous woman who has decided to cause my family harm. Here I am with my wife." He turned and gestured, and a woman took a step forward, looking miserable. "That's my wife, Sheelah, yes. And that's my daughter, Brandy." He gestured again, and the young woman took a step that landed her mostly hidden by her mother. He turned to the audience. "And you know what? From here, I can see that Miss Rochambeau and Miss Nez are here with their camera and microphone, again stirring up division, messing with our calm and honest community." He glared in their direction. "No questions this time, ladies."

Some in the crowd grew restless and shifted over, leaving the reporters alone and exposed.

A few began to boo.

"Now, now, none of that," Morrison said. "I actually want to thank Washington News-Herald and World Reports for discovering my true name. Working under a pseudonym was hard. Being two people was psychologically draining. I did it because I'm a humble man, and I didn't want any of the grace and gratitude to come to me. So I made up a persona. Now, I know you may have all read some heinous accusations. But the judge thought it was all kind of silly and let me out on a little bail. He didn't see it necessary to stop our charity from doing its good work for the Marines. So that's a blessing. Now, I am free from a jail cell, thanks to the generous donations that paid my bail, and thanks to the Washington News-Herald and

World Reports for clearing the path to using my given name. Life is simpler and life is good."

The crowd cheered.

"Like I said, I asked Mayor Early for a moment of your time at the beginning of his speech introducing your new representative. I think that going public is the best way that I can stay safe—me, my wife, and my daughter there." He stretched out the flat of his hand to indicate the two women, shrinking into the shadows to prevent their public exposure.

"You all might hear in the next day or so that there are accusations that I have a second family." He shook his head. "I don't know about you, but keeping food on the table for one family, keeping a roof over one family's head, is hard enough. A rich man might could get away with having two wives, I suppose. Someone of my mean circumstances could never even dream of such a thing."

He let the crowd's susurration blanket the field.

When silence fell, he said, "A woman is claiming that I'm her lawful husband and that I have given her two children. The man's name on her wedding license is Weseley Price, one more 'e' in the given name Weseley than in my pseudonym. We've already determined that's not my legal name. I am devoted to the family that stands here with me, showing their full support." He raised his voice to a shout. "This *other* woman is a dangerous lunatic. She's mentally ill. She has threatened me and my wife. Threatened my child." Morrison shook his fist in the air as if to show that he would pummel anyone who meant to harm his family.

To Auralia, it seemed performative.

Rehearsed in the mirror.

Morrison dropped his voice to sound pained. "This woman's gotten her family involved, and her brothers have threatened my life. They want me to—quote unquote—come clean publicly about my behaviors and to make arrangements to care for their sister and the children she claims are mine. A claim that is easily disproven by a DNA test that I fully expect to have done at a reputable company. This is a terrible scam. Do you know what I think, folks?" He pulled the crowd along with him by coloring his words with chummy, hurt, confiding hues. "Knowing I have my day in court on the horizon, these scammers, these swindlers, these frauds chose a low time in my life to blackmail me with made-up charges. They think I'll pay to keep them quiet." He held the mic between his two hands, as if in prayer, lowered his head slowly, and moved it back and forth. He raised his gaze and let it sweep across the dell. "What they want me to do is give them a huge sum that is derived from the HONOR charity, thereby depriving Marine veterans of the help that we provide them."

Auralia's mouth literally hung open.

What in the actual hell was going on here?

"That's why I'm here publicly today, claiming my true family, claiming that the money I pay myself from my charitable work is barely enough to make ends meet. Just look at how my family is dressed."

Auralia had been positioned at an angle, ready for Doli should she pan the camera over for commentary or a closure line. But now Auralia swiveled to face the stage squarely, focusing on what the two women were wearing.

It was too far a distance for Auralia to see the details. Since Doli was twisting her lens to zoom in and pick up that information, they could look at them later.

But from their position, Auralia thought that Sheelah looked like someone's neighbor. She looked like someone you'd run into while running errands. She wore a loose-fitting dress made of a fabric that might be too lightweight for a day like today. It clung to her legs when the breeze picked up. It had better styling than a caftan, but it gave off muumuu vibes. Over that, she seemed to be wearing one of her husband's hunting jackets.

In contrast, Morrison dressed in a well-tailored suit.

Auralia would bet good money that Mrs. Morrison had planned to listen to her husband talk from backstage, and somehow, he had coerced them onto the stage for this humiliation.

The daughter was in that hard-to-tell age range. She could be anywhere from twenty onward. This was particularly true when her long hair was blowing in her face. She didn't brush it away or tuck it behind her ear. It was as if the hair was her sanctuary, and that's how she preferred it.

Dressed in loose sweatpants, an exercise cami, and a man's hunting jacket. She, too, looked like she'd been dragged onto the stage against her will.

"Look at my wife's hair. She cuts it herself. She gets her makeup from the dollar store. There's nothing fine or pretty or high quality about either of them." Morrison once again hung his head and shook it slowly back and forth.

Dead silence in the field, bated breath.

Morrison said, "Grifters are going to grift," before raising his gaze to the audience. "I'm sorry this woman and her family are so deranged. I pray every night that they will find their way to healing. But beyond that, I have nothing to do with it. And I'll have nothing to do with them. And as far as I'm concerned, I'd sue that woman into oblivion for defamation, but since she hasn't got anything of value, if I sued her, I wouldn't even be able to buy my wife a new dress." He looked back at his wife, who was compressing herself into the smallest package she could, cowed under these circumstances.

"Now, listen here—"

Then the air snapped just over Auralia's head, followed by the whizz of a bullet's shockwave. A mad hornet racing by.

That noise triggered both reporters to sprint for the trees to their left and hide behind the hardwood.

While a human brain isn't built to process events that unfold at the speed of a flying bullet, a human's preservation doesn't need that much to make out the sound of a bullet zinging past and then throw their body out of the way of any follow-up shots.

Auralia's gaze immediately scanned for Creed and Gator, knowing that they were trained to do the opposite.

They'd be running toward the danger.

9

———

Creed

IT WAS A SINGLE SHOT THAT RANG OUT.

A crack of fire power rode the wind. The bullet hit the speaker that screeched and sizzled, filling the air with a painful cacophony of noise mere feet from the people who had gathered on the stage.

Even as Creed jumped into action, his brain was assessing.

His first thought was for Auralia.

From his security post, he had kept an eye on the reporting team and knew that they had stood up to record when the speeches began.

When the shot rang out, the women, seasoned in battle conditions, didn't play around. They were there filming, *CRACK*, and they slipped seamlessly behind the broad trunk of a hardwood.

Was that gunfire caused by something Rou had missed?

Creed and Rou had spent their time stationed at the security table, where the local sheriff's deputy continued to check the bags of any stragglers as they arrived.

Then Rougarou gave them a sniff.

Creed had felt certain that Rou had been on her game. The search had turned up three ankle holsters, a few kidney holsters, an interesting garter holster, and a bra holster. Rou had one hit that wasn't a weapon, but the woman said she'd just been at the range, so she had gun smoke residue on her clothes.

Creed told Rou, "Good hit," and Rou got her tug-of-war game.

When Creed asked the folks to lock their weapons in their vehicles, he had anticipated pushback from the attendees, but Rou had that handled. With her puppy charm and sweet affection, her whole body was wagging with excitement each time she got a hit and alerted to the scent of ammunition; folks didn't get bent out of shape. Generally, they'd chuckled as they returned to their trucks to lock up their guns and then came back to present themselves to Rou for a sniff test that cleared them.

Creed had documented Rou's good work and had been looking forward to reporting their success.

He had no idea where that shot had originated.

Now that he and Rue had found cover, Creed waited for Striker to assign roles to each of the operators as they facilitated the situation.

Creed had his eyes on the stage. Interesting what happened: Mayor Early and Representative Braxton curved their arms over their heads and curled over. They were older men, in their seventies, and probably had limited experience being fired upon. They started to jog left, then turned and jogged right, then left again and off into the wings.

The cooler head was Morrison, though Auralia had said he had never been in the military. He simply held his arms wide to herd the women and walked off the stage.

Training or not, everyone at the scene assessed the situation, and by design or by the insistence of their limbic system, everyone acted in survival mode.

There was a clear demarcation in the audience.

Those who went to school after the Columbine shooting followed their live-shooter training.

Older generations startled, cast their gazes about; then they did the lemming thing, which was good. If you didn't know, follow behind someone who did. Many of them, though, couldn't get off the ground, so they rolled to their stomachs and covered their heads with their hands.

Babies were dragged from strollers. Parents threw their bodies over their children.

Some lay flat, others ran for the back of the stage, where the tree line would afford them concealment and some cover.

Creed bet that a lot of the stage-runner group were remembering the Las Vegas mass shooting when survival was much more likely behind the scaffolding.

What didn't make sense—and what was a "what in the actual hell are you thinking?" response was what Auralia and Doli were doing right now.

They'd emerged from behind their tree, and there was Auralia, reporting like it was a day in the life, and Doli was recording.

And, yeah, it was just a day in their life. They were a hot-spot reporting team.

But seeing it in real time tied Creed's guts in a knot.

Did he want to race over there, tackle them, and get them clear?

Hell to the yeah.

Even though it was the wrong damned thing for him to do —interrupt their work—was he considering it?

Must be, because he'd grabbed up Rou's lead and slid a foot forward.

Who the hell was he? What the hell did he think he was doing?

The command in his ear was to hold his position while Jack, who had commandeered some kid's drone, searched the area for the shooter.

Creed wasn't some kind of macho shit running in to save ladies in distress.

Flip this around: what if she ran in and interfered with his work?

Yeah, that would go down badly.

Creed sent his gaze three-sixty until it landed on Gator. Creed sent his thoughts out like an arrow, the way they'd done on the battlefield. Gator was pulling children into his arms as their mother scrambled to her feet. But he stopped to meet Creed's gaze.

Creed turned in the direction of Auralia, with her mic in front of her face.

Gator assessed the women and then turned back to the children. He must sense that they were fine. Good call on the ballistic vests, though.

Had he and Rou missed anything? Had they let a gun into the crowd?

The thought cycled again, only to be discarded when Creed heard Striker come over his comms. "Strike Force. The shooter was on the roof of an adjacent property. Now that he sees the drone, he's climbing down. Jack is tracking the shooter's progress, but has only about fifteen minutes of battery time. Let's make sure that there's only a single shooter. In a minute, once everyone's nervous systems settle down, there's going to be a stampede for the cars. Creed, stay in place at the security gate and try to get folks moving slowly to avoid causing injury. Over."

"Creed. Wilco."

"The rest of the team," Striker continued, "those who are

frail or have low mobility, along with children, are to go into the woods until the agile have dashed out. We need to protect the kids from getting trampled or separated from their adult. No one is going to be thinking clearly. I'm heading to the parking lot, that's about to become a traffic jam if not a pile-up. You have your assignments. Over."

The comms filled with "Copy, moving. Out."

Since Creed was in position, he took a moment and sent a quick text to Auralia.

Creed: **Get out of the parking lot now before the stampede.**

And that was it.

Creed wanted to be in action. But here he stood babysitting the sheriff's deputy who was leaning against the tree, wheezing and grabbing his chest.

"Hey man, you're not looking good," Creed said, not taking his eyes off Auralia as Doli pointed behind Auralia, and Auralia spun her head to follow the finger.

There were three men in suits and two women running.

Auralia and Doli fell into step behind them.

Shit.

He preferred not knowing.

Just go do your job and come home safe, *chérie.*

Which was the same sentiment Creed's mamma said to him. He had aged his mamma with worry while he was deployed. She was married to a man damaged by war. Of course, she knew what could happen to her son.

Now he felt that darkness himself, and he was sorry for what he'd put his mother through. He wouldn't have changed his choices—not that he'd change Auralia's decisions—but he did have a newfound sympathy.

Creed had seen that Auralia had parked at the very front of the parking lot area, nose out. It was Auralia's mentor, Remi, along with the others in her WOMBAT sisterhood—women who worked in dangerous jobs in deadly areas—who made sure Auralia always positioned herself for success and safety. And when he saw Remi's experience put into play by Auralia, he was always grateful.

Creed followed their progress with his monocular.

Auralia and Doli were side by side with the men.

The daughter was falling behind. The wife was doubling over to catch her breath. One of the suits turned back, grabbed her hand, and dragged her forward. Based on the guy's height, Creed thought that was Representative Braxton. Had to be. Morrison was out front. And Mayor Early was beginning to struggle, falling back toward the daughter, Brandy.

As people in the woods saw the politicians race away, they began to run in the same direction.

If they stopped and thought about it, the target was probably one of those guys. If the sniper was repositioning for a second shot, the crowd would be running toward his rifle scope.

Auralia and Doli were rounding toward the car. They merely needed to pull the steering wheel to the left, head up the dirt road, and they'd be out on the rural highway, good and gone.

Creed swung his monocular around to get a visual on his teammates' positions. He wished someone would pull the plug on the speaker system with all its noise. It jangled the nerves, and calm was the best thing for these people.

As he thought that, he spotted Gator scrounging around by the stage.

A moment later, the silence was as startling as the screeches had been.

The air, void of sound, held its own kind of danger, like the inhale before a scream in a horror film.

A sudden boom of thunder was the jump-scare that dragged shrieks from people's throats.

The low rumble stretched menacingly across the blue sky.

Back to the west, there was a wall of sooty swells that rolled past the horizon like a wave across ocean waters.

Nerves were taut.

The air became thick with humidity.

There was a moment of silence, and then the sound of hundreds of terrified people rose like a plague of locusts that swarmed toward the parking lot, looking for a way out of the holler.

10

———

Auralia

Stick around for a sniper?

Maybe. That calculus depended on the situation.

Doli was filming and obviously had no intention of moving.

Sometimes, Auralia wondered if there was a part of Doli's survival brain that was underdeveloped. The weapons of war never intimidated Doli. Drone, RPG, bullet strafe, they were nothing to her. She'd stand out in the middle of a hailstorm of falling debris and incoming shrapnel without the slightest flinch, not a *soupçon* of inquietude.

It was eerie.

People might watch Doli and call her a fool. But, honestly, in the places where they were reporting, it was always luck of the draw who survived and who didn't.

Doli said she walked through the rain the same way she did rifle strafe. She sensed the movement and made sure she flowed in the open spaces.

Auralia had her talents. Walking through live fire wasn't one of them.

With that in mind, Auralia had to keep checking in with her own gut to make sure that Doli's poorly developed survival muscles weren't influencing Auralia's personal choices.

After the sniper's bullet rang out, they filmed the scene. Doli pointed at the running politicians. It would be stupid to run after them. They were the target, and it didn't look like the gunman was a sure shot. The politicians would jump into their cars and roar off to regroup in private. It was better to stay and film the crowd.

That was the plan up until the point when Doli swiveled toward the horizon. She leaned down to grab up her camera bag, yelling, "Now!" and took off at a sprint.

Auralia was tight on her heels.

They were moving as fast as they could. Their movement spurred others to their feet.

In crouched postures, parents wrapped their bodies around their children or snatched the poor kids off their feet as they hustled off the field; they all seemed to get the message that if the war reporters were racing for the parking lot, they'd better be hustling there, too.

The first drips of rain tapped Auralia's forehead and nose. "Do you feel that?"

"Run between the drops," Doli called out. "I've told you this."

"I'm not made of sugar. A few drips of rain aren't going to make me melt."

"But it will turn this parking lot into a slip and slide. We need to be in our car first."

They were clear of the crowd, and their feet were moving fast. Working where they did, Doli and Auralia took their fitness seriously. They needed to be able to outrun anything deadly heading their way. This race to the car was second nature.

The shouts were growing louder, and without turning

around, Auralia could feel the heave of bones and flesh. In her mind, she played a game that she used to spur herself along on a lonely, boring run and pretended they were zombies. If they caught her, she'd be a goner. It was enough to kick her adrenaline into power mode. "Go. Go. Go." She put her hands on Doli's shoulders and spun her toward the car.

Right now, as she and Doli raced after the three suits and the two women they dragged with them, Auralia sensed that the shooter had accomplished his goals by shutting Morrison up.

And that was unfortunate.

The two families thing—wow. That was surprising.

It certainly hadn't shown up in any of her interviews or research dives. Had he used an alias with vital stats? Apart from hacking, in the computer age, how was an altered birth certificate possible?

But in this moment, the bigger question was: Who would try to interrupt?

The second wife? She might have someone up in a hunting blind taking a shot. Her brothers? Was there a life insurance policy that would make whatever the court awarded seem like a pittance?

It could be someone having a vigilante outburst, getting Morrison for his scam.

It could be a disaffected young white male who fell down an algorithmic rabbit hole and became a nihilist looking for chaos.

Hell, Morrison himself could have had someone up there taking a shot to garner sympathy in the court of public opinion before the judge heard his case.

If it bleeds, it leads.

In Auralia's mind, the shooter was trying to get everyone's attention, maybe make Morrison pee down his leg. If that was an assassin's shot, the guy was either drunk or high. It was either a terrible damned shot, or someone was making a point by blowing up that sound system.

Until someone—thank god—shut it down, the high, shrill resonance coming from the speakers had echoed around the dell and set the fillings in Auralia's teeth into a sour vibration that she'd never experienced before.

"Whelp. We can always count on Gator to send a girl the right kind of gift." Doli knocked on her bullet-resistant vest.

"He's married." Auralia fobbed her car locks open as they came within sight. "You need to find someone else."

"I know this will surprise you," Doli said, rounding to the passenger side of the car. "Finding a psychic hero demi-god like Creed or your brother is not an easy task."

Auralia ducked into the driver's seat and slammed the door shut. "Doli, were you using your wide lens?"

"I tried to catch where the guy was shooting from." They dragged their safety belts across their chests and clicked them into place. "It was farther away than we would normally guess from the crack of gunfire. Given the wind blowing the sound in from the west, I think that's why it sounded so close because the dell amplified it."

"Bingo. My thoughts exactly," Auralia pressed the engine button but waited to pull out as two black SUVs raced toward the road. Auralia had shifted to drive and was ready to spin tires. The hordes had revved their engines. Get out now or get stuck in the mass confusion.

"Kamar's gonna be pissed."

"His decision. Also," Auralia flicked on her windshield wipers. "I don't think we were wrong about the clay and the mud bog. And I think as people start gunning their engines and churning the clay and water, that it's going to be a damned mess in the next twenty minutes or so." She turned her wheel and smoothly pulled out behind the second SUV. "Did you see that?" Auralia asked.

"Got it on tape. Mom in front, driving. Daughter in the passenger seat, and a coward lying down in the back seat. He must think that he was the target. Both the Mayor and Rep Braxton were sitting tall."

"He's using the women to keep him safe?" Auralia asked.

"When I heard the shot, I thought it came from the building back over there outside of the security ring Iniquus is monitoring," Doli said as she watched her footage.

"Who told you about their security ring?"

"Blaze was walking by while you and Creed were talking to your brother, and I asked him."

"Because you had a hunch?" Auralia asked.

"I'm wearing a goddammed bulletproof vest sent over by one swamp Gator with a third eye. I think it's reasonable for me to know the edges of the damned parameters."

"Yup."

"Also, he's single," Doli added.

"He's in a long-term relationship with Faith."

"Long, long, long term, and he hasn't put a ring on it is all I'm saying. Hey, this is kind of weird."

"What's that?" Auralia didn't look over because the rain was falling in fat drops, but the sun was still shining, making prisms that were hard to focus through.

"The reaction from the stage. Morrison was damned calm. For that matter, so were Sheelah and—what's her name?" Doli turned to Auralia.

"The daughter? Brandy. To be fair, if they were hearing about family number two for the first time, they might have been in shock."

"True. Where's Strike Force in this picture?" Doli asks. "Shouldn't they be moving the mayor to safety?"

"The sheriff's department was supposed to watch the mayor and the rep. No one was assigned to the Morrison family. Iniquus was here to lend a hand and make sure that damage to the venue is limited and there's no bad publicity from things happening, like reporters getting beaten up."

"Oh, okay. That went well," Doli deadpanned. "Did they have someone watching us in particular? I mean, Iniquus is known for its fidelity to family. And I assume I'm family by proximity."

"Deep was back a bit so he could cover all three of the news teams that stayed. He went forward to help KDRF because their team didn't stand up. He was checking to make sure they weren't shot when we ran for the tree."

"You sure?" Doli asked.

"I've helped them out on some training evolutions, and that's what it looked like to me. But it's a guess, not a given."

"How far are we going to follow?"

"I'm not so interested in the mayor and Rep Braxton. I'm planning on following the Morrisons until they park and get out. I have questions. But we'll do this slow and smooth, so they don't think that we're the shooter on the hunt."

"Yeah," Doli said, "how about you hang back just a tad so if the shooter is still gunning for someone or has someone out ahead that we aren't confused for being part of that posse."

"Yeah, I don't mind that suggestion," Auralia said. "There's nowhere to turn off until after the bridge. I'd like to know if they stay together. This whole thing is pretty curious, don't you think?" Auralia bit at her lower lip. "Gator gave us bullet-resistant vests. It can't be because a rifle was going to take out a speaker system." She flicked a glance toward Doli. "Grab my phone out of my right leg cargo pocket and text Gator and Creed for me. Just tell them what we did and what we're doing."

"Did you see the text from Creed?" Doli asked.

"No, what did he say?"

"We should go before everyone races out. Good counsel."

The car was silent except for the faint tap of Doli's thumbs on Auralia's phone.

Auralia had a white-knuckled grip on the steering wheel.

There was a good story just waiting to be told. She needed to find it and report on it.

Danger shivered in the air.

Yup, something sinister had Auralia by the craw and wouldn't let go.

11

———

Creed

Bedlam.

When the survival mind turned on, logic flew away in the gust.

If the crowd had been stunned into silent stillness, that phase had come and gone.

It was worse for the rain.

It had started shortly after the rumble of thunder when fat droplets danced through sunrays. It was the kind of rain that painted rainbows across the sky,

But then the dark rolled up.

It went from day to night in the snap of a finger.

Temperatures dropped as the rain hit with stinging velocity, and the men of Iniquus pulled on their ball caps, then the rain-coats that covered their winter jackets. Hoods came up, and the cord was cinched down. In this way, they could stay dry and maintain a clear visual field.

Rou was positioned between Creed's legs. His all-weather

tactical pants and the bulk of his torso could shield her a bit from the wet.

He pressed his sternal mic. "Creed for Striker."

"Go for Striker."

"These cars slipping around on the clay make me worried for Rougarou. I'm going to chat with this woman who looks like she's in some distress, then take Rou up to the highway and put her in the crate in our transport. Over."

"Striker. Copy. Out."

Creed had been watching a woman move to her car, two middle-school-aged kids in tow.

She'd been standing there for a while now, hand on the door, searching around, shivering.

He wondered if she was missing someone or perhaps she was dealing with adrenaline. When Creed called out to her, she didn't turn his way. And when he touched her elbow, she jumped, then clutched at her heart.

"Can I be of assistance, ma'am?" He pulled one of the emergency ponchos from the side pocket of his pack. It was a cheap, clear plastic deal, but it would keep this woman dry as they spoke.

"I'm from Arizona." She unwrapped the poncho and worked to unfold it with trembling hands. "I don't drive in the rain, and everything's flat where I come from. I don't know how to get up the hill in this mess."

"You can't stay here." Creed reached out to help guide the poncho over her head as it whipped in the wind. "Things are going to get worse instead of better."

Hand on her head to keep the hood in place, her eyes went wide and unblinking.

"Do you know where you're going once you get out of here?"

"I'm heading south over the bridge. I thought if I could get to the next town, we'd just pull over at a fast-food place and hang out until the weather passed. I think I saw a motel there. If it keeps coming down like this, I'll go there. Better safe than sorry."

"How far are you from home?"

"Forty-five minutes on a dry road. I just moved here. It doesn't rain where I'm from. Well, not never. It's infrequent, and most people I know stay in. I guess it's like driving in an ice storm here. It happens, but it's dangerous if you don't know what you're doing." She stared as a car started to slide sideways on the hill.

Horns blared, and the driver was able to regain control before hitting the car behind him. Creed was imagining dominoes.

"If you don't mind my dog in your car, I can get your car up onto the highway for you."

"Oh my god." She bent in half as she tried to catch her breath. One hand shot out and grabbed Creed's arm. "Oh my god, are you serious right now. I would be so grateful. You have no idea."

Because of liability, Creed wasn't sure he was allowed to drive someone else's car. "Let me get permission from my supervisor." He pressed his mic. "Creed for Striker."

"Go for Striker."

"I have a lady who doesn't have the skills to get her car up to the highway. Over."

"It's getting worse by the minute. We need to get her out of here. Patch her through to Logistics so they can get an oral agreement that she takes full responsibility for any damages. Then you get her up as far as the highway. Out."

Creed briefed the woman, and they all got into the car to make the call. Legalities done. He signaled Deep, and Deep held back traffic. Creed edged the car around.

He chose not to drive where the clay was moist and slippery, but kept the left tires near the scant vegetation and rocks. He put the gear in low and kept his foot steady.

"I was in the car with my husband during our first rain-storm, which was last week. It was coming down so hard, we didn't know what to do." The woman's teeth were chattering. "We couldn't see. When the people ahead of us put on their hazards, we could kind of see where they were going by following their flashing lights."

"Which is fine until they're driving off the side of the road," Creed said as he felt for the conversation between the tire tread and the road surface, giving just enough gas and no more.

"Yeah. I hadn't thought of that."

"If you can't see when you're driving, I'd pull over. And if you're under an overpass, then drivers can see that you're there and parked. You don't want someone to plow into you as they get off the road themselves." He turned off the dirt road up over the bump of pavement.

"Yes. You're right. That could happen."

Creed pulled to the other side of the highway and put the hazards on. "You good from here?"

"Oh my goodness. You are a guardian angel. Truly, thank you so much. I'll keep you in my prayers all day, that you get home safe and warm."

"Thank you, ma'am." Creed got back out of the car and jumped Rou down beside him as the woman came around to take over the driver's seat.

The traffic surging out of the dell was nuts.

He patted his chest so Rou would jump into his arms. Creed would have to dash across the street when there was a break in the line created by someone heading north.

As he turned his head to watch for a blinker telling him to go, Creed thought that those turning south were damned lucky. And a chill snaked its way up his spine.

12

Auralia

"Where do you think the speakers are heading?" Doli slid the phone into Auralia's jacket pocket and zipped it up.

"Not home. They all live to the south. North is an interesting choice."

"We're heading toward the highway on the other side of the northern bridge, then?" Doli tapped the navigation panel.

"That's what we planned, right? Find a BBQ joint?"

Doli narrowed the screen. "This takes us toward West Virginia."

"Beautiful area, but nowhere near a population center. If I were running away, I wouldn't head to the country."

"Why's that?" Doli asked.

"Think about your family. What would happen in a small population when strangers show up?"

"I grew up on Native lands. So there would be a group that went out to have a chat about why they were there and how soon could they be gone."

"Yeah, those are different circumstances. But it's the same in theory. In a small town where everyone knows everyone, an outlier takes on significance. You suddenly show up in the Bayou and we start wondering if you're there to feed your dead wife to the gators."

"That's horrible. Does that really happen?"

"Could be. I know that Creed and Rou joined a group of search and rescue personnel who went to a pig farm to sift through the dirt in the hope of finding teeth. The police suspected the guy there of being a serial killer, and he'd strip the bodies naked and feed them to his pigs, then burn the clothes. They found a zipper in their fire pit."

"Gross."

"But a gator could do the same kind of damage. A few years back, we were down home for my cousin's wedding, and everybody was all stirred up. This five-hundred-pound, twelve-foot alligator attacked a Louisiana elder. A man."

"That one's as big as the one that gave Gator his name?"

"Same size. And while Gator's name makes it sound like it was kind of fun, it wasn't. They clamp on and put you in a death roll. You're not fighting your way out of that. No way. The only reason my brother survived was that he had had a suspicion that he would need my daddy's hunting knife, so he strapped it to his side in a thigh holster that thankfully had a release latch, so it didn't just fall out as they were fighting in the water. Still, it was a close thing."

"No shit," Doli said. "And the elder?"

"Yeah, not so lucky. His best friend watched it happen, too. He tried to help. Got him out of the water and up on the porch. But the elder was bleeding out, and there were no phones in that stretch. So he jumped onto his hydrofoil and took off, which must have been terrifying. I mean the size of the beast that was in the water somewhere."

"Can you imagine?" Doli asked.

"The best friend got to the volunteer fire department, and

they went out with lights and sirens. But by the time they get there, the elder is gone," Auralia said.

"Dead, huh? That's a shame."

"Nope," Auralia said. "Just gone."

"Is this one of your ghost stories?"

"No, you can look it up on the web. There was a big old alligator hunt by the folks in that area. It was just too dangerous, what with the family pets and children playing by the water."

"And grown men," Doli added.

"Exactly. So, they find the alligator and cut it open. Sure enough, they find human remains in its stomach."

"How do families cope with that kind of danger?" Doli asked.

"Alligators don't usually eat humans. They hunt something, then they stash it under logs and what have you until they rot, then take them out and eat their kill. That guy was attacked after a hurricane, so the alligator's caches were probably all empty, and he was extra hungry. The same thing happened to Gator. Besides his natural woo-woo, Gator probably had his antennae up because even though he'd warned his commander, the cake eaters decided to continue with their scheduled evolution. Gator was grabbed when he dove into the water in service to a fellow Marine with marginal swimming skills and no idea how to act in a swamp."

"Brave man, your brother."

"Still married."

"Yeah. Yeah."

Behind their car, the locusts were swarming; people headed both left and right out of the designated parking space. While they popped a little extra gas as they hit the pavement, they quickly slowed along with the traffic.

Horns bleated as people realized they were trapped on the slope.

The rain was coming down now with enough force that

Auralia adjusted her windshield wipers to the intermediate setting to see clearly. "We beat the clay pit."

Doli lifted her camera with its long-range lens still attached, and she spun around in the seat to look out the back window. "Not by much. This is the outer band, but the sky looks fierce. I'd be blaring my horn, too. This guy is about to touch your bumper. And I'd say he was being an obnoxious asshole, but it looks like he's getting pushed from behind. People are stomping on the gas." She turned back around and let her camera dangle from its strap. "Yeah, people coming out of the bowl are freaking out and pushing everyone forward."

"If they were smart, they'd keep their foot off the gas and give themselves some cushion. I say that once we get over the bridge, we find a good shoulder, pull to the side, and let them roar on by. You can get some footage."

"We'll lose Morrison," Doli pointed out. "We don't know why he's driving away from his house."

"True. Okay, scratch that idea." Auralia sat a little taller in her seat, not liking that she was in a pack of panicked drivers. The next stretch, there was silence in the car until the bridge rumbled under her tires.

Doli craned her neck, looking out the passenger's side window. "The river's running fast and high. I wonder if it might just flood the dell after all."

The sudden squeal that sounded like truck brakes came from out in front of them.

Doli grabbed her seatbelt to yank it tighter. "Incoming!"

Over the top of the hill on the other side of the bridge, a semi was sliding down the hill. Cab faced forward, his bed swung wildly from left to right, then decided it liked the north-bound lane best and pushed the cab down the hill, crunching the mayor's SUV and pushing into Auralia's lane.

Auralia jammed on her brakes, but the car tailing her had

left zero reaction room. She knew they'd get plowed. "Cover your face!"

What Auralia didn't imagine at all was that the car with Morrison would try to evade the pile-up by pulling hard to the right.

The screech of metal against metal as his SUV scraped along the ancient railings was agony. The pressure of the behemoth of a vehicle, pressing against the structure, made the railings bow outward. Finally wedged between the mayor's car and the bridge, Mrs. Morrison came to a stop.

And even though this whole scene played out in Auralia's mind as if she held a film under a light and could investigate the action frame by frame, she knew this was happening in the blink of an eye because a piece of metal rotated into the air and then hung there as if suspended.

Auralia was sandwiched between the Morrison family car that she had jammed into and the car behind her, which had slammed into her bumper with what seemed like full force.

Unseen by Auralia, a car had been in front of the semi. It slid along the bridge, hitting the Morrisons from a front angle at the same time that Auralia slammed into the Morrisons from behind.

The SUV flew through the railing, arced through the air, and dropped into the river below.

Auralia was thrown forward. Her face was bright with the sensation of stinging nettles, and she popped back upright as her head hit the rest behind her. Creed had adjusted it to be exactly the right height to prevent whiplash, she thought gratefully as she was thrown forward again against an empty airbag.

Doli swung her head toward Auralia like a dream-scape. Then everything popped into real time as Doli yelled, "We're going in!"

The car rocked back and forth.

"You okay?" Auralia grunted.

"I had an acid facial from the damned airbag. I'm okay."

They tipped down, and there was the river water churning below them.

"Brace!" Auralia yelled.

Filtering into Auralia's assessment of the situation they found themselves in was an article her newspaper had recently printed. It reported that when the legislature allocated money to pay for long-overdue infrastructure projects, this bridge had topped the list for emergency funding.

This bridge was bad.

Like the "collapse at any minute" kind of bad.

They tipped up and they could see the sky and trees.

"Shit!" Doli screamed, reaching for the grab handle.

They dipped down, and there was the water.

Auralia held her breath.

There was a scraping sound beneath them, and that's how the car came to a rest.

"Good," Doli said. "Are we good?"

Auralia patted Doli's arm. "Are your camera and bag still with you?"

"Yup."

"Here's a plan." Auralia reached for her armrest and pressed the toggles on all four windows to open them. If they were going in, they'd need an exit. "You are going to very slowly move from the front to the back seat with your camera. Go out the window, over that other car, and get a safe distance up that hill so you can film."

The car rocked forward another inch, and the undercarriage scraped again, sending vibrations through the cab.

Both women gasped and grasped.

"What about you?" Doli asked, breathlessly.

"I'm right behind you. But I have to get out from under the steering wheel." Her phone sounded. "It's got to be Creed checking on us. He'll have equipment. So when you're safe enough to text, can you let him know my situation?"

The car shifted forward another smidge, just enough to make Auralia's gut clench. She reached up and cranked her seat belt tighter and gripped the wheel with her elbows locked out. She'd been over the edge of a river bridge a time or two, but she was always free jumping in a known area with friends in the water to help if help were needed.

And then she realized. "Doli, we didn't break the rail. It was the Morrisons' car. They're in the water. Tell Creed that, too. They'll need a fast water rescue team."

"They'll need an all-hands-on-deck rescue team. This pile-up is crazy."

Doli swiveled her cross-body strap so her equipment was on her back.

She stopped talking as she fully focused on getting out.

"Slow," Auralia said with a level of calm she definitely did not feel. "You've got this."

Doli was supple and strong, and she moved with the grace of someone who grew up climbing cliff walls and crawling through cave systems. Her toes found purchase on the dashboard, but she didn't thrust her leg into it; instead, she moved her weight hand over hand on the backs of the seats until she could coil her fingers around the few inches of window that were still visible to Auralia in her mirrors.

"Slow and steady," Auralia encouraged as Doli's body was a silken ribbon being drawn from front to back.

Doli let her body bend at her hips as she thrust out of the window. As graceful as a yoga flow, Doli was brave enough to let her body fold at her hip joints.

From her side mirror, Auralia watched as Doli placed the flats of her hands on the glass-strewn road. She walked her hands forward, slowly, slowly dragging first her thighs, then her shins out of the car. Once Doli balanced her ankles on the lip of the window that extended past the door, she bent a knee, pulled it to her chest, and stepped down, one foot then the other.

Auralia's car hadn't moved an inch through all that. Maybe she'd stabilized.

Crouching, Doli sucked in a breath and panted as she came to stand beside the car. "Should I try to pull the frame back down?"

"I think we're balanced. If you tip it at all, you might break the thread holding it in place. Text Creed and Gator, then get to work filming. I'm going to be slower than you were."

Doli called out, "Doing it!"

And now it was Auralia's turn.

She had to get out.

She would. She could.

It was simply a matter of sliding to the side and working her way to the back seat, then out the window.

Doli did it.

Auralia only had this extra step, and she could do it too.

But just in case she was going to take a car ride over the edge, maybe she should first get rid of the extra weight of the ballistic vest.

13

———

Creed

"CLEAR THE NET. CLEAR THE NET. CLEAR THE NET. LOGISTICS for Striker Force," came the call. When that pattern was used over the radio, it meant that only Logistics and the commander were allowed on the radio frequency. The commander, Striker Rheas, designated his role by calling himself "Striker Actual."

Creed opened the back of the transport and loaded Rou into her crate. She stared at him and stomped her foot. He hadn't seen that before and wasn't sure how to interpret it other than that Rou probably wanted to check on Auralia. Creed would like that himself. Instead of her danger thermometer going down as she drove away, it seemed to be rising to a fever.

"Go for Striker Actual."

When Creed closed the crate door, Rou was barking angrily. "Sorry, Rou." And he shut the back doors, making sure the transport was locked.

"Striker Actual, Logistics began satellite surveillance of your area after shots were fired. Be advised, there is a serious accident on the northbound bridge, creating a pile-up in both directions. Our view is five minutes delayed. We are augmenting the visual with AI due to weather interference. At this time, AI estimates that there are fifteen or more vehicles involved. We have emergency response en route. Each car traveling on a northern path is adding to the numbers. We are standing by. Over."

"Striker Actual, Copy. On it. Randy, stay where you are and direct cars only to the south. Strike Force rally at the transport."

Creed did a quick calculation. Auralia and Doli had left over fifteen minutes before. He hadn't gotten a text that they were in trouble. He stilled and tried to get a sense of her. In response, he thought 'car' and then 'concentrating.' Both of those made sense in this storm, which seemed to follow a cycle of intense downpour followed by a light drizzle. The sun was just now getting swallowed by the tower of thunderheads.

The rain was just heavy enough that those traveling north would be hard-pressed to distinguish between a car that was moving and one that had come to a stop. Everyone would be riding their brakes down the hill, so a red light added nada to the equation.

With this kind of rain, the roadways became just slick enough for the tires to lose their grip. It was always the most slippery as the rain began washing the roads clear of accumulated oils and other fluids.

And it had been a long while since the last good rain.

And now that the torrent wasn't filling Creed's ears, he could easily pick out the scream of tires and the unmistakable sound of car bodies impacting way down the road.

Then the hits kept coming.

Creed locked eyes with Gator as he jogged up.

"Damned, it's like live-action dominoes," Gator said as he

rounded next to Creed and popped open the back. He reached past Rou's crate to grab up emergency response kits.

"Bowling pins dropping," Deep said as he accepted the first bag and handed it over to Blaze.

Gator handed a pack to Creed. "She feels like she's stressed out but not hurt. I tried to call her, but it went to voicemail."

"I sent Auralia a text. She hasn't answered. She never does when she's driving."

Gator held a hand up by his head. "You picking up anything?"

"Deep concentration?"

Gator stilled. "Yeah, that's about right."

Did that let Creed drop his worry meter? Maybe by a couple of degrees.

"Gentlemen, comms will be used uniquely amongst our Strike Force. Each of you has a Logistics professional dedicated to helping you accomplish your tasks that you'll contact via cell phone. When you call in, you will automatically connect with your support staffer."

There was another bash, and then another.

"Randy's trying to warn people, but their nervous systems are so fried, they aren't rolling down their windows, and they aren't following his hand gestures. He's even moved into the road with a high-vis vest on, and they're maneuvering around him like he's the escaping gunman, looking to carjack someone for an escape vehicle. It's a shit show." He turned. "Jack, you're our tallest, and I hope our most intimidating. Get dressed head to toe in a high vis suit. Get some flares going, run up the street to let folks know this is a dead end."

"That's not optimistic-sounding." Jack held his hand right in front of another car whizzing by. And all seven men waved and yelled, "Stop."

The young female driver looked over at them with fear on her face as she accelerated.

The team held its breath.

Fourteen was the number Creed used when he was a boy to tell how hot it was. Creed would count the number of cricket chirps for fourteen seconds, then add forty to get the temperature. Today, he counted fourteen and then got a bang as the young woman's car hit. From that measure, Creed could get a fair calculation of how long the pileup was growing.

The problem was that surviving the first impact meant you survived the first impact; as long as cars kept driving forward, the hits would keep coming.

"It's on us, boys," Striker said. "It'll be a while before we have support."

Creed reached past Rou's crate to grab the suit for Jack.

"The two sheriff deputies?" Jack asked, tugging on his neon limon coveralls with reflective tape stripes and zipping them up to his neck.

"Their patrol cars were at the bottom of the parking lot by the security entrance. I don't see how they're getting out of there," Deep said. "I didn't see either deputy around."

They were a team of seven that day, eight if you counted Rou. And as young and goofy as she was, Creed always counted Rou as a force multiplier.

Parked facing south, Rou was hard focused up the north road, her body tight. Creed knelt beside her to get her line of focus.

"It's the keening," Blaze said, "The wind is blowing the sound away from us. But Rou can hear it."

Creed knew what he was about to get into when he ran down that hill through a cloud of physical and emotional pain. The keening sound of grief and pain could crawl under your skin if you weren't careful. Then, it could come alive at night and strip you of any respite from the world's pain. Exhausted from night terror, that's when things could turn southward with a soldier's mental health.

Something Creed had noticed when he was a kid was that pain was manifested, and Creed would swear that once it had form, it didn't go far. It set up house and lived in that spot, forevermore.

When he was little, Creed could walk past a spot, and it would scare him something terrible. He thought that the centuries of Hoodoo and Voodoo that had been practiced in the Bayou might have put spotlights in dangerous areas, so people would know to walk the long way. Creed was never sure that pain wouldn't tail him home.

Creed felt it every time his team entered an area devastated by the acts of war.

Mrs. Moony, his high school A.P. science teacher, taught him the Law of Conservation of Energy, which states that energy can't be created nor can it be destroyed. The only thing that could happen is that energy could transform. Energy in the universe remains constant over time. It can change its type or its location, but it will never disappear.

When Creed thought on that, it explained a lot about what he sensed in the woods, and later, on the battlefields.

Fear and pain, anger and grief, have ridden the wind and saturated the soil since time immemorial. But so did love. So did kindness and hope.

As a child, he'd learned that putting on mental body armor was a poor way to deal. If Creed shielded himself from the atmospheric angst, his senses were equally insulated from his ability to be aware of his survival signals, both as a child of the Bayou and later a Marine Raider.

To stay safe as a boy, Creed imagined that there was space between his cells and that his body became porous. Like water running through a sieve, it came and touched on him, then left.

Yeah, Creed's trick meant he was freed of the miasma of haints, boo hags, and booger men so his soul could sleep safe at night.

He had taught Auralia how to protect herself that way, to open up the spaces in her physical body and mental space, and let the air and all the particles waft on through.

After that, she said she slept better at night, free from the spooks that haunted her dreams, but never free from the safety of her family's etheric connections.

Time to open up and let the pain waft through.

The team slung their own high-vis vests into place, buckling them at the waist. It not only helped keep them safe, but it also served as an identifier for the team to keep track of one another.

Next, they dropped their hoods to pull the headlight straps over their visored caps and set to red light. The hoods on the Iniquus raincoats were tightened down over their visored caps, keeping their light system in place and the rain out of their eyes.

With everyone suited up, emergency packs on their backs, Jack stationed up the road,

Striker rallied his team. "Gentlemen, here we go. Creed, you're learning the ropes, so I want you out front, a steady cadence as you jog the length of the crash. You need to establish a video connection with Logistics and narrate what you're seeing. As you pass by a car, read off the license plate if you can quickly see it. That information will help emergency services identify the owner. Count heads, guess at ages, describe obvious injuries on the run. That will be the first level of information for Emergency management to assess the types of resources that are needed so they can deploy the right number of people and bring in the right equipment." He looked down at Rou, leaning forward, ready to leap into action as soon as Creed gave the command. "Let's leave Rou in her crate for now. But in case we need her later, go ahead and put her shoes on so she isn't cut by broken glass."

As Creed crouched to pull Rou's socks and shoes from her

zippered tactical vest and signaled her to lift a paw to get dressed, Striker continued.

"Next out is Gator. Your job is visual triage. Fast and dirty." Striker lifted the strap and moved a box in front of Gator. Clasped to the strap were indelible markers. Inside were triage tags. "Use one tag per car, duct tape the tag to the right passenger's door if possible. Keep your phone on speaker. As you fill out the tag, you're simply saying it out loud. If you think it will cause undue stress to the car's occupants, then just say the number of passengers and their corresponding colors, which will give the responders more information about resources required."

The purpose of a triage system was to provide a quick and straightforward way of communicating an assessment. The sheet was a prioritization.

Red patients took transportation priority. Red meant that they had life-threatening injuries, but that if they got help fast, they could survive.

Yellow meant the person was seriously injured, but death wasn't imminent. They could wait a bit.

Green was for minor injuries, what they called "walking wounded."

The lucky ones who fell under the "White" category were fine.

Black meant they were dead or that their injuries were so extensive that treating them was performative for the family's mental health, like performing CPR when the subject had been face down in the water for ten minutes. Any attention given to a black tag meant moving resources away from red tags, who had a chance.

This was going to be hard on Gator. Essentially, at a glance, he was tasked with determining who might live and who would die. With the closed rural hospital and the urban hospital almost an hour away, even with lights and sirens, Gator would have to weigh that distance into the tag system.

Gator looked up and said to no one in particular, "Not much chance of getting medivac support in this weather."

Striker turned to Blaze. "Grab a roll of duct tape out of the back for Gator. And while you're in there, grab the bag of tourniquets and the window breaker. You'll go behind him. Your job is to tourniquet and move on."

"Sir." Blaze rounded to the back of their transport, and Creed was glad they were positioned effectively. Their equipment would undoubtedly save lives.

Another car barreled by them at full speed, and the men shouted and waved to no effect. Moments later, there was the screech and the bangs.

"Blaze, Gator, and Creed, as you move forward, tell anyone who can reasonably get themselves out of their cars to move up on the ridge that they need to move. Under normal circumstances, it's counseled that the safest place to stay is in your vehicle. But on a day like today, if Jack isn't able to get people to turn around, this will continue to be a bumper car situation. What might be a mild injury in this moment might become a deadly crush in the next. Better up the hill and wet."

"Hypothermia in this rain," Deep said.

"Yup." Striker raised his voice, "Blaze, pull out the box of Mylar blankets and hand them to Deep. Deep, you're ahead of Blaze, take the window breaker and pop the window or open the door so Blaze can get right in there for a fast tourniquet. Seconds matter. Hand a blanket to every person until you run out."

Deep accepted the box. "If I run out, that's going to be a bad sign."

"As you get them moving, Deep, make sure you warn them about the effects of the weather. They should crouch together and try to keep warm with body heat. Tell them to take shelter under those evergreens unless there's more lightning. Another thing," Striker said, "some of these folks might be in shock. Look for the most cogent, helpful people and put them in charge of those who might be at higher risk."

"Sir," the team said in unison.

"Gentlemen, people will see our uniforms and want us to stay with them and help. There are babies and children in the mix. It's going to be tough, but head over hearts saves lives."

"Sir."

"All right, Creed, head out."

"Moving," Creed said as he glanced at his phone. No text from Auralia. Had she followed Morrison and already crossed out of the danger area, or had she gone south on her way back to the bed and breakfast?

Creed was glad to be the point guy. He'd be thorough but move fast. He'd be the first to get to the bridge. Iniquus was all about family, and if he found Auralia needed him, Iniquus would stand one thousand percent behind his decision to focus on her, just as he would if any of his brothers needed him.

Creed pulled out his phone. Before he dialed into Iniquus Logistics, he took a moment to send a quick text.

Creed: **Cherished, are you and Doli okay?**

14

Auralia

With her jacket pulled free and resting on Doli's abandoned seat, Auralia's next big effort was to get the ballistic vest off.

It wasn't easy to pull apart the hook and loop closure without a significant jerk. If she were in the water, though, swimming through the current wouldn't be possible with this added weight and movement constriction.

The image of an armadillo came to mind. "Yeah, they can swim, but their armor doesn't include ceramic plates."

She edged her fingers under the flap and crawled them forward.

Waste of time? Putting herself in danger when she could simply follow Doli's performance?

Auralia's intuition told her that she wasn't going to make it out of the car while it was on the bridge. She could feel the frame straining to hold her in place. She was going to take a plunge.

Still, she'd act as if she still had a way to get out until the very last second.

As Auralia worked her fingers over the plates, she tried to be logical and methodical in her decision-making. Like, with her safety belt. She could crawl out with it attached, but if her car was to take flight, she'd want it to be holding her safely in place.

And then when she landed, if it jammed, that was a problem.

Auralia opened her console and pulled out a thick rubber band, a window punch, a seatbelt razor, and a high-lumen flashlight attached. It was a gift from her mentor, Remi, who often handed out little items like this to her friends and colleagues as if they were door prizes. Auralia always read that as a wish for their safety. It was warm and loving, and in this instance, might well be life-saving. The back window might end up being her egress.

While she pulled that onto her wrist, Auralia tried to imagine what would happen if she were crawling out the back window when her car plunged forward.

There was no help coming. The number of injured had to be mind-boggling.

The wailing. The screams. It tortured Auralia, and she had to focus on imagining herself as diaphanous, the way Creed had taught her to stay safe from nightmares when they were young. She used that technique as a necessary tool in her toolbox when off on assignment, so the energy that filled the air and was buffeted around didn't glue to her skin or seep into her psyche.

She needed to listen to her intuition to survive the day.

Iniquus was surely in the mix.

Emergency services had to be rushing to the scene.

She'd be low man on the totem pole, or in this case, high girl on the bridge.

"Here we go," Auralia said as she unclasped the belt for a brief moment to lift the ballistic vest over her head.

Afraid to shift the dynamic of the teetering car, Auralia set the weight on the console right next to her thigh.

Still, the move made the car sway. And Auralia quickly pulled her seat belt back into place.

The movement was mere inches forward and back, so subtle compared to the grand sweep of sky and water when the car was shoved into this position. Still, scary.

"Okay, think. What are the options?"

The back seat of her car could be pulled down to access the trunk. Auralia had practiced a few times after her sister WOMBAT, Kim, had been tied up and thrown into her trunk. When the kidnapper stopped for gas and a pit stop, Kim kicked out the back seat and was able to get out through the passenger door.

Granted, she'd still been bound hand and foot, but as she lay there writhing and yelling for help, the people around her became her protectors. The assailant took off, abandoning his car.

She could be like Kim in reverse and escape from the car trunk instead of the side window. Her weight back there might press her into a better position.

Okay, it wasn't her favorite, but it was on her list.

"Here's the plan," Auralia said aloud so that her brain was processing it in different parts, giving the plan a better chance of action, "If I'm going over, I'm popping the trunk. It might make a sail, it might make getting out from the back seat easier, and it might give me access to my supply boxes in the back, including a life preserver from my boat trip last week."

Auralia reached her hand up and felt for the trunk latch button. She put her hand down, then did it again, leaving it there as the car tilted downward and the frame slipped a few more inches.

Her weight pressing her into the safety belt, Auralia could see the water again. It looked damned far down there.

But now, quite obviously, she wouldn't be slinking over the back seat and out the window.

She was going to dangle there until help arrived or she was going in.

Wouldn't it be miraculous if Gator's team suddenly arrived at the scene and worked their magic, stabilizing the car and pulling her free, so she could walk away with only an abraded face?

The "if only" game came in handy sometimes when things were bad and there was no clear escape.

She and those she loved worked in dangerous settings, yet they seemed to emerge unscathed each time. That was fallacious thinking.

Which one would apply?

Maybe 'Appeal to Tradition'?

"Traditionally, I have survived life-threatening circumstances; therefore, I will do the same today."

It seemed a dangerous mindset for Auralia to call her survival a logical fallacy.

"I pull those thoughts from the wind, and I send them down into the water as fish food," she muttered as she pulled the safety belt back tight over her hips and tried to press back so her lungs had room to expand.

The rubber band around her wrist was cutting off circulation, and Auralia was glad because the burning sensation reminded her that she had useful tools at her disposal. "If the safety belt won't release, there's a sharp blade on the window breaker to slice through. Don't wrestle, slice."

The mental pictures were lining up. Auralia always found a plan of action helpful. If A happens, I'll do this. If B happens, I'll do that.

Unfortunately, there had been many a time when it was so

far down the list of possibilities that a G was happening, even P. And for that, she probably had no plan.

Still, plotting an escape helped to steady her nerves.

She considered her clothes.

If the ballistic vest could drag her down, so could her steel-toed boots. Letting her hands dangle straight down, she was able to remove them. It would be good if she could keep hold of the boots somehow because the only way out of the jungle of bent vehicles would be to hike to help.

She tied the boots together and shoved her socks into the toes.

Pulling her phone from her thigh pocket, Auralia inserted it in the waterproof bag she had had dangling at the ready since she heard about the possibility of rain.

She'd keep the cord around her neck as her get-out-of-jail-free card. If everything else were lost, she could reach Iniquus. She pulled her shirt and fleece out to make space, then thrust the plastic bag inside against her skin. Auralia reached under her top to position her phone in her bra under her boob, pulling the cord tight and putting the slack in her cup as well, hoping that it wouldn't get caught on anything and trap her.

Whew. It was hard to breathe.

In her mind, she tried to block out what she expected—the impact, the re-orientation, her escape from inside the vehicle, then the churning white water that would wrestle to drag her under.

Her goal was to stay conscious as she hit the water.

Get out. Get to shore. And there, her battle would be with the wind and cold.

Hypothermia was terrifying because the body's best survival tool, the brain, slowed and dulled.

Auralia felt for one of the large black leaf bags she kept in the console for emergencies and dropped her boots inside. Followed by her fleece, then her thermal shirt.

She needed to get out of her pants—windproof and fleece-lined, with her identification and credit cards in the zipped pocket. Yeah, she'd need her pants too.

Popping the snap, pulling the zipper, she had space to slide them over her hips because of the angle of her dangle. She let the rhyming words loop around as she edged her pants down by an inch on one side and an inch on the other.

Soon she'd be out of tasks, and that wasn't good.

Action was Auralia's counterbalance to fear.

Her pants slid to her ankles, and she scooped them up and put them into the bag. Auralia had to think through this next step. Before she tied off the clothes bag, should there be air or no air in the bag?

No air would make it easier to get it through the open window in the back.

Air could help the bag stay afloat.

Too little air in the clothes bag wouldn't be helpful.

Too much air, and she could rip the bag as she exited.

She needed Goldilocks air; it needed to be just right.

Auralia scooped the top through the air to trap a little more gas inside, then rolled the top again before tying it to ensure no water got in.

Water was weight, and the boots were heavy enough to drag through that current.

"You will float, you will hold me up, and you will stay with me," she told the bag.

She put that bag in the back seat by the window.

What would she do if she broke a bone or was injured?

Release the clothes.

Hypothermia?

She had another bag that she could use to make a flotation device, and once she was on the shore, she could crawl inside, just as they had taught her in the Hug-a-Tree Program at Sunday School.

All that rain from up in the mountains was rushing toward the ocean, ice-cold.

As she worked on the second bag, which would serve as her flotation device, the "Why me?" question was growing louder in her mind. A little voice that wanted to make her small and pitiful.

And then she remembered the story of how Creed's fellow Team Charlie operator, Halo St. John, had met his wife, Mary. They were strangers working together to save a family. His wife had shown up in that city for a singular reason: Mary's horoscope said it was her responsibility to be there for the greater good.

Talk about leaning into the woo-woo.

That story didn't quite fit Auralia's present reality.

Fact: Auralia was in no position to be helpful to anyone, except perhaps herself.

Another small, selfish part of her brain was voicing astonishment that Creed and Gator weren't calling out to her that they'd have her down in a minute, hang tight.

But she also wasn't in dire need. Maybe Gator and Creed checked in the ether and saw she was okay, and trusted her to save herself, so they could focus on the truly vulnerable.

Auralia decided to go with that story.

They checked on her.

She was okay.

This was all going to be fine.

Now, to make herself believe it.

15

———————

Creed

It was bad. Really bad.

And the worst of it was that the cars on this four-lane highway kept coming.

Looking back over his shoulder, Creed could see massive Jack, nearly seven feet tall, standing at the top of the hill in the middle of the damned street with his high-vis neon limon—the eye-catching color that looked like a lemon and lime had a baby—rain gear pulled over his Iniquus uniform with flares in his hands, waving them as a signal, wasn't having much success.

Physics says a body in motion tends to stay in motion, and Creed would be damned if he hadn't seen it time and again. Someone comes upon something that doesn't make sense to them; perhaps their inner child got scared by what might seem like a giant asking them to slow down for no apparent reason.

Then, over the hill, they'd go, and all bets were off.

They'd see the pile up; they'd stomp their brakes.

Some were able to bring themselves to a stop. Some were even able to start a three-point turn just to get T-boned while trying to head back in a safe direction. BAM! They got bowled into the crisis by the next guy, who wasn't going to be dissuaded from their route by some guy in a neon jumpsuit.

Creed held his phone off to the side for Logistics to view and record the situation in real time.

When Creed was going through his orientation, the tour of Iniquus Logistics reminded him of something out of a sci-fi movie. The people sitting at their computers with large boards that could bring up real-time maps that locked in the movements of personnel—both human and K9—as well as vehicles, the satellite feeds that would make the intelligence communities salivate at the clarity of detail both day and night, and the systems managers that protected the operators' cover stories. "Movies and fiction novels," he repeated to himself as they showed how a call would come in to a dedicated line. The people who sat in front of those lines were not only trained as improv actors but also by the intelligence community to extract information while revealing little. They could be anyone that the operator had set up in advance to protect their cover story.

One of the stories they told was about Honey Honig, an operator in Panther Force (the first field operations team that Creed trained with after signing with Cerberus). Honey had the cover of being a high-dollar executive. When Honey was captured by terrorists, he had the kidnappers call the line to prove he was worth a great deal of money. Whatever the actor said was believable enough that the threatened decapitation was postponed. Iniquus knew this cover was for extreme circumstances, and they were able to pinpoint his location halfway around the world.

Strike Force was in the air, and Honey came out the other end whole and healthy.

"Stuff of thrillers and novels."

Iniquus Security ran on a golden reputation. Men and women were held to the highest of personal ethos and moral code.

All of it was damned impressive.

Creed was a lucky man. He had a dream job, his dream pup, and, most cherished, his dream woman in Auralia. Could there be anything deeper and more satisfying than loving someone all your life as smart and kind, rock-solid, and fearless, and then discovering there was magic laced beneath the surface that wove them together, like ribbons of gold and sweet like honey?

Those thoughts were the opposite of what he ran past.

This looked like the streets of Afghanistan after a bomb went off. The lifelessness in the eyes that turned toward him told him that the injuries were severe, and the passengers focused all of their energy on surviving the pain.

He wanted to pull open the doors and render aid to each one.

But orders were in place for a reason.

One thing Creed hadn't been prepared to include in his survey was, "They're going to need the jaws of life." And a step farther down. "This one's standing on end. They're going to need some kind of crane to get it off the one in front. I can't see how many were in that car."

Sometimes the computer couldn't differentiate Creed's voice from the wailing and the calls for help. He'd have to step back and repeat the information slowly and clearly so that it could be hand-entered into the system.

Looking over his shoulder, Creed focused on Gator coming up behind him with a much more challenging job. He had to look at each person and make the call. He might well be writing their death sentence and all from a glance in the window.

The men were used to this kind of life-or-death situation. But used to it didn't mean anesthetized. It was something that they'd need to process after the fact.

Creed could hear the snap crinkle as Deep busted a window. "Tourniquet," he'd yell toward his phone dangling in its waterproof pouch from a lanyard around his neck. His Logistics professional would put a pin in that exact spot.

Creed took another step. "Single male, sixties." Two more steps, he swiped his hand over the window to see past the raindrops. "Two middle-aged males."

With a squeal and crash, another car hit the pileup, jostling and repositioning the mound.

Creed remembered having a collection of cars as a child and how he liked to roll them into each other, making crashing, exploding sounds that mimicked what went on in his imagination. He liked to sling them along so they would flip and roll. It had been his goal to see if he couldn't get them to pile high like crawdaddy chimneys in the mud.

Creed moved further, pushed himself to go faster while getting the data right.

At least the storm seemed to have eased a bit. The sun wasn't out, but the rain that had come down in fat droplets at stinging velocity turned to a vision-obscuring mist.

His phone buzzed.

Doli was on his line. It was against protocol, but he had to break communication with Logistics to find out about Auralia. "Logistics, stand by. I have an incoming urgent communication."

"Standing by."

He tapped the line open. "Creed here."

"Doli."

"You two down the road?" he asked hopefully. "There's a pile-up north of the dell."

"Yeah, it started on the bridge. A semi-truck plowed into

the mayor's SUV. We were two cars back. I couldn't see in his tinted windows to assess. There are laws against that for a reason."

"But you're okay? Why isn't Auralia calling?" His heart stopped mid-beat, his breath clawed its way back into his lungs, unwilling to release. Gripped and suspended, Creed couldn't feel his body. He was momentarily unable to process the other side of the question, if it meant anything other than Auralia was alive and unharmed.

"Okay," she started, "you can't freak out on me."

Creed's soul left his body. He felt it fling itself free and then a moment later popped itself back like a rubber band, like his boyhood slingshot. And there he stood, as he morphed into a beast that wanted to race forward, ripping and tearing away anything that would keep him from Auralia's side.

"She's *unhurt*," Doli pronounced clearly.

The words sifted into his brain.

He repeated the word through a dry mouth, "Unhurt. You should lead with that one next time."

"Here's the situation, though," Doli said. "I'm going to put you on video so you can sort of see what I'm saying to you. The rain, though …"

His phone buzzed, asking for permission to take the encrypted video call, and he punched the button.

"Behind Mayor Early and Representative Braxton was Mrs. Morrison driving the family SUV. Her daughter was sitting beside her, and Shithead Morrison was crouching in the back so no one would see him leaving. I guess he thought that speaker bullet was aimed at him."

"I'm not getting much but geometric shapes and rain." Doli was talking to him and didn't lead with 'get here now,' so he planted his feet firmly on the belief that if Auralia was ever in need of him, he'd know it in his gut, and he'd race to her side.

He sent a feeler out in her direction, and he got "nervous"

and he got "busy," but he didn't pick up on any pain with what his battle buddies called his "mother's intuition."

That intuition had saved many of their hides on more than one occasion, so he didn't give a rat's ass what they called it.

"I thought that might be the case," Doli said. "There's not really a good way to show this to you right now. Just listen. When Mrs. Morrison plowed into the mayor's SUV, Auralia was swerving to avoid hitting them – it doesn't matter. It was more complicated than that. It was a mess. The point is Auralia's car hit Mrs. Morrison's SUV, and it went through the rails into the river."

"Okay, three people are in the water. Let me get that information to Logistics so they can send a fast water rescue team out here. The river's bound to be roiling from all that rain in the mountains."

"Yes. Creed, listen. Auralia's car went through the bridge rail. *Listen.* Before you panic, just listen. It rocked, then it stabilized. She told me to get out through the back window and start filming. I crawled out first. She's going to crawl out, too. I stopped to help some folks before I called you. Because … well, there are a lot of people doing really badly. Auralia, though, is unhurt. She's taking it slow and careful, and she asked me to let you know where we are and what's going on."

"List her injuries." Creed could sprint to the bridge and get to her in a matter of minutes. Were "minutes" good enough?

"Listen again. No injuries. Well, yeah, Auralia's face was abraded when the airbags went off. But no cuts, no complaints."

"She's okay." He pressed the words through a dam of agitation.

"She's going slow because she has to get out from under the steering wheel and over the back seat. And I saw her working on getting the bullet-resistant vest off. Which you'll agree makes sense."

"Perfect sense." Creed had shifted to a combat breathing cycle meant to keep his limbic system from going crazy so he could stay in the fight. "Her car's still on the bridge?"

"I was trying to show you a visual. It might be tipped to a sharper angle, but I can assure you it's still on the bridge."

"What about Morrison's SUV?"

"By the time I got out and looked over the edge—at that point the rain was coming down hard enough to obscure my visual field—I didn't see the SUV. With the current, I think it got washed down the river. From the map Auralia showed me earlier, the waterway thins as it flows around the outside of the field we were in. If that's the case, the car should be stuck, and everyone probably can crawl out. I haven't looked again. I've been busy staunching blood. Not mine. Other people's."

"Can you look again? I need to let rescue know."

"No, I can't let go of this leg. Some lady is holding the phone to my ear. Listen, I'm not talking to you as a reporter here. I'm guessing at what happened. I got out of Auralia's car, looked over the bridge to the extent that I felt safe, as the cars continued to shift with each new impact. I didn't see the SUV that went over. I'm guessing it's downriver. I haven't seen Auralia, and she hasn't called me, so I'm assuming she's still in the car and is moving carefully as she gets out from under the steering wheel and over the seat, then out the window."

"How far is the drop?" Creed asked.

"The distance was obscured by the heavy downpour. Do you want me to guess?"

"Yeah, I do."

"Okay. It's far down. But not far enough that I wouldn't have jumped off the bridge back in high school. Creed, honestly, there are so many people in dire straits right now, I'd keep on with your task and let Auralia figure out her situation. She was thinking about you as I was getting out of the car.

She's sure to call you the second she's got feet on the ground, so you know she's safe. What is your team doing?"

"I'm counting cars and counting heads. Gator's on triage. We've got tourniquets going on where needed and mylar blankets all around. Since you two aren't in immediate danger, I'm going to work my way toward the bridge, gathering this information and passing it on to emergency management as quickly as possible. But, Doli, you have to call me immediately if Auralia's car …" He couldn't form the words. He pushed the picture out of his mind.

How many times had he been in battle when, just over the ridge, his brothers were in real trouble, but accomplishing his task meant lives were saved?

He just needed to speed things along.

"Shit," Doli said, "they'll be pulling emergency equipment from the entire region. I don't know how they're going to get people out of here."

The phone buzzed through.

"Gotta go. Keep in close contact," Creed swiped the line open. "Creed here."

"Striker here. My Logistics rep says you've stopped moving. Sit rep." he was asking for a situation report.

"Getting an update on Auralia. Her car's dangling off the bridge."

"She good?"

"Doli, her camerawoman, got out the back window and said Auralia was going slow and careful. Uninjured." He took a moment to relay what Doli had said about the SUV going in.

"Auralia's got this. Where are we with numbers?"

"I see babies in car number eighteen. The parents are trapped."

"I have a nurse here. Walking wounded, but she's trapped in her car. I'm going to stay here and try to get her out. Another set of medically trained hands is crucial. I'll send her to car eighteen as soon as she's freed. Heads up, no one is paying the least attention to Jack, his whistle, or the flares. The pileup will continue, and the impacts will have a ripple effect beyond their collision. What's true now of our headcount and triage will change quickly.

"They've got to have it out on the area radio stations," Creed said.

"Do you know anyone who listens to local radio?" Striker asked. "Incoming, get back from the road!"

The squeal of tires as they locked into place, the sound of treads fighting against the forces of kinetic friction, speed clashed with the slick surface and gravity.

The air smelled thickly of burned rubber and chemicals.

Creed jumped up the embankment. He was too far away to see the impact, but car parts flew into the air and rained back down. The car with the babies was pushed forward.

"Status?" Striker asked.

"They were hit, the kids look fine in their booster seats. This is one for the record books."

"Who are you working with in operations?"

"Mandy," Creed replied.

"Have her enter the new coordinates for the vehicle with babies so the nurse can find them."

A woman's voice rose in a tone that wanted to be heard by whoever was on the line. "The nurse is called Karen—keep your jokes about my name out of your mouth. Yeah, you need to get me out of here so I can be helpful. Now listen, my church is a few miles from here. I called over there, and they're bringing in the choir bus. They can park it at the top of the hill and be a dry place for folks to set, while they're waiting for emergency services to get their butts in gear. Tell your Jack fellow that they're on the way, and they'll park in the middle of the goddamned highway if necessary. You can't ignore a bus. Even a shortie like we've got, it's still big and yellow."

"Yes, ma'am," Striker said off the phone. Then he was back, "Creed, I'm out." And the connection ended.

Creed tapped the call on hold. "Mandy, Creed here."

"I'm set up on my end. You're a go."

16

—————

Creed

Looking uphill toward the Iniquus van, the scene reminded Creed of the pictures he'd seen in history books of the great northwest, where the loggers would roll the felled trees into the river, floating them from the forests to the lumber mills. Sometimes, things went awry, and the logs jammed up, piled up, and kept coming.

He'd always thought that it was where loggerhead came from, logs that came to a head and couldn't move farther. He was disappointed that it was the name of a turtle.

Moving forward on his assigned task, Creed could see the bridge now. There was the pile-up of cars, and above that, he could just make out Auralia's car over the edge.

Creed took a picture and spread it wide to see the details more clearly.

Auralia was inside. He could see the top of her head.

The car looked stable. "Mandy, I'm sending you a picture of a car balanced on the bridge. Can you have the engineers assess the situation and get back to me ASAP? Single female, twenty-five, Auralia Rochambeau. Mandy," he paused as his heart galloped; he didn't want emotion to color his words, "it's Gator's sister."

"On it," Mandy said.

In Creed's experience, an "on it" from any of the teams that supported operators in the field was swift and comprehensive. Iniquus employed the best of the best because their bread and butter was saving lives. The lives they saved first were those that sheltered under the Iniquus employee blanket. Labeling Auralia as Gator's sister meant every resource available would be pressed into play. Creed had to be patient as the cogs moved into place. "Mandy, give an update to Gator's support to loop him in. Make sure he knows Auralia is *not* injured."

"Not injured. Wilco," she said as Creed was distracted by, "Striker here."

"Mandy, I'm putting you on hold, Striker's in my ear."

"Standing by."

Creed tapped the button on his phone and dropped the plastic case to his chest as he pressed his sternal button to open his mic. "Creed."

"Randy is moving up to take your place. Here's the situation: a man, bleeding profusely from the head and walking, and I quote, 'like a zombie,' climbed through his moonroof. He fell down the west-facing ditch, and the woman reporting thought he'd passed out there, but then he crawled out and kept on moving and disappeared into the woods. She said, and again I quote, 'he looked like a drunken banker.'"

A *drunken* banker? "Copy."

"Suit, hard-soled shoes. She says there's also an elderly woman who got out of the car and seemed to be trying to follow the man. She made it to the ditch, but she slipped. And has been gripping her back. She's pretty hysterical. And, it's raining on her."

"How are you hearing about this?" Creed asked.

"A member of the walking wounded made a recording and brought it to me as they made their way up the road."

"What's the priority?"

"Throw a Mylar around the woman," Striker said, "so she doesn't go hypothermic. See if you can calm her enough to find out why the guy took off into the woods. The only thing I can think of is that he's concussive and doesn't know where he is or what he's doing. He might also have some substance in his system that's affecting his behavior, but it could be anything. Maybe he's afraid that the cops will detect something when they get to his car. That's not interesting to us. We just need the guy found and escorted to the road. If he's walking, we can put him on the choir bus, though the bus filled up almost immediately after arrival. It's about to go deposit these crash victims at the church and come back to collect more."

"I'll grab Rou. We're on it."

"Sending you the PLS," Striker said, referring to the point the man was last seen.

A moment later, Creed's phone pinged. "PLS received. Moving. Out."

Creed jogged by his teammates. Blaze was ashen and determined as he tugged off a pair of Nitril gloves and shoved them in a hazard bag. Immediately, he pulled on a new set as he moved up to the next car that Gator had smashed while he was doing his triage. That broken window was Blaze's visual cue that someone inside needed a tourniquet.

This whole dystopian landscape looked crazy and unsurvivable, but Creed kept reminding himself that it was by design, the result of decades of engineering work, testing, and reworking. This was what brilliant minds had developed to absorb the impacts into the bodies of the cars and to keep protective cages around the passengers.

The destruction was the beauty, the safety, and the hope for those going through this hell.

Creed jogged past Striker, who was walking with a child on his hip, and a woman was tightly holding onto his side. They were making their way toward the minibus. It was a vital resource.

The smells of burning rubber, the sobbing cries, and the moans of pain filled Creed's senses.

Creed was hyper-aware of how many people were trapped in their vehicles for myriad reasons, and beneath the surface of his assessment was a wave of terror: What if one of these cars caught fire?

The flames would leap from car to car, gas tanks would explode, the people would burn to death, and there was nothing that could be done for them.

He hoped that the regional airport was sending in its fire engines, which could shoot fire-suppressing foam over the scene.

Until then, the risk was high.

At the van, Creed stopped long enough to put a bowl of water out for Rou. When she was on a task, she was so focused on the endgame that it was all but impossible for Creed to get her to stop and drink. Here at the van, he might be able to fool Rou into thinking they were taking a break.

He pulled her collapsible bowl from his pack and poured some water from his water bottle. Knowing Rou, once she got her nose on the trail, she wouldn't let up. This was Creed's chance to drink as well, so that his shirt didn't ping Mandy and tell her that he was dehydrated.

The technology of the wearables was fascinating.

Creed had been watching a video about the dental guards that women's Rugby players wore on the field. When a specific head motion occurred, the AI in the tiny chip inside the mouthguard could interpret it. If certain parameters were exceeded, the guard would light up, and the athlete would be pulled for a brain check.

While many brain injuries in the military were caused by blast concussion, wearing a mouth guard like that might be an important tool for post-mission health checks.

A similar technology was also appearing in various products, such as shoes for seniors and smartphones, which used accelerometers and gyroscope sensors to detect sudden movements, like falls.

Right now, Creed would- guaran-*damn*-tee that loved ones designated as ICE—in case of emergency—in the accident victim's contacts list were getting text messages letting them know there had been an accident.

Creed wondered if that was actually multiple text messages as the cars took hit after hit, piling one on top of the other, quite literally.

The Iniquus tactical shirt he was wearing took that idea a step further, monitoring everything from his temperature to his hydration levels and heart rate, among other metrics. It fed that information back to Logistics so they could monitor the safety of each operator, as adrenaline or concentration on the unfolding event could cause the operators to be unaware that something had gone awry.

Another feature of the shirt, which Creed didn't like to emphasize, was that if an operator died, the shirt would enter death mode. To conserve battery, it would turn off. Then, every thirty minutes, it would come briefly back online to send out a signal. In that way, his body would be recovered, and his family would have closure.

Closure was imperative, and that's why, long after the rescue part of a search and rescue became a recovery, it was every bit as imperative as a live find. The searchers went after it with the same sense of urgency.

The pain of a distraught family was unbearable to Creed.

When he was fighting in the war, he'd seen horror and pain, and it wore on him.

It started gnawing at his guts at night.

Sleep deprivation became his norm, and the only reason he didn't drink himself into a stupor or take drugs to ease the mental anguish was a promise he'd made to his mamma on the way to boot camp.

His mom was a wise woman who had witnessed the effects of life as a military family firsthand.

She'd told him, "Son, proud of you. But I will take a mother's privilege and extract a promise from you to solace me."

The look on her face, anguish that she tried to disguise as calm, and he would promise her anything to ease the suffering he knew he was going to cause her.

"No alcohol and no drugs. Not a drop. Not a dribble. Not a dram. Clean and sober."

"Yes, ma'am." And because of that oath, he'd told the men who made fun of him that they wanted someone who understood what it was to have a set of guiding principles, to have a creed and live by it. And one of his guiding principles was that his word was his bond, especially when it came to his mama. And in boot, they changed his name from Honoré to Creed, and it stuck for everyone because it just seemed to fit him like a well-worn glove.

Creed looked down where Rou sat like a soldier at his feet. Her head tipped back, and her body tensed. She knew from the shift in Creed's posture that they were about to get to work. And there was nothing that Rou liked better than to head out on a search.

The point on his map would pull Creed farther from Auralia, but having seen the car looking stable and knowing that better-informed eyes than his were assessing, relieved some of the pressure that was expanding his ribs.

"Part of the problem, Rourou," Creed said, "is that even if we find a cut through in this mess—which I don't see happening—taking it would be too big a risk. We can't do it, not with the cars that are still slipping and sliding down the hill. We'll have to jog to the top." Though Creed had noted that it had been a while since he'd last heard the shriek of brake and the bang and crash.

Creed had tried to figure out how long it would take for a siren and a badge with authority to stop the traffic and turn them around.

He knew that the police in this area divided the county and that the cars were distributed based on population, not by area. That meant there was one lone officer tooling around in his car, waiting for the call.

He also knew that when that call went out, it would be all hands on deck and they'd be racing from everywhere.

While it felt like much longer, it had been only about thirty minutes since their mission had switched from dell oversight to rescue. Creed was just now hearing the sirens scream out in the distance.

Creed put the phone to his ear. "Mandy, Rou and I are rerouting to the point uploaded to my map system. We will be starting a search there. I'll be functioning as a single searcher. My focus will be on Rou, and cell connectivity is intermittent in this area."

"I'm inputting that data. I've already downloaded the maps to your shirt. If you're offline, you can still follow the directions. Are you at a good point to start the tracking?"

"I'm getting prepped." Creed twisted the top back on his bottle. "The engineer?" he asked.

"Looking at Auralia's car? They're putting it through computer modeling to include the local weather conditions and wind dynamics over that type of bridge."

The wind was steady with heavy gusts, and that was what he was afraid of. One big blow could come over the bridge and catch the undercarriage of the car, tipping it end over end.

Or, Auralia could have climbed free already.

That was the picture he wanted to hold in his mind for her.

He didn't want to conjure danger or pain. He'd hold her in hope.

He pulled up to the table of life, and he found sustenance. Not showy, not five-star restaurant fare, cause that didn't feed the body and soul the way a plate could be filled with an honest day's work. And around that table, there were places laid for all the people that he cared deeply for and who cared equally for his best.

And now, he and Auralia would tell all those people about how deeply they loved one another.

Gator's nonchalance about Creed's being in love with Auralia was a burden relieved. He'd felt that his secrecy was a lie of omission that he would never have taken on except that he'd been raised to allow the lady to decide what was publicly said about her and the relationship she was in. His mamma would have taken him to task if he did anything that might sully any woman's reputation.

His mamma, Creed shook his head, she was going to be thrilled.

Rich. He was the richest of men. He just wished to hell that Auralia would call in and tell him she was okay.

And as if he'd sent out an etheric signal, his phone buzzed with a call from Auralia's phone.

"Mandy, stand by." Creed switched calls. "Shit, woman!"

"Yeah," Auralia exhaled. "I guess Doli got hold of you."

"Are you okay?"

"Just hanging around for the moment. I wanted to let you hear my voice so you could focus on the people who need you most. Is Rou with you?"

"We're getting ready for a search. Somebody seems to be concussive and wandered into the woods."

"In this rain? Shit. Get out there, Creed. What the hell are you doing talking to me?"

He chuckled.

"I love you. Be safe."

"Love you. Be safest." When she hung up, Creed tapped Mandy. "Mandy, that was Auralia calling in. Let Gator's support know I heard her voice, and she's okay for now."

17

———

Creed

Creed scanned the horizon on the top of the hill before he sprinted Rougarou across the four-lane highway, slowing to check the distance to the red point on his topo map.

Rou was ridiculous in her little red shoes with matching socks.

The Cerberus trainer, Reaper Hamilton, had just introduced them to Rou's training, so on the upcoming hot summer days, standing on the macadam and sniffing out the crowds, little Rourou didn't scald her paw pads.

Rou hadn't quite figured out how to navigate the new sensation. To say she was clownish as she moved down the road was an understatement.

With a bit of time and a job to perform, Rou would shift her focus away from the odd addition to her paws, but so far, she wasn't yet distracted enough to forget she was wearing them.

As Rou ran along, each step went too high or too sideways as she hopped and popped and waggled, trying to figure out how to move forward in a straight line.

She was lifting her hind legs with a kick, kick, hop, then the other side, kick, kick, kick, hop, followed by some fancy prancing with her front paws that included a little wave, as if she were a movie star working the red carpet at a gala, greeting her fans.

Ridiculous and endearing, the teams would stop to watch and get a good chuckle during training.

Under these circumstances, while she was keeping up with Creed, she was burning energy. But with the glass and metal pieces peppered across the area, he wasn't risking an injury.

"That must be the woman up there, Rou."

She was sitting on the edge of the road, with her legs dangling down into the gutter below. The weeds, left unmown for months, spiked up around the thickness of her soft body. The kind of body that reminded Creed of summers on the porch, sitting with the neighborhood elders as he snapped beans and listened to them sing. It was the kind of soft body that gave hugs that he could remember wrapped around him like a blanket when he was lying in the desert listening to the bombs explode and wondering how he had found himself so far from home.

Creed made sure to call the woman's attention to his approach so he didn't startle her. In his search and rescue classes, he'd learned that Cerberus often got called out to assist on local searches, and there were three main subjects in this area—those with dementia, children with autism, and (to be frank) men doing dumb shit in the woods.

The elder had wrapped her arms around herself and was rocking side to side, making a humming sound as she self-soothed.

"Ma'am?" Creed said, warming his voice and adding a dash of confidence and capability.

She jerked, then shifted his way. Putting her hands on either side of herself, she rocked harder, this time to gain momentum to stand.

"No need to get up, ma'am. I'm coming to you." He put his hand to his chest. "I'm Creed Duchamp. This is my search and rescue dog, Rougarou."

"That little thing with her too-big paws? She's trained to look for people?"

"She's a star," Creed said with a grin, seeing that she was trying to tease, though her eyes were red-rimmed with crying.

"My grandson, Parker, was in the car with me, and we were in kind of a protected place there." She hitched a thumb over her shoulder to the sedan pressed at the trunk between the car in front and the one in the back.

"Looks like you almost maneuvered yourself out of that mess." He pulled out the emergency blanket, along with the disposable plastic poncho that he'd prepositioned in his pocket.

"I was doing a three-point turn, just not quite enough room or time. But I tried. Anyway, Parker, my grandson, hit his head pretty hard. I told him we needed to sit quietly in the car until the rescue workers came. Well, that only lasted for so long. He went out through the moonroof. He never could stand to be caught in places. Claustrophobia, you know. But when he got out, he wasn't himself. He walked in the wrong direction, out toward those woods. Silly me, I took off after him. Slipped on the gravel, now I'm down for the count. A man from further up in the accident was heading up the road. I asked him to get help, and he made a video. He said he'd seen earlier in the day that there was a search and rescue team at the event." She looked Creed up and down. "Beggars can't be choosers, but when I heard 'team' I thought something other than a man and his puppy."

"Star puppy," Creed smiled as he wrapped the Mylar blanket around the woman. "I want to get on Parker's trail as fast as I can. So let's go through a few things, please."

She held the sides together in a fist. "Ask away, and thank you. This here is a blessing."

"Your grandson's name is Parker. How old?" He pulled the poncho from its plastic packet.

"Oh, let's see, I think that one was thirty-six on his last birthday. Maybe thirty-seven. I'm an old woman, and I have almost a dozen grandchildren and four great-grandchildren. It's hard to keep track."

"I'm going to pull this over your head to cut the wind and keep you dry." He opened the poncho. "Can you tell me what kind of shoes he was wearing?"

"Flat-bottomed, go-to-church shoes. We were there for the late service, then stopped for a bite to eat at the diner back in town."

"Do you have a picture of him?"

She shook her head.

"Okay, that's okay. What was he wearing? Is it appropriate for a day like today?"

"He had on his church suit. He left his overcoat in the car."

"I'll take that with me." And as Creed found the man's dress coat draped over the driver's seat, he watched Rou give her coat a good shake. In this drizzle, Parker would be wet too. "Does Parker have a change of clothes and rain gear in your car?"

After Creed had gathered the information he needed, he offered Rou the coat to scent before putting it in his pack, then they went off into the woods.

Rou, nose to the ground, seemed to be tracking easily.

It was good luck that they were following before the weather had a significant impact on the scent cone.

The rain, as heavy as it had come down, though brief, dripped from the overhead evergreen needles and the bare deciduous limbs, still winter-naked. The forest floor was undisturbed for the most part. Parker wouldn't slip on the carpet of needles that tend to roll and slide underfoot when wet, threatening a twist or sprain.

The head trauma was Creed's biggest concern.

That, and if Creed found Parker non-ambulatory, there was no help to be had.

No sense in using brain cells to anticipate next steps; he had no idea what condition he'd find Parker.

While searching for Jeb in the woods earlier, Creed had found fault with the technology that allowed him to trace the zigzagging trail Rou had followed as she lost and then regained her scent. Now that he was jogging into more difficult terrain, he could see the benefit. During the search and rescue training sessions the team conducted in the Virginia mountains, Creed found that the leaf debris was thick and often hid naturally occurring pockets and holes in the ground.

How many times had he been on searches when his foot unexpectedly went down into a hole? It could easily take a searcher off the playing field, and worse, pull resources to him instead of focusing them on the lost person. A searcher's weight, plus the weight of the resource pack he carried, typically filled with bivouacking supplies along with Rou's needs and first aid equipment, meant that the body created a forward momentum that resisted stopping.

A body in motion—The sudden shift from go to stop meant wrenched knees, twisted ankles, and snapped tendons. A responder could train—and they did, they trained hard at Cerberus with athletic trainers who taught their bodies how to be both stable and dynamic—but a hole was a hole was a hole.

Nothing to be done about the hole other than hopefully shake it off and keep going.

This was more like war. Everyone was out on parallel missions, doing their best to handle the situation at hand.

Here, Creed was alone in his efforts to find and protect Parker.

Should he have a stick to prod? Yes.

Was he going to take the time to be prim about this shit?

Speed.

All else be damned.

Just like earlier in the day when Rou found Jeb, the howling "Come here!" bark went up.

Stepping around a massive rhododendron, Creed found a man, blood running down his head and soaking his white collar, sitting stupefied on the ground.

"Good girl, Rou," Creed said, approaching softly.

The problem was immediately apparent. The man had stepped into a trap. "Rou, wait." Creed took off his pack and laid it at his feet. Then he picked up a sturdy stick to probe the area and make sure that there weren't more traps that might cause harm.

It looked horrific as the teeth bit through the man's dress pants, now wet with blood.

"I'm Creed with Iniquus, here to help. You've already met my pup, Rou. I'm trained in first aid. Do I have permission to help?" He pulled out his first aid kit and pulled on gloves.

No response.

Creed began his mental orientation questions. "What's your name?" he asked as he pulled out his wound dressing supplies.

The man stared off as if he couldn't hear. His grandmother said she didn't know of any disabilities or health concerns.

"Do you know where you are?" Creed draped the sterile cloth over the wound.

"Can you tell me what day it is?"

Not a blink. Not a flutter.

"What happened to you?" as Creed wrapped Parker's head with gauze bandaging, he hoped to provide enough pressure on the wound that he could free up his hands for other tasks.

Not ideal.

Creed was recalling the time his family went inland to hunt deer to stock up the freezer with sausage meat. One of the boys from the farm stepped into a rusty trap just like this one. It was the first and only one Creed had ever seen. He'd known since he was a boy how to set out a snare made out of wire and sticks to catch rabbits, and other small critters to add to the stew pot, but that damned thing had been terrifying with its rusted jaws and sharp teeth.

When it snapped, his cousin's howl was otherworldly.

He looked the trap over and couldn't see the mechanism for release.

It clapped shut, he reasoned, so it couldn't be rusted to the point where he couldn't get it back open.

His first instinct was to grab hold and wrench it open.

The last thing he wanted to do was more damage.

Rou had squirmed into the man's lap, and then Parker, much to Creed's surprise, pulled Rou tight to his chest.

Rou seemed fine with that.

Creed pulled his phone from his thigh pocket and called Mandy. "Creed here. I've located the missing subject, Parker. Parker is conscious and oriented zero out of four."

"Is he ambulatory?" Mandy asked.

"Right now," Creed said, taking a knee to inspect the device, "his foot is caught in what looks like an old-timey bear trap."

"Creed, repeat last," Mandy said after a pause, "did you say the vehicle crash victim has stepped in a bear trap?"

"Yes, ma'am. This one has to be from back around the nineteen hundreds or so because it has teeth. Big ones. I've seen a modern trap opened. I need instructions on how to proceed. I don't want to make any mistakes on this one and have it clamp down on him, causing further damage. I'm opening my video so you can see for yourself."

Creed held his phone out, moving it slowly back and forth.

"Creed, standby, let me see if anyone has expertise. I'm not equipped to support this particular situation."

"That's you and me both," Creed said under his breath.

18

———

Creed

A LONG MOMENT WENT BY, THEN MANDY WAS BACK IN HIS EAR, "Creed, I've added Tamara Bailing to our Parker team. Be advised, I have communicated the situation to Striker. He has sent two teammates to your location with a stretcher. I'm handing you over to Tamara."

"Creed? Tamara here, I'm on the engineering staff. That's a vintage trap from around the nineteen hundreds. They are generally more dangerous than modern traps because they lack contemporary safety features. Mainly, the problem was that they are indiscriminate, catching anything that walks over top. And looking at the images, it's hard to see the damage to the victim's ankle. Is the trap attached to something?"

Camera in hand, Creed followed the chain to a stake that had been driven into the soil, and a tree had formed around it. "I have cutters that will probably go through this."

"That's the question. Hey, Doc," Tamara called, "I need you here for decision-making."

"What are we looking at here?"

Came a fourth voice.

"Creed, Cerberus team Charlie. I was on a search and rescue for a middle-aged male. He stepped into the trap that you see on your screen. He's wearing hard-soled shoes and dress pants. There is blood being absorbed by the pants. The question is how do I move forward, being of the most help and causing the least amount of trauma."

"Tamara," the doctor asked, "what can be done about getting the man out of the trap? What are the risks?"

"Looking at it, obviously, it's rusted. Medically, that can be handled when Parker gets to a hospital. Structurally, though, it makes opening the trap risky. My concern is that those old steel parts may be brittle, and an attempt to open the jaws may cause them to snap back, creating more damage."

"What kind of force are we talking about here?" Doc asked.

"One that size was made to hold a large animal," Tamara said. "Given the location, I'm assuming it was set out for a bear or a wild boar. The closing mechanism can crush bones, dislocate joints, lacerate muscles and tendons, and break the skin. Creed sees blood."

"Can you tip the phone up, please, Creed, and let me see the man's face?" Doc asked.

Creed thought the guy looked like he'd left his body. That happened sometimes on the battlefield. When their teammate Deep dove out of the way of the grenade and he was burned over much of his body, he had the same look on his face. It wasn't shock; shock had its own white-faced, slack look. This was like the man's body was vacant. Like his soul slipped away from its earthly vessel and was sitting off on a tree stump somewhere, watching.

Rou had settled with her chin draped over the man's shoulder, and Creed thought that if this was shock, his doggo's body heat would help.

"Given your present situation, you and your team will have to carry this guy out. Any instability of the trap can further damage the leg. I think if Creed can get it off, it's best that it come off. Creed, you'll want to have your first aid kit out. Any bleeding needs to be packed. The foot and leg need to be immobilized. Emergency management is bringing in lighting systems because they plan to be at this all night, so you won't get much help up on the road. Don't wait for the ambulance crew. If you can get him into a civilian car on the other side of the pile-up, he needs to be treated quickly. We need to get hands-on to preserve his future mobility. Tell his transport to take him to a hospital in D.C. Give Mandy a rundown of what you're finding, so they can get staff prepped for his arrival. Does he have support there?"

"His grandmother is among the wounded."

"Doc!" The call was urgent from the other side of the room.

Creed now had Mandy and Tamara as his support.

"Here's what you're going to do, Creed," Tamara said. "Go ahead and get your first aid station set up. Then get your leather gloves out. I'll hold."

"Tamara, if it's helpful," Mandy said. "My search indicates that's probably a vintage Bradly-McGuire long-spring bear trap."

"Let me read that," Tamara replied.

Creed worked on pulling his equipment from his bag and setting it up for a one-handed grab. "I'm prepped."

"This is going to take significant force," Tamara said. "You'll want to make sure that your body mechanics are on point. Make sure that there's nothing that's going to stab into your knee, nothing that is going to come loose and make you slip, or the ground give way. You'll want to position yourself straight on so that either arm of the long spring is lined up with your hands. Imagine that you're going to perform chest compressions. Straight arms, using your body weight as well as your strength. Do you think the victim will be able to pull his foot free once it's open?"

"No," Creed still thought Parker's soul was floating out in the tree branches overhead, watching all this.

"And no one's there who can assist? The grandmother?" Tamara asked.

"The team will be here soon. Parker's losing quite a bit of blood between his head wound and the leg."

"Give me a second, let me think this through," Creed said. "I need to rig something."

Creed and Parker were the only humans around, but he had Rou. In his mind, Creed went through the various skills that Rou had been developing with Cerberus, trying to figure out which ones could be combined to work in this circumstance.

He finally had a plan in place. He pulled a roll of tarred bankline from his daypack. He unwound a length and then tossed the line up and over a tree limb above where a branch was located, so the cordage wouldn't slip.

Creed took one end of the loose line and slipped it under the crook of the man's knee and tied it below the patella in the front. Walking over to the roll, Creed pulled more length free, then cut it and tied it to Rou's water bowl, setting it down a few inches away.

In his mind's eye, this was going to work fine.

Would he have liked to have tested the theory?

Damned straight.

Would he leave this man in agony for a second longer than absolutely necessary?

Hell to the no.

He was winging it. "St. Jude of desperate situations, I call on you again," he mouthed as he reflexively made the sign of the cross. "Alright, Tamara, I'm set up." He said into his phone that lay in the dirt, giving his helpers a view of the gray sky."

"Creed, you're going to use the heel of your hand and slowly exert pressure until you've compressed the bands of steel and they come together. That should open the teeth."

Creed talked to Parker the whole time. He told him what was happening, and though he hated doing it, Creed called Rou to him. Rou did as she was instructed, though it was with obvious reluctance.

"Rou, get your bowl."

Once again, aware that the strange red shoes still wrapped her feet, Rou side-kicked and danced, making her way to the bowl.

Creed shot a glance at Parker to see if her antics caught his attention. But he was still gone.

Rou picked up her bowl and turned to Creed for her next assignment. "Rou, hold."

With a final adjustment of his knees, Creed took a deep breath and pressed down, doing as he'd been instructed, keeping his arms straight and using his weight. And the damned thing didn't budge.

Not even a little bit.

Slowly, Creed released his breath and lifted his weight from the sides, easing back onto his heels. "Fail," he called out.

"Nothing?" Tamara asked.

"Affirmative. It didn't budge."

"Do you have any oil, a lubricant?" Tamara asked.

"Affirmative. I have a penetrating oil."

"Try that. Just keep it away from any lacerations."

Creed had reached for his bag and pulled out the small bottle, dribbling the formula around all the places that he wanted to move.

He checked in on Parker, and he was still out of his body. He hadn't even moved or shifted when Rou got down from her place in his lap.

Creed spun to look over his shoulder, and little Rou sat like a soldier with her bowl in her mouth.

"Going in again," Creed said as he once again adjusted, inching up a bit and curling his toes under so he could hike his hips into the air as if he were getting ready to dive off the high board.

Creed placed his palms down, and this time, as he pressed, he thrust into his toes, driving them into the ground with the strength of his thigh muscles, shoving everything he had into compressing the level.

It gave, and wobbled.

He'd hoped that once it was open, there would be a catch that held it in place. He hadn't seen a mechanism to do that; it just made sense to him that it would be part of the design.

Creed pressed harder into his toes as he growled and flexed his muscles into action, and the teeth spread out to release Parker's pants.

"Rou!" Creed panted his command. "Back up. Pull. Back up. Pull."

He couldn't see what she was doing, but the string overhead grew taut.

"Good girl, Rou. Pull hard. Pull. Back up."

And little Rou dragged and tugged until the string pulled Parker's leg up. Yes, there was an angle to it. No, it wasn't by any stretch of the imagination perfect. But Creed was able to shimmy and adjust the trap so that Parker's foot could come free.

Then, leaning his weight onto his left hand, Creed shifted his right hand under the man's slick-soled shoes to make sure it was clear of the trap as it snapped back in place.

"Good girl, Rourou. Release."

Once again, there was slack in the line.

Creed kicked the closed trap out of the way and eased Parker to the ground, laying him flat on his back.

"Rou, come cuddle." Creed snapped his fingers and pointed at the man. The day was chilly, made even colder by the gusts of wind. And Rou's warmth would help until Creed could get the man's leg stabilized.

Rou didn't have to be told twice, though the way she hopped and danced her way forward made her look like a court jester or the town drunk.

"Parker is clear from the trap."

From the phone line, Creed heard the high fives and sighs of relief from Mandy and Tamara.

With his rescue shears, Creed cut Parker's dress pants from the cuff to the knee. He carefully unlaced his shoe, pulled it free, and then cut into the sock.

Creed had already decided that he would treat this as a worst-case scenario. He was walking a tight rope here. With Parker being uncommunicative, Creed didn't know if he should call the man's attention back to the situation or let him cope as best he could in his own mind. Creed simply didn't have enough information.

He decided to narrate to the wind, to tell the tree what he was doing and what it might feel like. "There is a bleeding cut. I'm going to put gauze over the cut and apply pressure to stop the flow of blood. This is the gauze. Here is more gauze. And the last piece of gauze. Now I'm applying pressure all the way around the leg with my big hands. This pressure is to stop the blood.

Each and every step, he told the trees.

He kept his voice gentle but firm, conveying that he was there to be kind but dependable.

Was he doing the right thing?

He had no idea.

But the drips that the wind shook loose on the way in gave way to a sky that was opening back up.

Getting Parker stabilized and back to shelter took on a dangerous urgency.

And to Creed's deep relief, Jack and Deep moved into view, carrying a stretcher between them.

Deep called out. "The evacuation team is on the scene."

19

———

Auralia

"Here goes nothing," Auralia mumbled under her breath.

The car had been stable. The rain had shifted to a pitter-pat.

It had been her intention to be ready but stay put. Eventually, rescue workers would arrive on the scene, and she had an advantage in her position. She was close to the truck that had caused this whole thing.

Initially, this seemed like a good approach because the rescue workers would park on the side of the road and jog forward to assess the situation. And she was in a very visually precarious situation. They'd want to get lines on her right away.

As time went on, that hope dimmed.

First of all, what the heck was going on with these drivers?

Sure, it was country driving. And country driving was long and often dull. These were all roads that the folks out this way could drive blindfolded. The problem was that people were driving by rote, not paying a lick of attention to what was out in front of them.

From either side of the bridge, there had been a string of squeals and strikes.

Luckily, that had stopped.

By using her mirrors and phone, Auralia could see other cars sticking up at odd angles. It was like playing her beloved childhood game of pick-up sticks, only these results had to be devastating.

The pile-up was catastrophic.

That shift in the probability of getting some support was certainly one of the reasons that Auralia was rethinking her strategy.

The other was the wind.

It had picked up considerably. And her car, with its flat bottom sitting up there like a sail, would feel the sustained press. One good gust and she'd go over.

Over might be fine.

Might even be preferred.

With the passage of time, her calculations were changing. Not only were the water levels creeping higher, but equally concerning, the sun was setting.

In the water in daylight? A crisis.

Trying to survive rushing white waters under the dark skies of a new moon? Possibly cataclysmic.

Yes, over the rail might have been fine, unless her car flipped and she was trapped upside down in the cab.

Over the rail might have been fine when there was enough water to act as a sort of cushion to ease her down.

But she'd missed that window of opportunity.

Not only was the water higher, but it was also faster.

What she could see of the shoreline had been gobbled by munching waves. The water had risen to a point where the drop off was sheer and slick with clay. No one was moving up or down that slope. She'd have to find some bit of land that still rose above and perch there and make a new determination.

And because hypothermia fogged the brain quickly, she'd have to be aggressive about her actions to stay warm. And that meant she couldn't sustain any injury.

Now, like all the Rochambeau children, Auralia could swim before she could walk. But fast water with only a black bag of air shoved under her chest and held in place by her armpits, dragging her clothes along wasn't ideal.

She had her phone. Her phone still worked.

She'd avoided all but that one, brief check-in with Creed.

If she got hold of anyone from Iniquus, they'd stop what they were doing and prioritize her.

Did she love that idea? Yes!

In fact, no.

Still, she'd call even if it was selfish because she didn't want to die.

She was privileged in that she had the connection.

Auralia didn't want to go in. Survival seemed improbable.

She needed to chance the back window and see if there wasn't a handhold she could grab onto.

Bracing with one hand, she toggled the button that slowly, slowly moved the driver's seat backward.

She paused. Where the seatbelt had compressed before, it had been the anxiety she experienced in many yoga poses. She knew from her daily practice that the calmer she could remain, the better she would be able to navigate to the other side of this fiasco.

Whew, the anxiety of her precarious position lit panic in her brain like a match to dry kindling.

Auralia fought to stay in the moment and to process. Panic or freeze was life-threatening, and the danger of both had become a ratatatat at her temples and oddly in her sinus cavity.

She hadn't had an expectation for how her body would move in space while she adjusted her seat. The idea had been to keep things as even keel as possible. Moving weight in a straight line toward the back of the car seemed reasonable, but shifting to the side, out from under the wheel, and then back through the tiny crawl space seemed jarring.

Doli had done it, but Doli was serpent-like in her ability to move her body. She was as fluid as the ribbon of a rhythmic gymnast.

Auralia was athletic and trained hard for survival's sake, as well as for the pleasure of strength; she didn't have Doli's hypermobility. She wasn't convinced that she could slither to the back seat without causing the car to rock.

Pulling a knee off the ground, she wedged her leg against the steering wheel. She stilled and waited for the gust to still. The car seemed to handle one change agent; she didn't want to push the boundaries.

Slowly, she lifted her right hand to wrap around the metal posts of her headrest. It was a squeeze to get all four fingers into place.

So far, so good.

She raised her left hand and was able to wrap just her index finger into place.

She'd forgotten the seatbelt.

Auralia pressed her lips together as she scolded herself for forgetting a step. Every movement felt like she was taunting fate.

How to move forward? She was a little stuck.

Finally, Auralia wished she hadn't put both of the black bags in the back.

She'd done it for fear of the plastic getting over her nose and mouth, and if she blacked out, she'd never wake up.

It would be unforgivable for her to die and put so many loved ones into churning grief. Creed and Gator would blame themselves for not saving her, and that would become a life-long burden.

I'm going to survive this. I just need to think clearly and

choose wisely, and then hope that my guardian angel didn't go off on a damned coffee break.

She lowered her hand, knowing that she would take more of her weight onto it, and pressed her leg harder against the steering wheel.

The release came with a gust of wind.

Back and forth, back and forth she teetered.

The car slid an inch, and her stomach dropped with the lurch.

As the wind abated, she pressed her leg and pulled her hand until she could tuck her knees and swing both bare feet onto the steering wheel.

Crouched, she reached for the back window as she straightened her legs.

But she was stumped because she seemed to be dangling from her back tires. Yes, that last slip and slide seemed to catch or latch or something. Something was different.

She should have set the hand brakes to lock the rear tires.

Honestly, what would stop them from simply rolling over the rail?

Fatal mistake?

Breathe. "You can't fix that now." It hadn't even occurred to her until she tried to imagine if dangling from her tires was a good thing. The physics of this said no; this wasn't good at all, mainly because the rear window wasn't over land anymore.

The only thing Auralia could think to do was to turn over onto her belly and reach a hand out the window for the rail, let the bags go—there was no way for her to take her things with her—get the other hand out of the window onto the rail, pull her body out of the car to dangle over the raging river. Could she do a pull-up? Adrenaline might help, but the thickness of the rail meant that she would have to cup the top of it. They weren't painted, and they were wet, so they were probably slick. If someone was on the bridge and could grab her wrists, that would be helpful, but surely that was wishful thinking, because anyone on the bridge was either injured or actively helping someone else.

And it was dangerous as hell to be possibly half in and half out of the vehicle if it decided to drop into the water.

There were no easy choices here, but one thing she felt for sure was that if the car was going over into the water, she wanted to be face down with a firm hold on the headrest and her feet thrusting into the steering wheel.

And while the safety belt seemed like it was the safest bet, Auralia was glad she was free of it because traumatic asphyxia, caused by pressure to the chest and restricted blood flow, was deadly.

And dead was dead, no matter the cause.

Auralia started the process of rolling over. When she moved, she tried to counter her weight and keep her body from jarring the car loose.

It was so slow.

It sucked her attention like a sponge, and she was oblivious to anything else happening. There was no sound, no color, no fear. She had entered into a space of sensation alone as she asked her blood not to throb through her veins with such velocity so that the beat of her heart didn't tip her into the water and end the *beats* of her heart.

Once Auralia's hip bones settled against the seat back—perspiration dripping from under her armpits and in a rivulet down her spine—she tucked her chin and gripped the seat, working to pull more oxygen into her lungs.

This was better. She could stand here at this angle with her bags gripped so tightly in her fist that her fingers had turned white and her joints had locked into a claw.

But looking out toward the place on the rail where she'd hoped to put her hands, Auralia realized it was way too far away. She could make it if she were an orangutan, but even then, the splintered metal would slice her.

Devastating.

It felt like a blow.

A loss.

A personal spit in the face by the Fates.

And when the next gust blew across and under the bridge, the wheels turned.

And as the car plummeted toward the roaring waters, in her mind Auralia screamed, "Creed!"

20

———————

Auralia

THE MOMENTS FROM UP TO DOWN DIDN'T EXIST IN AURALIA'S brain.

She had no sense of time or her body in space.

If she were injured, adrenaline had masked it.

Somehow, her knees were in the seat and her elbows were on the back of the seat that had been lowered to its full extent when she was dangling from the bridge, and her ass was pressed into the steering wheel, the yoga "child's pose" of car accidents.

Outside, the water boiled a few inches below her open window.

Auralia came to her knees and leaned as far as she could out of the window, dragging the black bag with her clothes and phone out into air as thick and heavy as a wet sponge.

She flung the weight toward the front of the car and whipped it back toward the trunk, which had popped open in the tumble. She let the velocity of her swing carry the clothes bag into the bowl of the trunk. Once it successfully landed, she let go of the knot and worked to catch her breath.

This moment was replete with anxiety.

The way the current broke at the back of the car, the roiling foam along the sides made her worried that it would form a suction and pull her under.

Sitting around bonfires, entertaining each other with stories, the adults used to scare the children with tales of those who drowned in the Gulf and how their spirits washed up on the shore. There was always the story of the person who survived the original impact but was drawn under the waves by the suction of the boat.

Creed's dad told one of those stories to explain away the *feu follet*, the ghost lights that could sometimes be seen over the water. They were glowing orbs that appeared at night in the Bayou. His Mémère said that *feu follet* were spirits playing tricks, trying to spark people's curiosity, enticing them deeper and deeper into the winding Bayou until they were hopelessly lost, and there they died. The lights just tested naughty children to see if they could be lured to their death—a cautionary tale.

Creed's father, whom everyone called Papa Jacques, said, "No, the *feu follet* weren't to be feared; they were to be pitied." He believed the lights that glowed bright and hung in the fog right where a lantern would hang from an outstretched arm were the souls of unbaptized babies trapped in limbo, and of course, the souls of drowned folks who went out to catch dinner and never went back.

Auralia remembered that when she heard those stories, she'd started to cry. She was a little thing in this memory, maybe seven or eight years old. Creed had come over with a blanket and wrapped her tight, kneeling to look at her earnestly. "You know, Jean-Marie and I were talking about this. And you know that your brother is supposed to see clearly, that's what Miss PittyPat told us, you remember that day?"

She'd nodded her head with a wobbly chin as she tried not to cry because she wanted to seem brave to Honoré

"Jean Marie says they're part of the fairy realm, and they show up to cast protection on the land and sometimes try to lead a lost person to safety. So they weren't leading them to their death but showing them the way home. I'm thinking Jean-Marie's right and that the lost person was just too far away to get to safety before the morning came and the light dimmed."

"I'm not scared," Auralia had whispered. "I'm sad for all the families who cried."

Why the hell am I thinking about *feu follet*?

That memory shifted through Auralia's mind as she, gripping her bag of air tightly in one fist, brought her right leg out the window and down into the water.

Something in the river wrapped her ankle and tugged.

HER BRAIN, primed for something otherworldly, shrank into a tiny ball in her cranium.

A scream ripped from her lungs, and she sent it winging out in a cloud of horror that was whipped through the air and sailed downriver.

Auralia's arm spasmed out as she reflexively caught hold of the headrest on the driver's seat and clung to it with an iron grasp.

Something had grabbed hold of her ankle and was walking up her leg.

She squeezed her eyes shut. There was no obvious explanation for the weight that wanted to drag her from the car.

Something was hand-over-hand moving up her leg.

With her memories already tuned to Bayou legend, her

imagination conjured the rotting flesh of a drowned person come to life.

That Auralia didn't piss herself was a miracle.

She couldn't fathom this sensation.

She screamed again as a head emerged beside her, the current shifting to make way for this new obstacle on its journey.

A man, hair streaming with water, clung to her knee.

In shock, Auralia couldn't move. Couldn't register. Couldn't breathe.

The man, holding tight to her leg, swung his head around, gauging, assessing, and planning, before he pulled harder on her calf to leverage his own feet onto the side of her car and launched himself out to the side toward the opposite shore, some ten or fifteen feet away.

Did he realize she was there?

Did he register that her leg was the rope he used to climb to safety?

She sat there in shock, willing herself back in her body, back to the present, back to reality so she could understand this scene.

Had he been whipped down with the turbulent waters and happened to catch on to something?

Perhaps he was half-drowned, and he, too, had adrenaline brain, where everything that wasn't connected to survival disappeared.

He pulled himself onto a rock and stumbled forward. Barefooted, in dress pants and a button-down shirt, Auralia realized that it was Morrison.

And only then did Auralia remember that the family's SUV had plunged over the side of the bridge railing ahead of her car.

The current must not have washed their vehicle downriver the way she'd imagined.

As she'd dangled over the edge, there was nothing in her

visual field that was beneath her other than water. In her mind, the family had been fine following the plunge. Modern-day high-end vehicle engineering being what it was with the surround of airbags, she thought that as they plunged, they'd float off. And as they did, the family followed the four steps for surviving a car in the water: putting the windows down, unfastening the seat belt, exiting the car, and assisting the person in the vehicle.

Or, if not that, then the family took a crazy ride around the curve that made the dell. They hit the shore and climbed out just fine.

To her horror, Auralia realized that from her vantage point, dangling in her car, she simply couldn't see them below, where the family was fighting for survival.

She had been yards away as a family struggled to stay alive.

When her own car went over the edge, it hadn't landed on a rock outcropping or a sand bar as she'd assumed. She must have landed on the Morrison's vehicle.

Auralia's body contracted as if she braced to take a blow. She stuck her head through the window and pushed her neck around until she could see the bridge the most clearly, making sure that another car wasn't about to be jammed forward and come down on top of her head as she escaped her own predicament.

It seemed clear.

No bumpers were visible, at least. Also, no one came and leaned out to see what the screaming was all about.

Two cars over, and the injuries up top must be significant if there were no bystanders and no curiosity. After all, it wasn't every day that two cars flew off a bridge.

The dad escaped.

There he stood on the bank with his hands on his knees, sucking in air to fill his lungs, coughing and hacking, and spitting out water.

When he stood, he looked up the hill, planning his route out of there.

He didn't look up and around to see if any helpers could get involved in a rescue.

Most confusing to Auralia, he didn't look back at the cars in the river. He didn't see Auralia in the back seat of her own vehicle, with her leg dangling into the rushing waters.

That meant one of two things. Either Morrison's family was dead and he knew it, or he left his family to die.

Auralia's instinct was to go over the side and check for herself.

But some inner warning system reminded her that, as hard as it was, slow and steady was the way to win the race.

She needed to get to the shore. There, she could better assess and make decisions about a rescue effort.

Though time was precious, her mentor Remi's voice was the little bird in her ear, "*Thinking* saves lives, especially yours. Take the time to evaluate and plan, then go."

Auralia decided the fastest thing to do was to follow her original plan.

Auralia's next task was to get herself into that cavity.

One of her roadblocks would be that there was no room to step into the trunk cavity. In there, she kept two bins. One barely had anything in it; it was simply her day-hike pack with "Survival Ten" items that she'd never go into nature without. She'd heard a hundred tales of search and rescue missions that would have been successful had they just gone out prepared. And if only to save herself from becoming an ancestral cautionary tale whispered around the bonfire back home with the tree frogs singing their lament.

Once she reached shore, that pack might be extremely help-ful. That, and the bin it was packed in was watertight. Bonus.

The other bin taking up space back there was from a recent camping trip with a bunch of friends. She hadn't yet had time to take the things out and clean them up to repack; the items would be grungy, for sure, but they were usable. She just didn't remember if this was the box with the pop-up tent and sleeping bag, which would be helpful, or if this was the clutter box.

Auralia wanted to use both boxes as floatation devices. She was fairly positive the lighter one should float. She'd have to test out the camping box and see if it was friend or foe.

Edging farther out of the window, that one foot still in the water, both hopeful and horrified that someone would grasp her leg again as a lifeline, Auralia's next battle was to get the air-filled plastic bag, which would serve as her flotation device, out the window. She had done an okay job of guessing how much inflation would work. But still, it was too much when she was taking up space in the opening as well.

Not wanting to take the time to unknot and start again, Auralia pressed the air to one side of the bag and held it there with a tight fist. After feeding the limp side of the bag through the window until it reached the bulge, she then reversed the effort, pushing the air to the side of the bag outside the window.

It worked like a charm.

Now, Auralia realized that as she was presently configured, there was no room for her to wiggle and bend and snake herself out of the window.

Yoga was helpful because it kept her flexible, but Auralia was reminiscing about her youth when she would climb along the bald cypress knees and swing upside down amidst the Spanish moss.

She got her torso out the window and shoved her air bag under one armpit, then the other. It was stupidly cumbersome. Still, if she slipped into the water, it could be lifesaving. "Please, be lifesaving."

She flipped over onto her butt. The few inches of window

that never receded, and Auralia had to assume as some safety feature, stabbed her in the ass as she reached up over the hood, splaying her fingers wide, trying to get a grip—in every sense of the word.

Pressing into her feet, she hoisted her hips into the air, and here she could feel the immense pressure of the water behind the car, pushing, pushing, pushing against the frame.

She thought her car was safe as long as the SUV below her held.

She stepped a foot out of the window, then fished it over toward the trunk.

Fear clawed at her heart, snagging it with its sharp talon.

Her toes found the frame, then wiggled forward until they were on the box.

Auralia jumped her hand to the trunk lid and curled her fingers tight like she was climbing the rock wall at her gym. She had a vague idea of how to shift her weight over; she also had an image of getting stuck, neither in nor out of the car, neither in nor out of the trunk, and losing the capacity to move either way.

In her mind's eye, Auralia could see the image of two women underneath her, mouths held like little fish bubbles, craning their necks to suck the last of the oxygen from a pocket of air.

Don't rush, your falling in means you can't get them out.

Auralia closed her eyes and took a breath before sliding her foot along the box toward the back of the car, bringing her hips lower in an ice skater squat. Leaning her chest against the vehicle, she lowered her hand to the lip of the trunk, which felt like a better grip.

Ducking low under the trunk lid, she pulled hard and was able to jump her second hand over, edging them one at a time until her weight was entirely on the trunk.

Her right hand caught between the boxes, followed by her left.

Now one foot in the car, ass in the air, hands gripping the boxes at the center of the trunk, her air bag like two puffy black wings at her back, Auralia lowered her right knee to the box, gritted her teeth and made the same guttural rage noise that the power lifters made at the gym as she dragged her left foot toward her chest.

There in a bear crawl, Auralia paused to make sure that her jostling around hadn't shifted the car, and she wasn't about to slide into the current.

The slow part of the show was over.

Auralia wanted her feet on the shore.

Sitting on the back of the trunk, she opened the box containing her hiking supplies and put her clothes bag in before sealing it against the water. Then, she lifted it to the back lip of the trunk, spreading her thighs wide to balance it there.

She turned and failed at lifting the second box with a twisted spine.

Auralia wrapped her left hand around the handle of the hiking box. If she fell in, at least she had this. Facing away from the bridge, clenching her abs, Auralia jerked the second box to get the bottom onto the edge, and that was going to be about it.

She was stuck.

The little bird on her right shoulder said the hiking box was enough.

The little bird on her left said that the camping box could save lives, and she knew there was probably a rope inside. Auralia would listen to the bird on her left.

But she was out of ideas, and frankly, almost out of steam.

Adrenaline, she'd learned in her life as a reporter, ebbed and flowed. When it was on like a spigot, it often turned off without so much as a trickle.

Even a trickle would be helpful right about then.

She decided to pull a Morrison.

Releasing both boxes and being careful not to prick her airbag, Auralia twisted and squirmed, grabbing here then grabbing there, until her feet were on the bumper and she was facing downriver.

She wrapped a hand tightly around a tote handle on either side of her. Then, pretending she was back at the gym, she pressed into her heels like the squat machine and arched her head backward.

What happened next was total body chaos.

Water rushed into her nostrils.

Her wrists were wrenched this way and that until the totes figured out how to align with the current. Her airbag was airbagging to its best ability, though it had squirmed out from under her pits and was now a belt under her stomach.

Auralia was kicking hard because that's what her body knew to do from growing up on the water.

Still, it was a confusing, scary ride until one of the totes scraped against the river bottom, dragging along behind as Auralia's arms were pulled wide, and she was able to get her knees under her.

Twelve inches is all the muddy water necessary to sweep a car away.

Six inches was what it took to drag a human off their feet.

The eddy calmed the waters a bit. And the tree trunk just a few yards away would act as a stopper.

Still holding on to her resources as if her life depended on them—because it did - Auralia came to her knees, then got a foot under her.

The thick clay squished up between her toes. And there she stopped. Winded. Just a moment of rest.

She remembered Papa Jacques taking her along with his family when they went to a friend's house to go out on the pontoon. The pond where he kept the boat was at dangerously low levels, and the group had to wade out about twenty feet in the low water to reach the boat. The guy simply kept tying a longer and longer rope to keep the pontoon afloat.

That was all fine and good on the way out.

But on the way back in, that was a whole other story.

The kids hadn't been allowed to swim in the pond because the man said they had an infestation of cottonmouths, also known as water moccasins. They were a type of pit viper that could be lethal. The smaller you were, the deadlier.

At the end of a day out on the water, each of the big boys worked to get the coolers and other paraphernalia that had made their day so nice off the boat and onto the shore, and as asked, Auralia had sat out of the way.

Now that they were all on shore, they called for her to follow.

She jumped off the boat and sank ankle deep into the silky silt. One foot was flat, the other foot curved over a solid form that slid out from under one foot and over the other.

In her mind, the only thing she could think of was that it was a water moccasin and that at any moment it could pull itself far enough out from under her foot, that it would turn and strike, taking retribution for the thing that had attacked it. And when it bit her, she would die.

Auralia remembered that at the moment those images came together in her imagination, it was as if a great hand came down and snatched her out of the water. Somehow, to this day, she couldn't conceptualize how she leaped from waist deep in water and ankle deep in the mud back up onto the pontoon with a shriek that spun the entire group in her direction.

"What's she doing out there like that?" Papa Jacques had asked Jean Marie. Before they attempted to answer, Papa Jacques cupped his palms around his mouth and called out, "Cherie, what gives?"

She had no words.

She didn't, in fact, know what happened.

She was yanked out of the water by an unseen hand. That was even more shocking than the possibility of death by snake bite.

Auralia erupted in laughter and tears, trembling from head to foot.

Eight, maybe nine, still a girl but not a small girl, is what Auralia remembered.

Honoré and Jean Marie were both in the water, coming out to her, racing each other to see who would get there first.

Auralia was crying and shaking her head, wishing that words would come to her so she could tell the boys, "No, don't come out here! I angered the snake!"

But there they were standing under her, their arms outstretched.

The only way she could think to protect them was to get down to them fast, and then everyone could get out of the water.

The boys turned their backs on her and put their arms around each other's waists.

Jean Marie held up his free hand, "Come on, Lia, hold my hand and climb on our shoulders. You don't have to get in the water."

This was a practiced move, she'd realized. They must have saved others this way in the past.

Auralia clambered on and was carried like a swamp princess out of the water to the shore, where Papa Jacques lifted her for the dismount. "What happened?"

She didn't answer because she didn't know, and Auralia had already decided that when she grew up, she was going to be a reporter. So, when she reported on something that happened, she had to be neutral and honest. And she was neither, so she stayed silent.

Blading a hand over her brows, Auralia lifted her chin to scan the bridge, expecting to see either Creed or at least Gator standing there looking down and trying to figure out how to help.

But to her surprise, the bridge remained empty.

They hadn't come.

Creed hadn't heard her call as she'd gone over the edge.

Unfathomable.

Not Gator, not even Rougarou the swamp beast, who seemed in her ultra cutie-snooty doe-eyed way to sense where someone was rather than sniff them out.

What happened that Auralia was within the same catastrophe, but her tribe didn't pick up on her distress and find her?

That squeezed her heart with what wanted to be self-pity. No, it was different than that. From a lifetime of Creed and Gator showing up if it was at all in their power, in places and at times when they wouldn't know she was in need, Auralia had a deep conviction that she was loved and cared for, and she could depend on the psychic thread that seemed to bind them.

Then she reminded herself that the air was opaque with grief and pain.

The people with damaged bodies and, possibly, alas, *probably* new and disoriented souls, all would attempt to get attention on every plane of existence.

It would overwhelm anyone with a sixth sense.

Her little whimper of need was selfish.

"Brush it off, girlfriend, and let's get to work."

There were probably two women trapped in a car, thinking they'd never again see the light of day.

Auralia needed to refocus.

This was on her.

21

———

Creed

Creed, Deep, and Randy had just handed Parker off to an ambulance team.

No rest when there were so many in need, Deep and Randy were already off on their new assignments.

Creed had walked Rou into the woods to go to the bathroom and play tug as her reward for finding the search subject.

Suddenly, she released the tug toy, and her nose went into the air; the lamenting howl that she released was a vibration that brought Creed's blood to a rolling boil.

Every molecule in his body screamed Auralia's name.

Poor little Rou, hunkered low, stretched her nose long. Red shoes forgotten, she sprinted out ahead of Creed.

Creed's feet never touched the ground as he flew toward the bridge, where there was no more car dangling from the rails.

Since the moment at Gator's wedding when Creed saw Auralia as someone other than his best friend's little sister, when he saw her as a person that he wanted in his life as his own to love, Creed had wanted to yell it from the mountaintops that he cherished Auralia dearly.

But Auralia's answer was always, "No, Creed, not now, not yet, we're tempting Fate." Always the temptation of fate: What was given could so easily be taken away. And given his childhood in the Bayou where magic hung like fog over the shoreline, he knew Fate was not to be tempted.

So he agreed, every time.

They'd give it time, and Fate wouldn't turn her head in their direction.

But this last time he said it, it was because Gator would see them, and he'd feel how the energy wove around them. He'd be a gentleman, for sure. But he wouldn't bald-faced lie to his oldest friend. Gator would know for sure. Better to come clean.

And Auralia agreed.

They revealed themselves

And Fate had arrived.

"Be good to us," Creed whispered. "Be kind."

But the keening lament and moans of pain all around him made it hard for Creed to hear hope's whisper.

Creed reached the embankment and realized there was no way to get himself down there without adding to the danger of the situation.

He raced up onto the bridge and looked down.

He tried to call out past numb lips.

With a thrumming heart, Creed saw Auralia, dressed only in her underwear, dragging her two trunk totes out of the water. There was a black plastic garbage bag, full of air, clamped under her armpits.

"Shit, woman!" He bellowed. "Good job! You are glorious!"

God, his heart was pounding so damned hard he might just die from relief. He clutched his chest to calm the assault.

Auralia opened a bin, pulled out her winter jacket, and tugged it on.

Creed cupped his hands over his mouth and yelled her name.

She didn't turn in his direction. The wind was whipping his words and scattering them about.

He scooped up Rou and jogged off the bridge over toward the trees above her.

Below him, Creed found her standing there, bare-legged, her feet in the narrow swath of wet sand before the sheer clay-slick bank, staring at her car. Creed couldn't fathom why she wasn't doing something more to save or protect herself. She grew up on water. She knew how dangerous the cold could be.

Just that morning, when she'd pranced out of the bathroom in her sexy little lace panties and the bra with the sweet little pink ribbon, he'd thought about how beautiful she looked then. But now she looked miraculous.

Creed whipped his phone out and dialed Gator.

"I see you. I'm almost to the bridge," Gator reported. Of course, Gator would have felt Auralia going over the side, and he would have been in motion, too.

"I've got eyes on her, brother. She's standing on the shore. She has a dry coat on. And she brought along her two car totes, where she keeps her outdoor supplies."

"Safe?" Gator was breathing hard in Creed's ear. "Say it again. Safe?"

"*Safe*. She's out of the water. I'm looking at her with my monocular. She looks like she's trying to catch her breath. No visible signs of blood or other injury. She looks clear-eyed with a churning mind. That look she gets when she's strategizing her next move. I'm not worried about her being in shock."

"WoooEEE! Hell to the yeah!" Gator yelled out. "Alright, brother, if she's good, I'll leave you to bring her up. I'll keep working on helping these folks."

"I've got Auralia. I'll get her up the banks."

Creed had given his word. And while his word was his bond, his heart was the reason he wouldn't stop until Auralia was in his arms.

22

Auralia

Auralia stood and looked along the bridge and the bank.

She would swear that Creed was there, but as she scanned, there were no human silhouettes at all.

And she felt sure that when she'd screamed his name as she went over the edge, he'd heard. She believed, with every cell in her body, that he was racing toward her. Gator, too. Of course, Gator.

But she couldn't wait for their help with the women in the SUV.

She wasn't even sure how they'd get down the slick bank.

Her intuition had been correct; the second bin that she'd almost left behind was the important one. She had her boating vest, her full-face snorkeling set, her kitchen tarp, and a bicycle helmet.

Auralia unfolded the tarp to find the long nylon ropes. With a practiced hand, she secured it to the tree and then around her waist. She lopped the other rope and looked for a way to put it on her body without losing it to the current. She decided to stuff it into the life preserver, tying one end with a figure eight knot to one of the survival loops.

Finally, she slapped the bicycle helmet into place and tightened the straps.

The car was only about ten feet away, but wow, that was a long ten feet.

Auralia took a moment to watch the current. If she entered the water well above the car, she could swim toward the opposite shore, and by the time she reached the car's body, the river current should wash her down toward where she assumed the SUV was resting below her vehicle.

If she missed, the eddy would angle her back to shore, and the tree would stop her from going too far. She could get out and try again.

Taking off her coat to stand all but naked and wet in the frigid wind was hard, and stepping into the racing ice water extra sucked.

Auralia was terrified.

She was *terrified.*

But despite her terror, she didn't wonder if she'd follow through or not. This is what humans did for each other.

Pulling on the life vest, Auralia hoped that its buoyancy would allow her to do both things she wanted to: dive into the water and stay above it.

Ridiculous, sure, but that's what she needed.

The one thing she knew for sure was that she couldn't stay in the river for more than a few minutes, or she wouldn't stay cogent. The water was just too cold.

Auralia checked to make sure she still had Remi's thick rubber band on her wrist. She had a window punch tool and a mini, waterproof, high-lumen flashlight. She went ahead and turned the flashlight on.

She stepped into the water up to her knees, and her feet came out from under her.

Auralia had to dig deep and kick hard as she swam back to her car. There, she clung to the door handles, with her knees beside her ears in a crouched position, the water trying to drag her away.

At the front of her car, she dropped her foot into the water. An antenna of sorts, she felt along the SUV with her toes.

It wasn't positioned as she'd supposed. Her car wasn't stacked directly on top. Her car had landed on the back half of the SUV, which was pitched at an angle. Auralia felt certain that, had there not been a meeting of the rushing waters at the front of the vehicle, the hood would have been visible.

The window in the back was open; that meant the SUV would be flooded.

Well, yeah, she reasoned. Morrison had to get out somehow. There would have to be a window open. So maybe he left them without a backward glance because they were dead.

Auralia's whole body shuddered.

If they were dead, she would get back on shore and tend to herself. A swift water team could retrieve the remains. That was the plan. But for now, she had to be sure.

Auralia couldn't reach her foot as far as the SUV's front window.

She took a moment to imagine what to do with her hands. If she reached down and held onto the SUV through the back window, letting her feet drift down with the current and lift toward the surface, she should be able to get them onto the side mirror.

Then she could feel with her right hand and see what was going on in the front passenger seat where Brandy had been sitting.

She could hear Remi's good counsel, "Make the whole plan, not just the next two or three steps. You don't want to be in the thick of it and flailing."

"Fine, Remi," Auralia said aloud. Once she had a clue,

Auralia decided she'd pull the whole-face mask into place without lifting the snorkel, so it would remain airtight. She could hold her breath and, clinging tightly with her hands, push hard with her feet to get down and see what was there to see.

Auralia tried that out, and the life vest was less than cooperative.

Auralia found herself foot on the mirror, arm looped through the window, floating alongside the submerged SUV.

Finding the front window down, Auralia was ninety-nine percent certain that Brandy had not survived.

Sliding her right hand along the inside roof, Auralia found the grab handle. Memorizing that position, Auralia pulled her hand out of the water, sucked in a deep breath, and lowered the mask over her face. And against her inner guardian angel's best advice, Auralia reached for that handle and pulled hard, so she could duck her head into the SUV.

Her emergency flashlight lit the interior. There was a bubble of air.

A pretty big one.

Brandy had pressed forward, eyes open, head angled, mouth wide and gasping.

Sheelah, draped over the steering wheel, seemed unconscious, but her nose and mouth cleared the water.

Auralia didn't feel a surge of victory.

She quickly pulled her head out of the opening before a drowning Brandy could grab her and kill them both.

Auralia pushed the mask back and sucked in great gulps of air.

A plan.

A plan.

Absolutely nothing was coming to her.

She put herself back on the banks of the Bayou. What had she heard? What did she know?

Brandy's being conscious was dangerous to her rescue because drowning people are out of their damned minds and will pull you down, so you can die together.

Be that as it may, Auralia would persevere.

How much energy did Brandy have? Auralia couldn't figure out, with the window down, why Brandy hadn't just swum free.

Then Auralia remembered the seat belt. Had it locked? Was she stuck?

Okay, step one: saw through the belt with the razor.

Next, take off the life vest and hand it to Brandy? Nope.

But she had the extra rope.

What if Auralia untied it from her vest, so her fate wasn't literally tied to Brandy's?

What if she wrapped that rope around Brandy's waist and handed her one end while Auralia held the other? Then, once Auralia got herself back to shore, she could guide Brandy in?

That was a lot of 'ifs.'

As Auralia prepared to plunge again, the seatbelt razor pinched between her thumb and index finger, and she thought of Brandy's father swimming away.

How cruel.

How monstrous.

But she didn't have the space to consider him beyond that.

23

———————

Creed

THIS DAY REMINDED CREED OF WAR AS HE JUMPED FROM ONE critical mission to the next. His mind and body were inured to heavy task loads.

As Creed and Rou jogged toward the Iniquus transport to grab ropes and pulleys, his gaze caught on a minivan that was one of the last vehicles he'd called in to Mandy before he was rerouted to find Parker.

Creed had knocked on the window and said, "If you're walking wounded, get out. Get the kids out. Get up the hill." The family seemed fine. For them, it had been a fender bender that set off their airbags, but they'd looked no worse for wear.

But the dynamic had drastically shifted. The front of their minivan had rammed under the frame of a jacked-up truck in front of them. Without the airbag there to cushion the blow, they'd taken the full force of the impact. And even with an airbag, it didn't look survivable.

"Mandy, it's Creed. Pin this location."

"I have you on the board."

"The parents in the van were walking wounded. I don't have the doors open. Their new triage ranking should be red or black. They're trapped under this guy's tailgate. Male and female in their late-twenties or early-thirties. We need a first responder to assess."

"I have a minivan in that location with three children, about five, about three, and an infant."

"Affirmative. The children are in their car seats and seem unharmed."

He was going to get these kids out of here. They couldn't be in the back seat calling for mama when her mom was dying in front of them. They needed to eat and drink, get warm, and the baby probably needed a diaper change.

Frustrated by the delay to get back to Auralia, damned straight. But he wasn't conflicted. Auralia had the resources and know-how, and she had her feet on solid ground. She wasn't in danger; the babies were.

"The infant is in an infant carrier?"

"Affirmative."

"Any access to a stroller?"

"No. I don't see that. There's a diaper bag. And a woman's purse on the back floorboard."

"We'll need to get the children forward to support. See if you can't get a diaper bag and if the woman has a purse so we can try to identify kin."

Creed moved Rou to the other side of the ditch, took off his pack, and told her to down-stay.

The doors were locked, and Creed decided to break the mother's window to protect the babies from the glass. Surely, if she were conscious, she'd agree.

He reached in and felt for a pulse, but from the angle of her head, the fact that he couldn't find one wasn't definitive. Creed wouldn't call that in unless it was certain, lest it put her name on the black triage list if it didn't belong there.

Reaching in, he pressed the door unlock buttons and heard a click and a shift at the doors.

Pulling up on the handle, Creed was surprised it had no give. He checked again to make sure the locks were unlatched. Next, he placed his booted foot on the side of the car and thrust out with his leg as he yanked on the door, but the vehicle's body was too buckled.

He reached into the mother's window again on the off chance that he could roll down the back window, and to his great surprise, that worked.

Creed grabbed the purse and diaper bag and flung them toward Rou, taking a moment to assure himself that she was on task.

From there, he unlocked the doors.

The oldest child was facing front and was positioned behind her dad. There was no access to their car from that side. The car had buckled inward from the pressure of the other crash vehicles. He wouldn't be able to reach her.

She had stopped crying and was blinking overly wide eyes at him.

"Sweet girl, do you know how to take off your seat belt?"

She gave him a solemn nod.

"Could you show me how you do that?"

She reached between her legs, pressed the red button, unlatched the belt, and pulled her arms out of the loops.

"What about your brother's seat? Can you do your brother's seat belt?"

Creed might be able to reach that one, but he wasn't sure of the mechanics of the rear-facing seat, and this was easier.

It also gave him a chance to assess the girl's well-being.

"Thank you, sweetheart. Hey, I have my puppy dog here.

Her name is Rou. Your car is pretty smashed up. How about you come sit with Rou so you don't get hurt?"

"Mommy!" she keened.

"Mommy got hurt in the accident, sweet child. We need to get a doctor in to help her. Right now, mommy wants you to be safe. You think mommy would want that, right?"

She squeezed her lips together into a tight pucker as her chin wobbled. She was holding back her sobs.

Creed leaned as far as he could into the car.

"Put your feet on the floor for me. Can you help your brother out of his seat and help get him into my hands?"

"What about Charlotte?"

"Charlotte is your baby?"

The girl pointed.

"Yes, I'm going to get Charlotte, too. And we're going to see my doggy, Rou. Then, I'm going to take you to some friends who will keep you safe and warm while we get help for mommy. Is that mommy and daddy in the front seat?"

She pointed forward.

"Okay, help your brother. What's his name?"

"He's Joey, and my name is Marybelle." She reached for her brother's hand and pulled. "Come on, Joey, we have to get out. The car crashed."

"Nice to meet you, Marybelle. I'm Creed."

As the children clambered out of their seats, Creed picked up an umbrella and the plastic bags from an earlier trip to the dollar shop that lay on the floorboard. He shoved those in his pocket. He reached his hands under Joey's armpits and pulled him through the window.

He put Joey on the ground and held him in place by sticking out a leg and sandwiching the boy between his shin and the car. Balancing on one leg, Creed reached back in. "It was a little easier for Joey because he's so small. If you held my hands, could you climb to me?"

The infant carrier was a problem that he wasn't sure he could solve. Marybelle was going to have to come over the top.

"I've got you, sweet child. Listen, I want you to stay crouched down like that on the seat, but turn and face Daddy. Good girl. Cross your hands over your chest and tuck your chin down. That's right. Now, I'm putting my hand on your back, and I'm going to put a hand under your bottom. I want you to just lean back, and I'm going to pull you out the window over the top of the baby. Here we go. Here are my hands. That's right, just keep leaning back. I've got you. I bet you learned how to swim like this."

"Mommy's teaching me to float on my back."

"That's right. That's what we're doing now." He eased Marybelle out of the window, and she seemed happy to find Joey standing there waiting.

Creed had hoped to get the infant carrier out just as it was because he wanted a paramedic to assess the baby in place, lest she had suffered a spine trauma. The baby wasn't awake and crying, and that concerned him.

The kids weren't safe along the road if he wasn't giving them his full attention, so Creed lifted Joey onto his hip. Joey held his bright yellow boots with rubber duck faces out to either side on straight legs, and Creed knew from his nieces and nephews that this was the way to keep his boots from sliding off. He reached for Marybelle's hand, which she slid trustingly into his. Her boots were black with bright red ladybugs, and he was glad that they were dressed to survive in the rain.

"Joey and Marybelle, look, here's my puppy Rou. Do you see she's wearing her red shoes? She has little red socks, too." Creed spread the plastic dollar store bags on the side of the hill, one on either side of Rou. "This is Rou's lead. She's still a puppy. I was hoping that you could hold on to her lead and keep her safe while I go get Charlotte. Would you hold Rou for me?"

Creed pulled off his pack and set it behind Rou. Then, he opened the umbrella he'd found in the car and ran the post through the pack's loop, sticking the hand loop under the weight to keep it in place.

He gave it about a twenty percent chance of being there when he got back. The wind was steady with sudden, powerful gusts. "Marybelle, I need you to do me a favor. We need to keep the rain off of you three. Can Joey hold onto Rou, and you keep your hand on the umbrella? It's too cold to be out here and get wet."

Her hand wrapped the umbrella handle, and Creed stood. "Back in the shake of a lamb's tail. He picked up the diaper bag and purse and walked them over to them, partly to keep the bags from getting sodden—there were probably diapers and formula that the baby would need—but also to check and see what the kids did when his back was turned.

All was well enough.

Back at the car, Creed took a moment to make sure the baby was breathing.

The relief he felt at the slight exhale on the back of his spit-dampened skin felt like guardian angels hovered close.

Creed pushed and pulled, pressed, and cursed until he got the carrier separated from its base, and then repeated all of that as he got the handle folded down.

He took a moment to assess the padding before unclipping it around the edges and folding it over the baby.

With a trained eye, Creed measured the width of the carrier versus the space in the window.

He took off his jacket and laid it over the baby as he broke out the short lip of glass that stuck up past the door. He felt that gave him the space he'd need if he could swivel the carrier.

The cursing he kept under his breath, but there was a point

at which he had to put his foot against the door and press himself back as he compressed the plastic sides that absolutely didn't want to give.

A blessing and, quite literally, a curse, with lots of curses.

He ended up on his ass, then flat on his back as he rolled to keep the infant as cradled as possible. That babe had been jarred enough.

When he got to his feet, he turned to check on the children, only to find Marybelle chasing the umbrella into the woods. He watched to make sure she didn't get out of sight as he reattached the baby's bunting.

"Okay, Marybelle and Joey, come on down. I'm going to take you up to get you warm and comfy. It's too far for you to walk, so we are going to become a great big giant together. Should we do that?"

Neither child answered. "Marybelle, I'm going to put you on my shoulders. It's your job to hold the umbrella. Joey goes on my hip, and the baby stays in her carrier. Joey, I need you to keep holding Rou's lead. She has trouble walking in her little red shoes. Throwing on his pack, slinging the mother's purse, then the baby bag across his chest, next came Marybelle and her umbrella, Joey with Rou, and finally, Creed scooped up the baby carrier.

Creed didn't know how to keep the kids' attention away from the destruction that they passed alongside. All he could do was keep pointing out things he saw off in the woods.

At one point, he needed to walk in the ditch to avoid the rescue workers, who were using heavy equipment that threw a shower of sparks into the air as they cut people free.

Creed noticed they hadn't applied a layer of fire-retardant foam, which seemed okay for the moment because the sparks landed on wet macadam. And the foam wouldn't help if the wind carried those sparks off into the tree line. When he'd gone after Jeb that morning, he'd seen how dangerous the drought conditions were in the surrounding woods. It reminded him of his emergency response training evolution in Nova Scotia, which had come to an abrupt end when the government deemed the risk of forest fires so severe that it banned people from entering the woods province-wide, with a $25,000 fine for those who ignored the rule.

Though here, just in a few hours, things had—at least in terms of fire danger—improved with the downpour. By the time Creed had gone after Parker, the top surface was damp.

Still, it was a risk. Especially because fire helicopters couldn't fly, and the logistics of circumnavigating the wreckage with equipment would be daunting.

But Creed knew the teams were moving as fast and as hard as they could to save life and limb.

Everyone who could lend a hand was elbow-deep in helping.

Mandy had told Creed that a nurse, Mrs. Simpkiss, was waiting at the Iniquus transport to take over care of the kids.

Since Mandy was tracking his exact position on her Logistics board, he wasn't at all surprised to see a woman in scrubs standing in the drizzle with a plastic bag tied on her head like a bandana.

"You happen to be Mrs. Simpkiss?" Creed asked.

"That's me. I'm supposed to take care of Marybelle, Joey, and Charlotte."

"I'm Marybelle. And that's Charlotte. Joey is holding onto Rou."

"And he's doing a mighty fine job of it," Mrs. Simpkiss said.

"Where are we heading?"

She ushered him to an ambulance to put them all down. He told Marybelle and Joey how brave and strong they had been. And that he'd never played great big giant with three better kids.

And as Mrs. Simpkiss leaned in to ask them questions about

how they felt and if anyone needed to go potty, Creed headed over to the fire engine to ask for ropes.

Since no one was around, Creed dug through the side bins until he found the necessary equipment and loaded it into his pack.

If there were *mea culpas* to be said, he'd do that later.

Right now, he needed to get to Auralia.

24

Auralia

Auralia had to be pragmatic. She was one person, and she was exhausted.

She had Brandy under the armpits after she'd made last-minute adjustments to her rescue scheme.

The seat belt took three separate dives to cut free.

A fourth dive, and Auralia watched Brandy inhale, then she pinched the woman's nose and drew her through the window. In her imagination, that process had been smooth and quick, and in reality, it had been neither. Auralia was out of breath. Her lungs screamed. But if she let go of Brandy, even to rise to the surface for a quick gasp of air, Brandy would drown.

Auralia fought against panic.

She caught the woman under the arms, pulled her halfway out, then placed her feet on the window ledge and thrust upward with enough momentum to help the swim vest get them both to the surface.

It had been Auralia's plan that while Brandy swam, Auralia could float into the eddy with the buoyancy of the life preserver and pull the rope she'd wrapped around Brandy's chest to help the woman out of the current.

Brandy was loose-limbed and slippery. She had no energy in her arms or legs. Just dead weight. Auralia thought the dead part, then, in her mind, struck through it with an imagined editor's mark, just weight.

Auralia's lungs screamed for air, and she had the facemask on. If she were on her belly, she could flip the snorkel up. But configured as she was, Auralia had to release Brandy long enough that she could pull off the mask, and grip it tightly as she hooked back under Brandy's arm, all while fighting the white waters that pulled her to the front of the SUV.

As Auralia kicked her legs and dragged Brandy, she thought about the next steps.

Sheelah was not going to fit out the same window that Auralia was able to drag Brandy. She was unconscious and unable to give even a little bit of help. At least Sheelah hadn't turned her head and sent Auralia one last long stare before she went on to her just rewards.

That's how a ghost can attach itself to someone and haunt them for the rest of their days.

Auralia shook off that childhood terror.

There was nothing Auralia could do about Sheelah.

She wasn't even sure she could save Brandy. She had kicked them into the eddy and now her butt, in the black lace panties, grazed along the bottom of the river. Auralia pulled her knees up and planted her feet, trying to press up from the squat, but it was impossible on the ground, which gave under her weight, sinking her up to her shins.

Auralia let go of Brandy and stood, then reached down to clasp the woman's wrists and dragged her backward onto the sliver of land between the rising river and the rise of the slope.

Brandy was out of the water.

She was out of the water.

Winded and with legs shaking so hard she couldn't stand, Auralia looked over to Brandy and for a moment wondered if she'd dragged a dead body from the car. But when Brandy blinked, then blinked again, Auralia clapped a hand to her heart and started crying.

She needed an emotional release valve to open for a minute.

This had been a stressful day.

Auralia crawled to her bin to retrieve her daypack, which contained the things she carried in case of an emergency. She pulled out a Mylar blanket to spread over Brandy. "This isn't it. I can do more to help you. I need a second," Auralia said as she spread the blanket over the prone woman, using rocks to hold the edges down so the wind didn't blow the resource away. "But there are things that Creed, Gator, and Remi keep preaching about, like saving myself first. You don't know them. They're—look, my mind is overwhelmed right now, I'm going to follow their counsel." She placed the last rock. "I'm sorry about your mamma."

When she looked over the woman, it looked like she was wearing a shroud, and Auralia was preparing the woman for burial.

Auralia reminded herself not to conjure any bad juju that might manifest between then and a rescue.

She pressed her hand under her breast to be sure she still had her phone, which would be their lifeline in just a moment. Auralia had to get warm first.

Pulling out a bottle of water, Auralia swished it through her mouth to clear it of the grit that had gotten into her mouth from the river. Then, she gulped some down.

The next thing she pulled out was her small, rough, and highly absorbent camp towel while she eyed the contents of the bin. There was a MOLLE bag that she knew contained a change of clothes, which she could use for Brandy.

First thing was to get Brandy out of her wet outfit.

With shaking hands, stiff with cold, Auralia battled with her bra clasp, finally feeling it give way; it was full of mud when she dropped it to the ground at her feet.

She pulled the phone bag lanyard over her head and set it in the bin before sliding off her panties. She'd call as soon as she could get herself and Brandy stabilized from the wet and cold.

Lifting the liter bottle of water, she let it drizzle down her body. With her free hand, she swished and swiped over her skin to remove as much of the sand and grit as possible. When she dressed, Auralia wanted all her attention to be on keeping the woman alive until rescue could reach them, and she didn't need the distraction of her clothes rubbing against her like sandpaper.

Her mentor, Remi, had talked to her on many occasions about how taking care of things at the front end would keep her safe and comfortable enough to keep their focus on the story. She had learned that things like rinsing off might seem like a time suck, but functionally, it was more along the lines of a "stitch in time."

Using her camp towel, Auralia rubbed herself vigorously not only to absorb the water that helped the wind wick away her body heat, but also to generate some warmth back into her system. Her teeth were chattering, she was goose-fleshed, and her feet were purple with cold.

The extra panties and bra that she carried with her in her day pack were chosen for "shit hits the fan" scenarios, figuratively, of course. Covering, supportive, modest, and comfy, all Auralia needed to do was pull it over her head and adjust the girls into position.

Wet as she was, the bra rolled itself tight, and she was struggling to get it into place.

Note to self, front closure next time.

Knowing that she planned to dress Brandy in her emergency clothes, Auralia pulled the tactical pants she'd been wearing that day from the black plastic leaf bag and sat on the lid as she got her socks and boots on.

And that's when a little black nose shoved under her arm. "Rougarou, you startled the crap out of me, girl." She saw a rope tied to the handle of Rou's vest and traced it along the empty shoreline. Her eyes searched up, and she found Creed on a rope system, walking himself down the slippery incline.

Without Brandy, she could have gone up that line and left this mess.

Without Brandy, this could be over.

She cupped her hand around her mouth. "About damned time you got here." She tapped the side of her head. "I've been calling you for a while now. I thought you or Gator would come. Good thing I wasn't twiddling my thumbs waiting to get rescued."

"I heard," Creed called back with a tap to his own head. "I saw you get out onto the beach and called Gator, who, by the way, dropped everything to race to you. I turned him around." He continued to walk himself down the slope, jumping the last couple of feet.

"You call this a beach? The ground is only about five feet wide." She caught his eye. "Thank you to you both."

"You find an extra person?" Creed twitched the rope and released it. "Was she with you in the car?"

Auralia pushed Rou away and asked her to sit on a box top before pulling on her shirt and fleece.

"She was in the SUV under me. This is Brandy Morrison. Mom's still under there. I can't figure a way to get her out."

"Brandy came through the window?"

"Yeah. And mom won't fit. I didn't try. She's breathing in a pocket of air. That can't last much longer. It's mostly carbon dioxide by now. I made sure her tongue wasn't obstructing her airway, and then I brought Brandy up."

"You need help with her?" He coiled around his hand and elbow.

"If you can just help me get her over onto the tarp, I think I have it from there if you can figure anything about Sheelah."

"Sheelah's unconscious?" Creed asked as he crouched by Brandy, moved the rocks, and scooped her into a fireman's carry, Mylar and all, and moved her as requested.

"She could be dead," Auralia said. "I don't know."

He placed objects from the bin on the Mylar to hold it in place. "The good thing is, Sheelah can't haunt you if she didn't turn and look at you." He strode the short distance between them.

"Please let's not with the dark humor." Auralia pulled on her jacket and tugged a beanie over her wet hair and down over her ears. "I don't need you to jinx me today."

Creed reached for her. "I just need to feel you in my arms for a second. Woman, do you know how many times you've stopped my heart today?"

It felt so good to be wrapped warm and safe in Creed's arms. It felt so good to know that he had indeed known when she was in trouble and had come running. He said he saw her come out on the shore. He must have gone after the equipment to get her out of there. She had been so focused on what was happening down here that if he were calling, it would have been a completely useless effort. Adrenaline had a tunnel-vision design that could harm as much as it could serve.

Looking down at Brandy's face, Auralia rose onto her toes and kissed Creed good and hard. "I have to take care of Brandy." She snapped her fingers, "Rou, snuggle." And Rue came over and lay against Brandy's chest.

"Give me a picture of what's going on down there." He stood with his hands on his hips, facing Auralia's car, assessing. "How'd you even know to go look?"

Auralia told the story of being Morrison's lifeline.

"You remember that time we were out on the pontoon and you stepped on something in the silt, and it scared you silly?" Creed asked. "I never saw anything like that before or since."

"I remember. I actually thought about that very story. But over here in the silt. Over there," Auralia pointed at her car, "I thought about drowned souls finding their way out of the depths."

"You are so grim." He walked to a tree and set up his rope and pulley system, which he had pulled from the pack on his back.

"Did you figure something out to help Sheelah?" Auralia dug through the box of supplies, fishing out her first aid kit, which included a notebook and an all-weather pencil to write down any notes that might help a doctor, along with her rescue shears to cut Brandy's clothes free.

Auralia would work from the waist down to begin with, then she'd let Rou warm Brandy's feet. But Brandy's core temperature must be very low after being in the water all that time. Better to let the emergency blanket and Rue's body heat start to bring Brandy's temperature up.

Auralia had a fire starter kit with her, and for a moment, she considered starting a bonfire as soon as she had the woman dried and dressed, but then she remembered the drought conditions and decided that wasn't a great idea.

"Tell me about Sheelah," Creed said as he sat on the tote to unlace his boots and take off his socks. "She was breathing?"

"I'm guessing. I can't say for sure."

Creed stood to pull off his clothes, dropping them into one of the boxes. He used a magnet from his kit to fish his ear canal comms out and put them in a bag with his sternal comms button. He was no longer a tap away from his team.

"What's the plan?" she asked.

"Two-pronged," he picked up the life vest and pulled it on. He had to adjust the straps, and even then, they barely closed.

"I'm going to try to open the door a crack to shove a wedge in." He pointed at a delta-shaped rock. "Then I'll tie off the door and swim back." He put the bike helmet on. "Then, I'll use the pully system to drag it wide and tie the rope off, so it holds open. Once I can get it angled so the current does the work, that should be easy enough."

"I have my snorkel mask there," Auralia pointed out. "It's the only reason I could see inside the SUV."

"That might help. Third, I'm going back in and tying the rope around Sheelah. Angling her out, I'll swim to shore a second time and use the pulley to drag her in. There's no time to finesse this."

"She'll drown."

"I know. But she'll drown if she stays there, too. So I bring her to shore and do CPR. My phone's there." Creed pointed at his pants. "If I get her to shore, call it in. Tell them to bring the defibrillator." He tied a rope around his waist, then picked up the rock and the loose rope that would secure the door. "She's going to have a rough ride. But if she's unconscious, I don't see another way, not in these white waters. And to be honest, if their SUV was any farther out than the three meters or so, I wouldn't chance it. We called in a white-water team. They were training in the Shenandoah. They got on the road imme-diately, but when I checked with Logistics, their ETA wasn't for at least another hour."

Auralia stood and gripped his arm as she leaned her head back for a kiss. Her heart was squeezing so hard that her voice creaked when she said. "Try but don't die."

"Sage advice." He chuckled before scooping her tight to his body and kissing her hard. "I love you deeply, wholly, completely. Get yourself warm. Stay safe."

25

———

Creed

CREED'S OWN CHEST WAS HEAVING AS HE SHOVED HIS PALMS DEEP into the flesh over Sheelah's sternum.

Chest compressions required serious stamina, and in the military, he had trained to switch out every two minutes to avoid fatigue, which meant that he wasn't pushing deep enough.

Auralia provided breaths every thirty compressions, and he was glad for the mini-breaks while she sealed her mouth around Sheelah's and pushed the air in.

He'd keep going for as long as it made sense.

But they were nearing the point where brain damage was a serious consideration.

He hadn't known Sheelah's status when he'd pulled her out of the SUV. She might already have been dead. Auralia was right; the pocket of air in the vehicle wasn't enough to keep someone alive for long, and both women had been using it.

"Seven minutes," Auralia called, as Creed said, "Twenty-eight, twenty-nine, thirty."

She leaned over and felt for an exhale on her cheek, nothing. Bending over, she tipped Sheelah's head back, pinched her nose, sealed her lips, then pinched Sheelah's nose and bent over to administer a breath.

In Creed's head, he had a thirty-minute mark. He thought he had enough gas in the engine to go that long. He looked over to check on Rou, who lay next to Brandy with her head resting on the woman's chest. Brandy blinked regularly, which was the only sign she'd given of life, and to be clear, Creed found it pretty disturbing. He'd never come across that before and had no idea what to do in this situation.

Auralia lifted, and Creed went in "One and two and three —" There was a sudden convulsion below where he'd posted his hands. "Auralia, come to the head." Creed pushed the woman's hip and shoulder, shoving her over on her side, where she vomited brown water.

In both the Rochambeau and the Duchamp families, the drowning protocol had been hammered home and practiced on the regular. The children were allowed a somewhat feral existence, but they had to do it with skill.

This wasn't the first time Creed had done CPR; it was the first time he did it on someone who had drowned.

Creed put a hand on Sheelah's back and felt it expand and contract in a regular pattern. "I guess next we need to get her warm and dry." He reached for his trauma shears and began to cut the hunting jacket and dress.

"Do you have any other clothes with you? Another Mylar blanket?"

"No, do you?" Auralia asked as she grabbed her camp towel and rubbed it over Sheelah's purple skin.

Creed had packed an extra regular Cerberus compression shirt without the technology, and even though Creed had broad shoulders, it was still a struggle to get the fabric onto an unconscious woman with wet skin. The fabric kept rolling and clinging. He kept at it. It was the only thing he had to offer her.

"We have the black garbage bags from my car escape. We can make a shirt out of the one bag and then pull the second bag over her feet and legs, and duct tape them together."

"If we cut the Mylar blanket from Brandy in half and share it between the two women, it'll help. It's good the rain stopped, or I'd be out here building lean-tos." Creed looked through his bag, hoping there was a hand warmer or other item that he'd shaken loose throughout today's rescues. "I have a beanie," he said, coming up triumphant.

"Can you get dressed, please?" Auralia handed him the towel, which, despite being damp, was designed to keep wicking away water.

He started by reattaching his sternal mic and dropping his magnetic comms into his ear. "Creed. Back online."

"Striker. Copy. Out."

While he dressed, Creed looked at the slope slick with clay, at the women, and at the sun disappearing over the horizon. Some people would call the rescue a *fait accompli*. Everyone was on shore and stabilized, and as much as possible, they were sheltered from the elements. These types of people would climb that hill, walk over the bridge before it washed out, and hike to a nearby house to call a ride-share.

It would be a case of self-preservation.

But Auralia would never have considered the possibility of walking away until she was in a position of do or die.

Creed had considered leaving the scene to get Auralia up and out because of his military training, where every possibility was on the table. Auralia and Rou were his family and his priorities. He wasn't about to have them stay here, trapped between a rising river and an impossible slope in a dark moon.

It wasn't going to happen.

If nothing else, he could get Auralia and Rou up top and then descend to tend to the victims as best he could.

Would Auralia go for that? He pulled his phone from the box. "Creed here, Mandy. Do you have our location up on your map?"

"I have you pinned on the southwestern side of the river, twenty meters ahead of the bridge pilons."

Creed turned upriver to assess the distance. "That's correct. I'm with Auralia Rochambeau. This is a sequence of events: At the time of the crash, the SUV ahead of Auralia Rochambeau's went through the rails."

"We have that documented. The white water rescue team was put en route."

"Next, you should have Auralia's car going in."

"Affirmative," Mandy's voice was crisply efficient.

"Auralia's car landed on the SUV. After shots were fired at the dell, Auralia witnessed three people get into that SUV. Eugene Morrison, wife Sheelah Morrison, daughter Brandy Morrison."

"Copy."

"As Auralia was affecting her self-rescue, Eugene Morrison from the SUV beneath her car, grabbed her leg, climbed himself to the surface, and swam to the north shore."

"Copy."

"He left his wife and daughter in the vehicle. When Rou and I arrived on the scene, Auralia had saved Brandy, the daughter, from the car. Here are Brandy Morrison's vitals." Creed took a moment to read off the notes that Auralia had been documenting, including breath count and pulse. "Brandy has her eyes open, but she's non-responsive to verbal cues. She has a zero times four orientation. She presents as being in shock and hypothermic. We've done what we can, given our limited supplies. After being in the water for so long, her core temperature is likely in a dangerous zone. We've considered a fire." It wasn't a great idea for so many reasons. But down here, if they built it right next to the water, they might be able to get away with it.

Auralia had moved up and wrapped her arms around him, her head to his heart, squeezing him tightly.

It was the balm and respite he needed.

"Negative," Mandy said. "There is a small fire in the woods beside the accident site. First responders are attempting to extinguish the fire. With the wind gusts, it's a game of whack-a-mole. Negative to a fire."

"Negative to a fire," Creed repeated. He didn't disagree, but these were desperate conditions, and choices could be life or death. "Our situation includes a second victim. We were able to extract Sheelah Morrison from the car. She is unconscious and has been since the time of our interventions. We don't know if she was breathing before she was pulled to land. Once on land, she received CPR and artificial breath for seven minutes before she vomited and resumed breathing on her own. She hasn't regained consciousness. We had to make-do dress her in trash bags, she's in recovery position, and we are out of ideas and out of supplies." Creed read out the notes that he had for Sheelah's status, moving through his list of vital stats and describing what he saw.

"Thank you, Creed. I'm adding the two victims and their status to the triage list."

"Auralia was also in the car accident, and then her car went off the bridge. She has been in the cold river several times. She needs to go to a hospital for a check-up. I can get her out, but that would mean abandoning the women. Our situation is devolving. The river waters are running fast and cold, and are rising. The embankment is a steep-angle rescue, possibly a high-angle rescue. This situation necessitates a rope system and gurneys for evacuation. There is no way that Auralia and I can move these women to higher ground."

"I am documenting your condition," Mandy said.

"Do you have a Search and Rescue team available with technical capability?"

"I'm putting those parameters into the system. A search and rescue team is on hand, but it is not a technical rescue team. We do have a supply van headed toward Strike Force. We have a call-out for any employees with technical capacity to report for duty. Should I put through a call to emergency management and ask them to bring in a team from the Blue Ridge?"

"That's hours away, Mandy, we don't have hours. The river waters are *rising*, and there's no place for us to go."

"Hold while I review assets. The Strike Force team is working on life-or-death scenarios and is unavailable. While I put this into the system, I have some better news. Parker and his grandmother arrived at the hospital. They are being seen by the emergency room. She's been released, and Parker is up and speaking. He will be admitted, but his condition is stable. I also have an update on the children."

"My babies, Charlotte, Joey, and Marybelle?"

"Yes, I have the notes set aside for you, so you'd know right away. The three children were evacuated to the local church, where they are reuniting with their family. The nurse who took charge of them accompanied the three to the church, where emergency management was bringing in off-duty and private nurses and doctors to assess the walking wounded and decide whether they should be transported to the hospital or treated by the local fast clinics. With the closure of the rural hospitals in the area, the distance is problematic, especially since the helicopters can't be put in the air. All three children were evaluated by a pediatric emergency room specialist, who made the final decisions. All three were deemed safe to be sent home with a follow-up with their pediatrician. The nurse was also assessed as safe to go home and has opted to remain to care for the three children. They followed through with the

ICE—in case of emergency—contact information from the diaper bag, and their aunt is en route. They expect a family reunification in the next two hours. The aunt is coming in from Maryland."

"That's fantastic news, Mandy. Thank you, I needed that."

"Understood, sir. I'll stay on top of it for you. So that's the good news. The bad news is that the computer has generated an approximate time for intervention. Nobody is coming to help with these two patients, not before dark and probably not until mid-morning tomorrow. I'm looking at the topo map. The bank on the far side seems to have a lower incline and a wider beach. Is it possible to get to the other side of the river?"

"Let me consider the possibility, Mandy. I won't tie you up. I'll send video of our location and our victims. Text receipt confirmation. Out." Creed wasn't just going to spit out a "no." That's not what Marines did. Creed's favorite Internet meme was a drawing of a rat maze and a Marine plowing in a straight line through all of the obstacles rather than wending around to find the easy path.

Could he get everyone from this bank to the other?

Creed shifted over to the camping bins that Auralia pulled from her car with her—brilliant, intuitive woman that she was. He looked through the possibilities.

Anything they did to evacuate these two women would be dangerous. He had to consider whether his actions would be irresponsible.

In the first bin, he pulled out a folding saw. Now, that would work especially on some of the tall, slender pine trees. Softwood was made for easier cutting. There was a cluster of them that were straight, with few lower branches and a suitable diameter for creating a stretcher.

He looked up the slope. Getting from down here to up there was going to take more than equipment; it was going to take a lot of trained hands. Good Samaritans who might be here trying their best weren't going to be effective here.

Creed pulled out a spool of bankline. What could he use that for? Physics was physics; the dynamic strength wasn't great, so the rope could snap with a shock load.

"We used that in my wilderness first aid course for making stretchers," Auralia said as she crouched beside him. "I bought enough for a single stretcher based on the design I learned." She leaned in and pulled out a roll of 100MPH tape, the military-grade duct tape. "Could this do anything? I'm thinking if we put the bins together, wrap this around and around the outside, and tie the handles together. They did a good job of floating even with some weight."

"Not much weight, less than fifty pounds per bin."

"Still in the water, some flotation is better than none."

Creed had been with a bunch of recruits who were trying to win an extra day of leave by beating the other teams across the finish line by outsmarting them. The team used their tape by rolling it into a strand and braiding it. With that, they were going to go up a slope and save themselves four miles of a ruck run. Clever ideas didn't necessarily lead to good outcomes.

The first guy made it up.

The second guy got a trip to the hospital with two broken ankles from the fall.

The time to try it wasn't when lives were on the line.

She placed the roll next to her saw. "Are you thinking about a raft?"

"Raft? No."

But Auralia had survived her own list of near misses and brushes with death throughout her childhood and career, and she might have an idea that had saved the day. "Can you tell me that thought?"

"You remember those teens that were sailing in the Gulf when—" she pressed her lips together. "You wouldn't know this story. You were deployed. There were these two boys who were sailing when a squall blew in and capsized their boat. It sank, and the kids stayed alive for thirty hours by gripping each other's elbows over the top of a cooler. Bonus points that the cooler had some sandwiches left and ice cubes, so every once in a while, they'd open it up and pop a cube in their mouths. They were sunburned and exhausted but otherwise in good shape. That and the cooler was lime yellow so the helicopter could spot them."

Creed picked up the top and looked the bin over.

"It's waterproof. And I tested that on the way over. One of them held my weight and the weight of my equipment when I rode it to shore. However, if we were trying to float, that tape could be wrapped around the lip," she slid her hand out to show what she meant.

Creed looked out at the river. Three meters to the car. Three meters on the other side of the vehicle. The water was thick with mud and debris, capped with white foam. "The water pressure is pretty intense, and if it presses a side in, it could open a gap, fill with water, and lose its buoyancy."

"Okay. Well, I hope it doesn't come to that." She looked at a stick Creed had stuck in the sand at the shoreline before he went out to get Sheelah. The water had moved about six inches closer to them. "How long do you think we'll have a shore to stand on?"

Creed shook his head. His bigger worry right now was that it would soon be dark.

"I saw you had your trash bag full of air that you were using for a flotation. So maybe we just do that?"

"Brilliant, don't you think?" Auralia asked.

"I think everything about you is brilliant. Sometimes I don't love it—like when you're standing up to report while there's a live-shooter situation."

"Long shot that he'd be gunning for me."

"Haha, funny girl." His system tightened and primed with the image of Auralia in danger.

"Speaking of reporting," Auralia said. "I haven't heard from Doli."

"She's up there getting footage of this mess."

"How did we get here? I mean, I know how we got here. But the number of people in the accident," Auralia shook her head. "It's almost unprecedented, I'd imagine."

"It started with the shot taking out the speaker. Crowd control was us shouting at people who couldn't hear because their systems were so adrenaline-spiked. We had no way to get their attention."

"You all didn't have a bullhorn?" Auralia asked.

"No bullhorns allowed at the event. It wasn't on our equipment list."

"Surely that rule was for the average Joe looking for a pork sandwich and a fried pickle. Which, by the way, Doli was very sad to miss out on."

"The rules were mandated for everyone. And Doli missed out. The fried pickle was delicious. But in the end, our crowd control was about as effective as our road control."

"How is this?" Auralia asked.

"Jack was in head-to-foot hazard limon gear, reflective tape, the whole bit, waving flares around trying to get them to stop and turn around. And they sped up and went over the hill."

"Yeah, well, if Sasquatch were out there trying to get me to slow down in the middle of nowhere, Virginia, and I'm going to speed up too."

"No," Creed kissed the top of her head. "You're not."

"No, I'm not. Look at Rourou. What's she doing?"

Rou's nose was up in the air, sniffing hard.

"Do you smell that?"

"Striker," came through Creed's comms. "We have a fire on

one of the cars. They put a fire extinguisher on it, but the sparks jumped into your woods."

That's what Mandy had said earlier. Above them, the pine needle beds were thick and dry. Though the rain sifted through the evergreen branches, the substrate was still a mix of patches that were slippery and wet, and others that were dry as kindling.

"Creed. We have an unconscious patient and another who is unresponsive. Auralia and I looked at the maps. Getting off this bank means taking them approximately twenty-five feet across the river. It's a high-risk scenario."

"Striker. Prep your plan. Contact Logistics before execution. All hands are dealing with a life-or-death situation. I can't spare anyone. Concerning your victims, it will be your call until the last minute. By that time, Auralia Rochambeau will be safe and sound on the other side of the river, and you and Rou will be with her. Heroics, yes, but only up to a point. You, Auralia, and Rougarou are the priority. You will survive. That's an order."

26

Creed

From the time Creed was a tiny boy, he had learned that hide and seek with Gator was a waste of time. Gator could snatch a thought straight from the air and read it like a map.

The one person who could do it better than anyone was Mamma Rochambeau, who knew if you were breaking the rules before you knew you were doing it yourself. She had her whole passel of kids and all their friends dialed in on her antennae. The house phone would ring, and whoever was closest would answer it. There would be Mamma Rochambeau, wondering what you were getting yourself up to, and maybe you had better stop in your tracks and think about the consequences. Then she'd always say what time she'd be back. "I'll be home before supper, and I had better find that you all were listening to your better angels the entire time I was gone." No threat. No violence. Just a timely opportunity to reflect and change course.

When he was about to make a poor choice, his subconscious would ring a warning bell. And sometimes, it straight up told him what was coming, if only he could read the tea leaves or interpret the signs.

"I dreamed of bonfires last night," Auralia whispered. "Bonfires and clanging pans."

Creed tipped her head to search her eyes, then leaned forward to plant a kiss on her forehead. He rested there for a long time. Long enough that Auralia asked, "What's this about?"

"I have the same memory from my dream."

"How did yours turn out?" Auralia's voice was barely audible. It had the pinched sound of adrenaline bracing the ribs, making an inhale nearly impossible.

Creed shook his head.

"Yeah, I don't remember what happened in mine either."

They held still, as Creed gripped Auralia's hands. The screams from up the hill were wild to listen to.

No one from this side of the river would be able to reach water unless they did what Creed had contemplated when he saw Auralia coming out of the water. For a flash, he thought to get to her in any way possible, and jumping off the bridge seemed the closest route. Luckily, the thought came and went. And he was able to obtain the necessary equipment to escape.

Creed released Auralia and moved to the bag he'd nabbed from the back of the firetruck. Back up on the road, he'd looked in, seen lengths of rope and climbing equipment, thought "good enough" and took off before someone told him to leave it alone.

Now he was pulling out the pieces one by one, using his phone to take a video of the information.

His phone buzzed, and Creed answered on speaker. "Go for Creed."

"It's Mandy. I have two pieces of information. First, please be advised that several members of Panther Force are en route from the north with first aid supplies and tactical equipment.

Honey Honig with a stretcher has been assigned to your situation. Their ETA is approximately fifty-two minutes. Gator has been assigned to your situation after he gets his patient to the transportation hub. No ETA available."

Too late. Night would be upon them.

"Honey Honig, copy. ETA approximately one hour. Gator ETA unknown. Over."

"We have a drone overhead," Mandy continued. "I have an extraction engineer assessing your situation. I'm passing you to Javier. Mandy, out."

"Javier here. It looks like we need to get you across the water within the next thirty minutes. I have videos that you forwarded."

"Copy. Javier, I'm forwarding a video of my equipment."

"That'll be helpful." There was a pause then, "Received. Give me a minute to reassess. Already, this looks much more promising."

Creed was glad that Mandy was labeling people's roles since he wasn't with Iniquus long enough to have met Javier. He knew that an extraction specialist was on call because when Truffles made her finds in collapsed buildings, they had a structural engineer review the tapes recorded by the camera on Truffles' collar, and they would make recommendations on how to get the victim out or whether they should leave well enough alone until heavy equipment could be brought in.

While they waited, Creed asked, "What do we do here, Auralia?"

She plopped down on one of her storage tubs and went very still. "I mean, if this were a movie, we could save the daughter, okay."

"Why a movie?" Creed asked.

"Seriously?" She pulled in a breath. "Okay. You pull off your shirt and flex your muscles, then you swim out to the car all

Rambo-like. You get some tools, get the lug nuts off the tire, and get the tire to shore."

Creed grinned at the absurdity.

"We build a stretcher for her and put the wheel on one end."

"Holding it together with magic and spit?"

"Magic and *duct tape*."

"I'm following you," Creed said.

"Then through the magic of suspended credulity, we somehow get Brandy up that sheer, slickery mess that's going on with the river banks."

"Yes, I can see it," Creed said. "Once we're up there, we just wheelbarrow her a mile to get to some medical attention."

"Easy."

"And the mom?"

Auralia frowned at the woman in an Iniquus beanie and a black trash bag suit. "I don't see a way to save the mom."

"We need to prep our bodies for a big burst of energy." Creed pulled out three protein bars for each of them. He then brought out his water bottle, dumping in electrolyte packets.

They ate and drank and watched the air quality above their heads deteriorate with smoke and soot.

"Now what?" Auralia asked.

"Now we rest and wait for Javier to give us our marching orders." Using a lid to keep their butts dry, Creed and Auralia curled into each other's arms.

And for a blissful moment in time, there was peace amidst the chaos.

———

"HERE WE GO," Javier said over the speaker. "It's a plan. It's dangerous. And I will advise you that the likelihood of successfully getting everyone across is less than fifty-fifty."

"Compared to the risk of staying here?" Auralia asked.

"Staying has a significantly lower chance of a positive outcome. Almost nil. Your route has been cut off by the fire, and the equipment and efforts to protect the people stuck in their cars."

Jeezis. The sheer panic of being trapped and seeing the fire out your window. The heat. The thickening air. It had to be a hellscape.

"So we chance it." Auralia sat tall. "We do our best. Tell us what to do."

"I've put various scenarios through the computer. This is the one that gives you the best numeric probability. But you're on the ground. I'm going to walk you through the action list, and you tell me when it can't be done."

"Go," Creed said.

"I'm suggesting a variation on a Tyrolean traverse."

Creed had come to the same conclusion. "Auralia, that's the fancy term for crossing over something like a gorge or a river. You run a line across, then use a pulley and harness."

Auralia looked at Sheelah and shook her head.

"Modified in your case. Creed you'll use boulders on either side as your anchor points. We start with a setup. You're burning daylight, so you'll have to move fast. Empty the bins. Place them end to end and zip tie the handles of the bins together. Use the duct tape to secure the lids, then attach them together by running the tape around both horizontally and vertically, as the tape can easily rip. This is your stretcher."

"It's not long enough."

"The computer measured, and they should be able to fit torso through thigh. From there, you'll have to bind their feet and put them in a loop."

"Bind them, that seems—"

"Dangerous. It's a risk you'll have to assess. The rope then loops into a three-wheels in your system: Two ropes run under the bins and attach to the wheel above the third wheel is for the foot loop."

"I can see it," Creed said. "We're floating the bins?"

"We're relieving some of the downward force by using the water. But this isn't a boat. The current has its own force, which complicates the calculations. My suggestion is that Sheelah go first. Creed and Auralia position her on the stretcher in the water, the rope and the pulley wheels in place. Then Creed uses his descent rope to get up to the bridge. Creed, you can't use the surface of the bridge to get across, but looking at the structure, you should be able to get across using the structure. It's either that or swim. I suggest you try climbing first. I'd attach Rou to your pack."

"Copy."

"You have the main rope, and you have a second rope with you. The second rope is attached to the front handle of the stretcher. You need to set up a block and tackle pulley system. I noticed that you have a stop capture device. That'll enable you to pull the weight through toward you without losing ground."

Auralia sat there staring at the width of the river. She wasn't blinking. Blood was throbbing at her temple.

"Once you're ready, Auralia uses her legs to shove the bins into the water, and Creed pulls Sheelah across. Creed gets the mother off the system. Auralia has a rope tied to the back handle, and she pulls the stretcher back to her."

"Okay," she sighed.

"Auralia gets Brandy onto the bins."

"This is like the game of river when we were kids, when you have to go back and forth to get everyone across."

"I don't like that Auralia's there alone."

"She gets on the bins third, and you pull her across, and you're done. The river is reading twenty-five feet across."

"She'll be coming in the dark," Creed said. "No."

"To Creed's point, that sounds doable on paper," Auralia said. "But is it impossible, given our time frame?"

"Push comes to shove, Creed has orders to get you, Rou, and himself to safety. If you don't believe this scenario is possible," Javier said, "you need to adjust accordingly."

"Do you have any other options?" Auralia asked.

"I do. This is the only one that the AI's predictive outcome gives a yellow light," Javier said.

Creed hovered his thumb over the disconnect button. "We'd better get on it. Out."

27

———

Auralia

CREED TOOK HER BREATH AWAY—THE STEEL OF HIS MUSCLES, THE ease of his movements, the application of his intelligence, the bigness of his heart.

For the last five years, Auralia had been in dangerous situations all over the world. She had seen how people behave. They might extend a hand, give a helpful push, throw down a line, but there were few who could or would do more.

Creed had never once said, "Let's save ourselves." And Auralia could only imagine him saying that in circumstances where significant harm would come to his friends or family, then he'd insist on protecting them. Protecting her.

As he moved like an orangutan, hand over hand, his legs dangling and kicking below him to give him momentum, trailing his ropes like vines in a jungle, Creed must believe they could be successful. He wouldn't allow anything bad to happen to her. She trusted in her heart that he wouldn't.

Maybe that was part of his calculus. Perhaps he didn't believe this mission was possible as much as he thought that she was so invested in the outcome that she wouldn't walk away, and he decided not to take up time trying to argue.

He might think that they'd do what they could, but, in the end, he had a command that superseded his own choices.

He would drop everything and everyone and save her.

There was a little dark angel that whispered in Auralia's ear that this was a futile task. That dark angel wanted Auralia to remember that both of these women were tied to one evil, cold-hearted man. Had the women known that all along? Had they participated? Had they turned a blind eye because they benefited from Morrison's exploitation of Marine veterans?

Would it matter?

Auralia imagined turning her head to the dark angel and saying, "Shut the hell up."

If Sheelah and Brandy had sins on their souls, Auralia wouldn't taint hers by doing anything less than her human best to help them survive.

Creed was the same.

They'd help until the bitter end, if for nothing other than selfishly not wanting to live with the torture of regret and self-recrimination.

Rou was such a good girl dangling from the D-rings on her work vest below Creed's backpack. Luckily, she was little. If she were a German shepherd, this wouldn't be possible.

Dropping from the bridge onto the opposite shore, Creed stayed in a crouch longer than Auralia thought he should— possibly just catching his breath, hopefully not hurt.

She sent her concern winging across the water, and he lifted an arm and waved at her. And she waved back like a fisherman's wife as he set off to sea. The kind of wave that held a longing that she was back in his arms, and that she hated the water for getting in her way.

Auralia stood over Sheelah, who lay on her back, with

Auralia's blue life vest buckled in place, helmet on her head, eyes closed. Her breathing was faint, her pulse fainter still.

As Creed tied the rope into place and winched it tight, Auralia made sure the line ran in the indentation on the pulley wheels. The loop around Sheelah's ankles lifted, and her body was held in a straight line. That rope supporting her ankles couldn't be comfortable.

When Auralia went across, she planned to lie on her belly.

A moment later, the loops of rope that wrapped under the totes drew taut. The whole system—woman and bins—lifted higher so Auralia could almost get her hand underneath. Another inch and Creed was making circles with his hand, pulling a knot into place. Every bit of this he'd done with the ease of a dancer.

He had been training in this since he was eighteen. And to Auralia, there was *nothing* sexier than watching a competent man in action.

Creed stood at the shoreline with the guide rope in his hands. He gave it a tug, and the bins shifted in the gravelly sand.

Auralia reached down and shoved until Sheelah was out of reach.

While it made sense on paper that Sheelah went first so Creed and Auralia could work together to get her onto the apparatus, it was also true that Sheelah was closest to death, and possibly brain-dead. And since they had no time for testing, if things were going to fail …

Auralia hated that a thought like that was blooming in her mind.

And hated that it was probably a big part of the AI's predictive outcomes. If there had to be a sacrificial lamb to test this escape route, it should be Sheelah.

If it were just her and Creed, Auralia thought, none of this would be necessary.

Saving the daughter had to be part of the AI's calculus.

Did she like thinking that a machine was weighing survival ethics? Who trained those ethics? Who reviewed the parameters? Auralia would talk that story over with her editor when she got back to the office.

"This tastes like a good story to bite into," Remi would say. In dire situations, head over heart was painful but necessary. Possibly the AI helped stay out of emotions and fully into the reasoning part of the brain?

If she were Sheelah, though, she'd want to go first, a mother's sacrifice to ensure that her daughter had a safer route.

Auralia would revisit those thoughts later with Creed and Gator.

Right now, she needed to put her hands on her knees and suck in some deep breaths as relief flooded her system. Creed had his hands on the tote and was dragging Sheelah farther onto the shore. He quickly unloaded her, still dressed in her black leaf bags.

He pulled off the vest and helmet, attached them to a loop with a carabiner, and walked the totes into the water. There, he signaled Auralia to pull the stretcher back to her side of the river.

That part wasn't as hard as she thought it would be.

The next step was going to test her. Auralia needed to get Brandy up, over, and on.

But when she turned, Auralia was surprised to find Brandy standing behind her, holding the Mylar blanket tightly around her shoulders.

Auralia needed to make decisions now. The sun had moved over the horizon. If Brandy came willingly, excellent. If it was a struggle, Auralia would go ahead and leave.

"Brandy, I'm so glad to see you standing up. Did you see your mom go over the river?"

No response.

"We have to get off this shore. There's a fire." Auralia pointed up the slope. "There's flood waters." She pointed toward the bridge. "There's night falling." As Auralia pointed toward the sky, she used her news reporter voice —slow, clear, steady, and believable. "It's your turn to go across. Can you come lie down here?"

And to Auralia's complete astonishment, Brandy did.

"You have to be very still." Auralia pulled the life vest on, clasped it, and tightened the tabs. "I have you on my rope. Creed has you on his rope. He's—" she almost said "a Marine," but thought better of it. Brandy might think a Marine might seek retribution. "He's been doing this kind of thing all his life. You're safe if you lie very still. It might feel rocky. Close your eyes. Hum a tune. We'll have you across pretty quick."

It was a charmed extraction.

Everything aligned.

Brandy went over.

Auralia went over.

Creed pulled Auralia into his arms and held her tight against him. Her hands clasped around his neck. To say she was surprised this worked was an understatement.

Auralia felt hot, tired tears of relief spring to her lashes.

Rou pulled her attention around with her whining, and when Auralia leaned down to tell Rou what a good girl she'd been, hanging off the back of Creed's pack as he moved hand over hand over the water, she found Rougarou staring down at the curve of shore that turned and continued behind the rocks —the place where Brandy had been standing.

And now all that was left were her footprints from where she walked away.

28

———————

Auralia

"This is a bad idea, Auralia."

"You have a better one?" She pointed to Rou. "Someone has to go after her. What if no one went after Parker when he wandered away in his stupor?"

Creed pressed his lips together.

"You know more about field medicine than I do," Auralia was trying to be pragmatic. "Honey should be here soon, and then you hand Sheelah's care over to him, and you follow your shirt's directions to Rou." She put her hand on her head. "That was such a strange sentence." She took a breath. "And if that doesn't work. She's wearing a tracking collar. Iniquus will know where we are. You can monitor everything over the video and comms on her collar."

"You'll hold on to her lead the whole time?" Creed was fighting some war inside himself; she could see it raging in his eyes. He didn't want her to go, and he'd never stop her from doing what she wanted.

"I can do that," Auralia said.

"And you press this button here if you need me." He bent down and pointed. "That signals my phone directly. I always look and listen before I call out. So if you don't hear from me straight off, it's because I'm following protocol."

"Yup. Hand me your headlamp." She opened her free hand. "I don't want to be down the river with just this thing." She shook her wrist with Remi's rubber band gift. "You have something to see by?"

"In my pack," he said, setting the headlamp to green before handing it over.

"Gotta go." Auralia rose onto her toes and kissed him. "I'll be back. Ten minutes tops."

Once she had Rou's leash in hand, Auralia held out her leg and said, "Rou scent. Scent." After all, Brandy was wearing Auralia's clothes, and if nothing else, they were washed in the same laundry detergent. "Rou search."

Rougarou's nose went up, her nose went down, then she shimmied and danced in her little red shoes as she tracked Brandy.

At this point in the search, Auralia didn't need Rou. There were only two sets of tracks that were visible on this stretch. There were the heavy boot prints of a man coming and going, and nearby were the smooth-bottomed tracks made with Auralia's swim shoes.

Now they added her hiking boots and Rou's doggie shoes, Creed would have no trouble getting to them even without his new technology.

At this point, ten minutes had come and gone.

They'd walked a much farther distance than Auralia had contemplated. She thought she'd find Brandy around the corner, and that would be that. But now Auralia was following Rou up onto the paved parking area of a public boat ramp.

There was a single jacked-up pickup truck parked there with a boat hitched to the back.

And through the windows, Auralia could see a man helping Brandy inside. "Oh! Hey!" Auralia called out.

The guy jerked around.

Good guy? Bad guy?

Auralia leaned down and pressed the comms button on Rou's collar so Creed would have a heads-up.

"Hey there!" she called out. If it were a good guy, he'd need to know what to tell the hospital. If he were a bad guy and he took Brandy away, thinking he'd get some from the girl who looked like she was on drugs, well, Brandy might die. "Hi!" She rounded within view but kept the hood between them.

"Hey," the guy said and glanced at Brandy, who might be up and walking but was eerily zombie-like.

"I'm part of the rescue effort." She pointed at Rou then up toward the highway. "Are you part of a first responder group?"

"Me?" He pulled the bill of his hat lower. "No."

Was he trying to hide his face, or was her headlamp shining in his eyes? There were parking lot lights here, so she reached up and turned off her green light.

Auralia wasn't sure what to say here. This guy wasn't offering her any kind of explanation for why he had his hand on Brandy. He simply looked at Auralia as if she were an inconvenience. The whole scene was off, and then it was even more off.

A second pickup roared into the parking lot, heading straight for the first guy's truck. He came to a squealing stop right before the two vehicles collided.

The door flew open. The man jumped down. "Shane, you no good son of a bitch."

"How'd you get here?" Shane asked, squaring off.

"'Cause your damned phone is in your cab and Brandy set it up so I could find her when she's with you." The new guy stabbed a righteous finger at Brandy, then waggled his own phone, showing a map with a red pin.

Brandy's set up a "find my" for this guy? So they all knew each other?

Auralia jumped back, pulling Rou around and picking her up. Auralia held Rou in her arms in such a way that the camera focused on the new guy's expression; it was one of red-hot anger and cold-hearted loathing.

"I know what you were planning to do, she texted it all to me. Brandy wants none of it."

Shane took a menacing step forward, blocking New Guy's line of sight to Brandy.

"Tough guy, huh? You think I'm letting you get away with this? You think I'm going to let you enslave Brandy? Hide her away until she's old and fat and dyes her hair?"

"You're insane." Shane hocked up a glob of phlegm and spat it toward New Guy's feet.

"Brandy," New Guy said plaintively. "Tell him. Tell him you love me. I saw you get pulled out of the water. I saw them try to take care of you. You should be headed to the hospital, not letting him take you away."

Brandy was vacant.

New Guy softened his voice to a warm and loving tone, the kind of voice Creed sometimes used when talking to Auralia — a boyfriend voice. "Your mom is fighting for her life on the beach right now," he cajoled. "She needs a hospital. Snap the hell out of it, baby. You haven't done anything wrong. This was your parents' scheme. Come with me and let's get you some help." He held out his hand.

Brandy, gripping her Mylar blanket tightly around her, started forward.

"Oh no, you the hell won't," Shane yelled, chest puffed out like a rooster, veins popping at his neck, spittle flicking with every syllable.

Shane shoved Brandy back, and she fell against the truck. He didn't even look to see if she was okay. Bent almost in two, he roared forward like a football player, driving his shoulder into the new guy, shoving him backward.

New Guy took the flats of his hands and slapped them together over Shane's ears.

A move that did a lot of damage with little effort.

Shane's head must be spinning.

Then they were at it, wrestling moves, football moves, probably things they'd seen in some kung fu movie.

The punches were real.

"Creed." Auralia was sidling over to get to Brandy. This was a shit show. This whole damned day had been a goddamned shit show. "We have a situation."

Rou had moved her body to drape over Auralia's shoulder, and that was good in that Auralia could hold her up with one hand. Though she had to shift her angle to keep the camera focused on the men. With her free hand, Auralia grabbed Brandy's arm to pull her out of the fray.

Brandy was slowly letting herself be drawn backward.

The men were fierce. And Auralia thought they were hell-bent on killing each other. To the victor would come the spoils. And that looked like Brandy.

Brandy had her eyes fixed on them when she froze. The woman had been pale throughout the situation, but now her lips were blue.

Was the new guy a good guy or a bad guy?

New Guy had Shane up over his shoulder and tried to throw him onto the ground, but Shane had hold of New Guy's pockets and held tight.

Neither shrank from the fight; they were going full bore.

Both of these men had tricks up their sleeves. Whether it was through their military training or a barroom brawl, it didn't really matter.

Even in war zones, Auralia had never seen anything like this. Shane made a move that put New Guy on his back on the ground, and as Shane straddled the man, he was hooking his thumbs into New Guy's eye sockets.

But New Guy responded by planting the sole of his foot on the ground and rolling his hip up just enough to rip his weapon from his kidney holster.

"Gun. Gun. Gun." Auralia said as the pistol barrel landed on Shane's temple.

Auralia spun on the spot.

"Lady, you move," New Guy panted out, "and I shoot you in the back. Easy as that."

Blood was pouring from a deep cut on Shane's head, dripping onto the gun barrel.

Auralia watched as the color drained from Shane's face. His lips looked white and chalky.

She'd only seen that one other time in her life. It was back home. The guy had been in the water going after his pole that was tugged in by his fish. He didn't see the croc, but the bite went into his femur, and he bled out right there in the water.

All the kids standing on the pier were pointing and screaming for help.

Her Uncle Sebastian was the one who got to the rowboat and got out to him first.

But by the time he got there, there was nothing that could be done.

Auralia had asked one of the elders from her neighborhood if seeing a man die like that meant she was going to be possessed by his soul? "Like, would he see that I was young and healthy and want to stick around and be part of me?"

"Now, child, why would you ask such a thing?"

"Because I felt him start to brush past me, then it was like he paused and looked really hard at the top of my head. And I didn't feel him fly off again."

Miss Cinnamon was her name. Wow, Auralia hadn't

thought about her in ages. Hadn't even thought about her when Creed and she were talking about Sheelah in the car.

But Sheelah hadn't died.

Was Shane dying?

When Auralia told her story to Miss Cinnamon, she got up and called Mamma, asking for permission to help. Mamma had apparently said yes, because Miss Cinnamon took Auralia out of the garden, sat her on a stool, and pressed colored stones into her palms. Out came the blue box of salt, and Miss Cinnamon traced her way around the stool three times, keeping them both within the lines.

There was a smudge stick, as Auralia remembered, and chanting.

Yes, she remembered that. She remembered that her eyes were closed and the skin on her scalp prickled and itched, but she knew not to move her hands to scratch at it. It felt like her hair lifted up like the childhood game of rubbing a balloon on your head and seeing the static.

She'd thought about how her brothers would shuffle their feet across the carpet at church and then reach out and zap her. She remembered how that was fun, but the zap she got sitting on the stool was not. With a zing, Auralia popped her eyes open and exclaimed, "Ow!"

Miss Cinnamon was sitting on the ground, nowhere near her.

She opened her lashes, too, and stared into Auralia's eyes for a good long time, then nodded. "That should do it, child. You sit still while I open the circle back up. Lord. Lord. I heard that you had a visit from PittyPat and that she said you had the gift. That's not how we use it, so I sealed you good. No one's gonna come hant you. Not in this lifetime. Miss PittyPat taught me herself. So I'm good at what I do."

Auralia had known that. That's why she'd hightailed her way over there to begin with.

When she got home, her mamma asked, "Did Miss Cinnamon take care of it?"

"I'm sealed tight," Auralia announced.

And that was the end of it.

But that wasn't the end of this.

Shane was hurt, possibly dying.

If he did die, Auralia was sealed tight; he wouldn't hant her.

29

Creed

HONEY HAD SHOWN UP JUST AS AURALIA CIRCLED BEHIND THE boulder.

Together, they were assessing the situation when Creed's phone pinged with Rue's collar connecting. *Auralia.*

When Auralia took off, it had been a pragmatic decision, and, in theory, the plan had made sense.

In his gut, Creed knew it was the wrong way to go about things. His instincts told him that there were unforeseen dangers. But what could he say out loud?

Auralia was correct. Something was terribly wrong with Brandy, whether she was in shock, bleeding internally, or any of a list of things that could be going wrong for her. Whatever it was, Brandy could easily and quickly die under these circumstances.

Sheelah, yeah, Creed thought Sheelah was fading. He expected death rattle breathing soon, or a sudden miraculous coming around, a last look around before walking toward the light.

Auralia wasn't hurt, other than being red-faced from the abrasive fabric of the airbag.

She was as capable as he was in this environment. She was a good tracker. She was fit. She was used to Rou and had been part of staged search missions, so Auralia could easily track Brandy's trail even if conditions for scent trailing weren't prime.

Still playing through his mind from this morning's rescue of Jeb: Six inches of muddy water was all it took to move a car. It was more than enough to sweep up a woman. Or two.

If they were good Samaritans as their families had taught them to be—or just humans with hearts beating in their chests—then these accident victims needed their care.

But still, Creed's gut told him it should have been inverted. Auralia would have done better and been safer here with Shee-lah, and he should have been off on the hunt.

And now, he had proof.

Rou's collar pinged just as Gator came leaping down the slope like his hair was on fire. "Where the hell is she, Creed?"

The three gathered around the video feed and watched.

Gator had his phone out. "Jeff. We have a situation." He looked up, "Creed, who's your support?"

"Mandy."

"Jeff, loop in Mandy to get the exact location of Cerberus Team Charlie K9 Rougarou."

Over the speaker, they could hear Jeff. "Rougarou is up on our board. I'm texting you her GPS coordinates and loading them to your shirts. We're updating Commander Striker Rheas. Given the AI data, we have advised police officials on the north side of the bridge."

"Creed here. Jeff, tell me about the AI."

"Our systems were able to extract still photos from Rougarou's video feed that included front, side, and rear pictures of the men who are fighting. The blonde-haired man is Shane Kirch." He spelled it out, "Kilo, Igloo, Romeo, Charlie, Hotel. Kirch is married to Brandy Morrison Kirch. He is identified by our systems, using the drone video that Jack captured, as the dell shooter from today's event."

"Creed. Copy Kirch is the husband and the shooter." Creed hadn't lifted his gaze from his phone with the real-time video from Rou's collar. Auralia had to be holding Rou in her arms. And she wasn't running away. Why?

"Jeff. The second man is identified as Kendal Cowan. Charlie, Oscar, Whiskey, Alpha, November. It found three connections to the accident. One, Cowan lives next door to the Kirch residence. Two, the truck that hit Mayor Early's SUV was abandoned, and witnesses described the driver as someone who had the same coloring and clothing as Kirch. Three, the semi that caused the accident belongs to a resident of that same neighborhood, and it was reported stolen."

Striker was in their ears. "Striker for Gator and Creed."

"Mandy and Jeff hold," Creed said.

Gator pressed his sternal mic. "Go for Gator and Creed."

"Striker. Get Auralia and Rougarou out of that situation. Brandy's with her husband. We are relieved of any duty for her well-being. The police will handle the matter from this point forward. I reached out to our FBI friends at Joint Task Force. They're on a call as we speak, moving agents to Rougarou's location. The FBI will detain Cowan and Kirch. Your assignment is narrow, Auralia and Rougarou. Over."

"Gator. Copy. Moving. Out."

The men didn't need the shirts for navigation. They raced along the shore until they were at the public boat launch.

There, they crouched in the vegetation to get a good read on the lay of the land and how the situation was playing out.

Rougarou let out a high, bright warning bark, and Creed,

with his heart beating so hard it had moved to his throat, closed his eyes and sent pictures of Rou being very still and very quiet.

The men could see two jacked-up pickup trucks nose to nose. The back one had a boat on a trailer. If that had been Shane's cover for the shooting, it was clever. As long as he actually took his boat out that day, maybe caught a fish or two, he could easily have hiked to the property and climbed up on the roof. Yeah, he could have circled back to get here and hang out, looking like he'd been there having a quiet day.

Gator had swung around so he could keep his attention split between what was happening over by the trucks and what they could see from Rou's collar cam.

The vehicles were enormous and blocked everything but the heads. Three heads—Brandy, Auralia, and the one with black hair, who had to be Kendal Cowan.

"So you know what I look like," Kendal said over the video feed.

"Me? No. I don't have my glasses on; they came off in the water when my car went into the river," Auralia lied.

Kendal held up three fingers. "How many?"

"Three. I'm not blind. I can see general shapes. Like if I had to describe you. I could say you had a brown shirt, you had face parts—two eyes and a nose. I can't make out your mouth."

"What's wrong with Brandy?"

"She needs a hospital if she's going to survive. Can you see how blank her face is?"

"Yeah, Brandy looked that way since you rescued her out of the water."

"You saw that?" Auralia asked. "Tell me how you know Brandy."

"That's not important."

"Do you care about Brandy?" Auralia asked.

"I'm here saving her, aren't I?"

"Brandy needs medical attention. Shock can be lethal. If you know about the day, then you know that her system might be in overdrive. How about you tell me why she's in shock, and I can see if I can add anything to what you know."

"Is Auralia buying time, or is she being a goddamned reporter right now?" Gator muttered under his breath.

"Both," Creed whispered back. "You go with what you know. That's her comfort zone."

Kendal must sense eyes on him; he kept glancing over his shoulder and into the trees. "Let's see," he refocused on Auralia, "from the texts I got, her dad surprised them with that story about the second family. And she was freaking out about that. But in the car, her dad said he made it up to add suspects to the FBI's list and get the feds off Shane's trail. Either way, that shook her up pretty bad. Then there was the shot. She knew about that, so while that might have been a plan—well, I'm a combat vet and when an actual bullet goes winging your way, it's still shocking."

"Then the accident," Auralia added, "and sailing off a bridge into storm-raging, ice-cold waters. That'll lower the core temperature pretty good. Oh, and then, Dad escaped the SUV, but left her there to die. Shocking. And then the surprise of being saved. Then, seeing her mom pulled out unconscious. Then back into the ice-cold water, which lowered the core temperature again."

"My poor baby girl."

"Physically and emotionally, Brandy's in shock. Shock can

be deadly," Auralia was using her reporter's voice. It was calm, respectful, and presented facts.

"Deadly, how? I mean, we warm her up." Creed and Gator saw the guy turn and look over at the fire pit.

"Cellular oxygen deprivation means that Brandy's not processing the air she's breathing in. Without oxygen, cells die, and she can go into organ failure. That can also lead to brain damage or coma. The damage can be irreversible. She could die." There was a flicking sound. "Don't even think of starting a fire," Auralia commanded. "First, the woods are on fire, and we're only safe because of the water buffer. What's dry over there is dry over here. And second, if she's oxygen-depleted, warm isn't going to help. An oxygen tent at the hospital will help."

"This is Shane's truck right there. We could get her in and crank the heat."

"The truck is a very good idea."

"You're that reporter woman."

"I'm the woman who saved your beloved twice. And I'm going to help you lift her into the truck. Do you have any medical training?"

"No," he whispered.

"Then I'm going to be the woman who keeps fighting to save Brandy's life. Does that sound like the kind of person you need on your team?"

"Yes."

"Then could you get the gun out of my face?" Auralia asked.

"Mystery solved," Creed whispered to Gator. "That's why she didn't run."

. . .

"Do you want to check you didn't kill that guy when you stomped on his face?" Auralia asked Kendal.

"Nope."

"Can I go check on him?"

"Nope."

"All right. Here, help me get Brandy up into the front seat. Do you think it lies back? Are there keys? Turn it on and get the heat going on high."

"Ma'am, you're going to do that. Remember, my gun is on you. I'm a damned good shot. Like I said, I've been to war."

"Were you a Marine? My brother is retired from the Marine Corps. My fiancé, too."

Good woman, *build that relationship. You're on the same side.* Creed sent his thoughts winging to Auralia.

"My fiancé was on the security team," Auralia continued. "He said that so far this wasn't the worst traffic accident in US history, but it might make the top ten, given the topography of the land and the rain, making it hard to see."

"A lot then? I mean, from this side of the river, there are a few cars that hit."

"Do you think there are any blankets or extra clothes?"

"He's got a jacket shoved behind the seat. You can't trick me into taking my eye off you. You can pull it out."

In the silence that stretched out, Gator put his mouth right next to Creed's ear. "We can't get around to them. Set out there in the middle like that. The dark of night isn't going to give us no cover, what with those streetlights. I'm gonna see if Iniquus can't get them switched off."

Creed lifted his thumb to signify yes.

Gator was typing out a text to Jeff.

Creed didn't move his eyes off the scene. He barely blinked.

On the video feed on his phone, Rou was now standing on the ground in her little red shoes. Creed had a view of two sets of legs.

"Yeah," Auralia said, "I don't think you understand what happened. There's a pile-up at the exit of the dell parking area. That's what, three-quarters of a mile on the south side of the pile up? People are severely injured. Life-threatening injuries, possible deaths. My fiancé pulled three babies out of the back seat of a car where the mom and dad weren't conscious. You're military. You know what happens to people with traumatic brain injuries. These are life-long disabilities that the pile-up caused. Possible deaths. Cars have been damaged. People who get out of this might not have a way to get to work without a car. How many people in that pileup don't have medical insurance? And if they do, how many insurers will cover people who need to take time off for extended periods of healing? Do you want to add Shane's death to this terrible day?"

"I was stopping a kidnapping. No law is going to hold me responsible."

"You figure?" Auralia asked. "If Shane's dead, it's Brandy's word against yours. If she dies, then no one can stand up for you. People might say it's you who's the kidnapper, and Shane stood in your way. If you're trying to steal the money back, you aren't Robin Hood. You aren't returning money taken by the rich to give to the poor. You're not the hero. You are the criminal who has created a catastrophe for scores of your neighbors by making them so frightened that they couldn't think right to drive."

"Ma'am, you have no idea what you're talking about."

Kendal's tone was icy. "None. I wasn't the one who shot the bullet today. That was Brandy's asswipe husband, Shane. No one knows about me. No one but you."

"Me and the satellites."

"Cloud cover," Kendal said.

GATOR BUMPED Creed's arm and showed him the text message.

Jeff: **Iniquus Command has reached out directly to the park's director of services. The director has agreed to shut off the lights. He can't isolate the shut-off to the parking lot. The lights throughout the park will go out. He'll do it as quickly as possible. If I'm given information about timing, I'll text.**

"WHEN YOU'RE IN A CAR ACCIDENT," Auralia explained, "your phone texts everyone on your in case of emergency list. They send the exact GPS coordinate to your loved ones."

"Everyone?"

"Yes."

"And tells them what?"

"I think that depends on your carrier," Auralia said. "Typically, it calls 911 and reports your location, stating that there has been an accident. And then texts go out to the people you listed."

"All carriers?"

"I don't know. I assume so."

"And it's automatic?" Kendal asked.

"HE'S REALLY fine-tuning this answer for some reason," Gator said. "He sounds spooked, but if he's telling the truth about being a combat vet, and he's got a gun on her, we need to take this slow."

Creed watched the video feed of feet while scanning the area for ideas.

"Too exposed. Too risky," Gator said.

Auralia picked up Rou again and was holding her in her arms. Gator and Creed could see that Kendal wore a camo hunting jacket, and every once in a while, they could see the gun. It was a no-joke forty-five. But the guy had his finger running along the trigger guard, not curled into position.

"WHAT YOU JUST SAID ABOUT the GPS, lady, that's not true." Kendal brought the gun back around toward Auralia. "Last week, they found a woman who drove over the edge of an embankment when she had a seizure, and her husband went out and walked the highway looking for her. Took him days, but he found her."

"Did she have her phone?"

Kendal was silent.

"Was the phone charged?"

AURALIA WASN'T BEING helpful now, Creed thought. She was reminding him of every relationship in his life where the woman could snatch details out of the air and leave him feeling inadequate. Now that Rou had shifted and they could see Kendal's face, he had that look. Creed had seen it far too many times not to recognize it. It was a man's face when he felt small next to a woman. And that was damned dangerous.

"HEY, just to stay up with the plot," Auralia said. "What was Shane's scheme? Why would he kidnap his wife?'

"The Morrisons put the charity money into an LLC so the courts couldn't find it. They was all going off to some property somewhere in West Virginia. Brandy sent me a text and asked me to save her. She didn't want to go."

"So your plan was to hold them at gunpoint?" Auralia asked

"No. I was going to block their path on the bridge, and she was going to get out and leave with me."

"But you didn't shoot the speaker system," Auralia clarified.

"No, that was the whole thing to make folks think a Marine with PTSD went after them. Then the whole family fled, and they disappeared. Or something to do with that cockamamie story her damned dad told from the stage—something about angry brothers."

"Yeah, well, I guess it's clever to have a list of possible people to confuse the authorities. Send them on a wild goose chase." Auralia's voice had become less "reporter" and more fatigued. "And they were going to West Virginia?" She paused. "So you have a gun. And we're all here. What happens now?"

"I'm going to jail if I stick around. Yeah, I can't have that."

"Too late."

"Yeah, but only you know."

"We've already established that's not true. There's you at the crash site, and you texted with Brandy. That's all discoverable with a subpoena to your phone company. That's part of your phone records."

"Okay. So I go to the property with Brandy, and we live together. I mean, her mom's probably dead, right? Or brain dead or something. And her dad's running."

"And her husband?" Auralia asked.

"Is passed out. I can move him to the river."

"And so you're doing to both of you what you didn't want for her," Auralia said.

"But there's a lot of money. Millions of dollars. Eugene can bitcoin a million of it to us, and we can get over the border. Get a boat. Go on foot. I don't know. I'll have to think on it. There are countries that wouldn't send us back, or we can lie low and use cash. Like I was reading about an island off of Bali that's super cheap. Sand and blue water. We can go there and be in love."

"That sounds wonderful," Auralia said. "You should do that."

For the first time, Kendal's voice sounded hopeful. "You think?"

30

Creed

"Sir, let me be clear and straightforward with you. The public knows about Eugene Morrison's crimes because I made them public. My fiancé and my brother are retired Marine Raiders. Their friends were impacted by this crime. I am a hundred percent behind Eugene being put away for the rest of his life and for every cent going to the causes that he had said he was supporting. But, sir, right now, I'm worried about his daughter. Brandy is going to *die* if she doesn't get help. You have to figure out what to do. I suggested you go to the property and lie low. Let me drive Brandy to the hospital, and you just do what you have to do. You can catch up with her after she's healthy again."

The lights in the parking lot flashed off.

"What the hell?" Kendal shouted.

"It's after hours in the park," Auralia said with a bit of boredom in her voice. "They turn them off so the teenagers don't come down here and hang out."

. . .

"We're up," Creed said.

"How are we playing this?" Gator asked.

"Seat of our pants, brother. Let's watch for a second and make sure Kendal's nerves settle from the sudden dark."

"Turn on the lights in the cab," Auralia said.

"People can see in."

"What people? Everyone is over at the pileup. Look, before the lights went out, I noticed Brandy's lips had turned blue. Remember, we talked about what happens if she doesn't get oxygen in her system? If you don't want to just jump in your truck and drive off on your own, leaving me to deal with Brandy, then you need to get this pickup on the road. I'll sit next to Brandy as you're driving and can give her mouth-to-mouth when she stops breathing."

"When?"

"When." Auralia insisted as she flashed a thumbs-up in front of Rou's collar camera. She knew Creed was there. "Before we can leave, you need to unhook that boat. It'll just slow us down. And you need to move your truck out of the way. How fast do you think you can get that done? And when we leave, you have to be careful not to drive over Shane's body."

"Body?"

"He never got up. It's been a while. I mean, you cracked his head open when you stomped on him."

Kendal was defiant. "Shane came at me. I wasn't gonna punch him, just wave my gun around."

"I don't care about him or you," Auralia said. "But I put myself in too much danger for too long today not to be invested in Brandy's survival. Chop. Chop. Let's go."

. . .

"Woowee, that girl's got some balls," Gator said. "Well, looky there, Kendal's rounding toward the boat. Let's circle around in front of his truck.

Creed turned his phone off. Gator followed suit. They couldn't afford to receive an ill-timed text that would give away their position.

In a practiced crouch, Creed and Gator hustled silently along the tree line.

The night was moonless. The clouds were thick. The soot and smoke, mixed with humidity, gave the air a strange, oily feel on their exposed skin. The nostalgic smell of pine and bonfire held the tang of electrical wiring and burned fuel.

While Kendal was working on releasing the boat trailer, Gator reached into the open window on the front pickup and pulled the keys from the ignition.

Creed thrust a boot onto the tire and rounded into the bed of the truck. He reached up and opened the sliding door, then moved to the front left corner, crouching low.

Gator went around to the passenger's side and slid silently to the ground, tucking his chin so his skin couldn't be seen.

"That's off," Kendal said. "I have to put Shane in the river."

"Leave him there," Auralia called. "Every second wasted is a second that could make the difference to Brandy's survival. Buddy, you know all about the golden hour. We are hours and hours into this hellscape, and it's at least an hour to the nearest hospital. Just move that truck and let's go!"

The command and the urgency in her voice pushed him along.

Kendal jogged forward.

When he pulled open the driver's side door and the interior light flashed on, Gator opened the passenger side with a "Hey there".

Creed leaped over the side and was at the window, grabbing

Kendal's right hand as he reached for the gun he'd shoved into his kidney holster, trapping his hand.

But Kendal wasn't going down without a fight.

And he had his own surprises.

With his left hand, he snatched a knife from his belt and flicked it open, twisting and stabbing at Gator. "Aw, come on, man. It's not like that. I don't have no quarrel with you," Gator said as he jumped back out of range.

Creed was having trouble getting control of the gun. The holster had a mechanism that he wasn't familiar with. And Kendal had a death hold around the grip.

"Who the hell are you?" Kendal flipped the knife in his hand so the blade lay along his inner forearm, and he brought his elbow up, trying to stab Creed behind him.

Creed wrapped his free hand around Kendal's fist as Gator reached back in and slammed Kendal's head into the steering wheel. Once. Twice. Three times.

A car was racing up the road toward the parking lot.

"Striker for Creed and Gator."

Gator pressed the man's head down with one hand as he tapped his sternal mic. "Gator here."

"Striker. The car advancing on your position is the police. The FBI is right behind them. Over."

"Gator. Copy. Kendal will just be hanging out with us until then. Out."

"Who the hell are you talking to?" Kendal asked, his cheek smooshed into the steering wheel.

"Never you mind," Gator said. "You'll see soon enough."

The single cop who exited the patrol car looked wrung out.

"I'm Creed. This is Gator, sir."

The officer shone his flashlight on the man lying on the pavement. "Who's this?"

Auralia climbed out of the pickup and came over. "He's Shane. Listen. Could you do me a favor and handcuff or zip tie or whatever restraint you'd like to use on that guy?" She pointed toward Kendal. "And could you get these two people into your car and take them to an emergency department? Seriously, I don't know about the guy on the ground, but this woman is going to die without care."

"FBI is five minutes out." He handed Gator two zip ties. "Creed is it? Sir, could you please lean back a bit? I know you have him constrained. For everyone's safety, I need this on my camera. Here we go. Kendal Cowan, I am placing you under arrest for aggravated unlawful restraint. You have the right to remain silent. Anything you say can and will be used against you in a court of law. You have the right to an attorney. If you cannot afford an attorney, one will be provided for you. Do you understand the rights I have just read to you?"

"Yes."

"With these rights in mind, do you wish to speak to me?"

"No."

"Thank you for your assistance, gentlemen." The officer made his way over to Shane and felt for a pulse. "That's it? The two of them?"

"Two," Auralia called out.

"Buddy," Creed said, "it goes like this. You release your knife and your gun. We zip you up. You get out of the car while we wait for the nice special agents to come get you. And you do it easy, or Gator slams your head into the wheel until you pass out, and it happens anyway."

"He's alive," the cop called from where he stooped next to Shane.

"I can help you get him into your car," Auralia said. "But he's the shooter from the dell. So cuffs first."

Creed took control of the gun and knife.

Kendal cooperated with the zip ties.

He was cowed as he stepped out of the vehicle, his head hanging low.

The police waited for the FBI to show up, even though it put Shane and Brandy in danger. It wasn't long, though. And they were off to the hospital.

The special agent was reading Kendal's Miranda rights to him again for good measure.

The day had been long. It had been physically and emotionally exhausting. There were the highs of overcoming terrible odds. There was the joy of seeing Auralia strong and capable, clever, brave. She was everything. Just flat out everything.

She walked over and slipped into his arms. "Today was one for the history books."

"Well, for the newspaper at least," she said.

Gator was rocked back on his heels. "The day's not over, we got us two more hours."

Auralia, uncurled from Creed's arms just long enough to smack Gator. "Don't you dare challenge Fate." Then she eased her arm around Gator and held all three of them together in a tight hug with Rourou curled up sleeping at their feet.

"All day long, when my spirit was flagging, when I was really scared, the one thing I held tight to was that I trusted you both. I trusted your instincts to be brave, and strong, and good. And most of all," she whispered, "I knew if I needed you, you'd be there. And you proved me right time and again. There is no luckier woman in this world." She squeezed extra tight. "Thank you both."

Auralia had no idea, none. How could Creed ever explain how much her love and trust meant to him? How could he show her how deep his love was for her in return?

Standing there in the black of night, he made a pledge to himself that he'd spend the rest of his life living up to her trust.

31

Auralia

Auralia sat next to Creed on the second leg of their flight from Washington, D.C., heading to New Orleans. Today was Mémère's birthday, and Auralia was able to budge her trip to Ukraine back by a few days so she could make the pilgrimage with Creed.

After telling Gator about their relationship, Creed thought this would be a good time to tell the rest of the family, who would be gathering in from far and wide.

It seemed that the Fates were on her side because she was able to book her ticket to fly with Creed and Rou without any problems.

Now, Creed was reading his book with Rou asleep on his lap, and Auralia was reading the paper on her tablet. Remi had told Auralia that she had updated the article about Morrison's craziness. Liu, their editor, said that Remi got this next one since Auralia would be mentioned.

"Hey, look at this." Auralia leaned in to share her tablet with Creed.

. . .

AFTER RECOVERY, Defendants Transferred to Jail as Charges Mount in Virginia Pileup Case

REMI TALEB,
Washington News-Herald and World Reports

VIRGINIA—SHANE and Brandy Kirch, along with Sheelah Morrison, were released from the hospital after recovering from injuries sustained in last week's massive highway pileup that left multiple people dead and scores of people injured. The trio was immediately transferred to the county jail, where they now face a litany of both state and federal charges connected to the incident.

EUGENE MORRISON, previously out on bail, was remanded to custody after a judge revoked his release. Additional charges are reportedly pending against him.

In related proceedings, Kendal Cowan has pleaded guilty to manslaughter charges and has received his sentencing date. Prosecutors are seeking four consecutive life sentences for his alleged role in the chain-reaction crash that stunned the nation last week.

INIQUUS SECURITY, whose tactical teams were instrumental in rescuing crash survivors, also coordinated the safe handover of the defendants to authorities. The operation included Strike Force, a Cerberus K9 and her handler, and Washington News-Herald's own reporter on the scene, Auralia Rochambeau.

Governor Abby Gail is expected to honor the team, along with first responder teams and private citizens who stepped in to help, at an upcoming ceremony recognizing their efforts.

"THAT'S AMAZING." He leaned to the side and kissed Auralia's hair. "Nothing will put this back together again. But it's good to see that there's going to be some level of justice."

"That was a very bad day." Auralia dropped her head to his shoulder.

"Only part of it," Creed whispered. "Focus on the bottom of that article. In the darkest of times, good people stepped forward and gave it their all. They put themselves on the line. They were tired and hurt, and kept pushing forward to save lives and give comfort."

"It was a day I'll never forget. Yeah, it was a dark and terrible day. But look what a village can do when we all work together." She reached out and laced her fingers with his.

There was more to say, but they both understood. That's the way it had always been between them—love and trust, and a splash of the Bayou magic.

EPILOGUE

"SEE THIS PICTURE?" MÉMÈRE HELD IT OUT. "THAT'S WHEN YOU announced your engagement."

Auralia and Creed bent over the picture of young Honoré sitting in a side-by-side baby carriage next to Auralia.

"She's eight months old. Honoré leaned around and held Auralia in his arms, saying, 'Lia's too cold.' And I said, 'Well, do your best to keep her warm until I can get you two inside.' And you wrinkled your brow up tight and said, 'Yeah. I'm always going to do that.'

'What does that mean, child?' I asked. And you smoothed the blanket over her lap and told me, 'I'm going to watch out for her. And then when I'm grown, and she's grown, we're going to get married.' You said it so earnestly, Honoré , with that tone that you get when you're not to be dissuaded. 'Are you sure about that child?' I asked. 'I guess I have to wait and see if Lia thinks that, too. But for me, yes.' And that was that. I have never known you to make a declaration without following through. Every blessed thing that you said you'd accomplish was checked off the list."

Auralia took the picture onto her lap and was smiling down at it.

"When you were off to war, that quality kept me sane," Mémère said. "After what happened to your daddy? I thought our family had done its share. But the first time you were deployed, you told me you'd be home in time to fix my roof before hurricane season. The second time you deployed, you told me that you'd be back in time to take me up north to see my sister for her birthday. The third time you deployed, I got nervous because you didn't say anything about anything. But then I heard from Mama Rochambeau that you said you'd be back in time to go to Auralia's graduation. If you said you'd be back, I knew it would be so, because it had always been that way. Yes, indeedy. Your relationship switching over like it did was something you predicted when you were about five years old. We've all just been waiting. And when you said you left the Marines and signed on where Gator works, we all said the time had come."

"Just sat around snapping beans and saying, well, it's about time for the young'uns to fall in love?" Creed laughed and reached down to rub Rou's belly.

"I'd be hard-pressed to call either of you young'uns. Both of you have seen too much. You've done our families proud at how strong you've stood. But even the very strong need a resting place. Better to find that with someone who can understand. I think that's where I failed your dad. I know that's how your mother's always felt. He has lived a life that we can't fathom, so it's impossible to know how best to be a support. Lord knows we've tried. It's a hard thing when you feel like you're coming up short for someone you love."

"Mémère, I'm a lucky man. Good woman, good dog."

"You're not done doing good, neither of you. And so it's wonderful that when you rest, it's in a place where there's no need to mask. You can talk plain and clear about your burdens.

Auralia, you've always been my grandbaby, every bit as much as Honoré . I don't need to welcome you to the family. You're already in our hearts." Her eyes misted as she reached out her hand, its tissue-paper-thin skin molded over blue veins and knobby joints.

And Auralia wrapped both hands around Mémère's, with an overflowing heart.

"But do let me tell you how much joy this news brings me," Mémère said. "It's just a wonderful birthday gift."

They all looked up as the sound of cars rumbled over the gravel.

"Look, everyone's here. time for food, music, and birthday cake." Mémère smiled. "It's good to have you home for a spell."

Auralia looked deeply into Creed's eyes. "It's always good to be home." And his heart knew exactly what she meant.

THE END

The Next Book in
The World of Iniquus Chronology:

Tank
Certified Cerberus Tactical K9

Make sure **TANK** is on your TBR list!

Readers, I hope you enjoyed getting to know Creed, Auralia, and K9 Rou. If you had fun reading Trusted Instinct, I'd appreciate it if you'd help others enjoy it too.

Recommend it: Just a few words to your friends, your book groups, and your social networks would be wonderful.

Review it: Please tell your fellow readers what you liked about my book by reviewing Trusted Instinct at your favorite retail store. If you do write a review, please send me a note at hello@fionaquinnbooks.com. I'd like to thank you with a personal e-mail. Or stop by my website, FionaQuinnBooks.com, to keep up with my news and chat through my contact form.

———

If you would like to know the reading order of the World of Iniquus books, flip the page to find a chronological reading list.

WORLD OF INIQUUS NOVELS
IN CHRONOLOGICAL ORDER

Year One

Weakest Lynx (Lynx Series)

Missing Lynx (Lynx Series)

Year Two

Chain Lynx (Lynx Series)

Cuff Lynx (Lynx Series)

WASP (Uncommon Enemies)

Year Three

In Too DEEP (Strike Force)

Jack Be Quick (Strike Force)

Relic (Uncommon Enemies)

Mine (Kate Hamilton Mystery)

Deadlock (Uncommon Enemies)

Instigator (Strike Force)

Yours (Kate Hamilton Mystery)

Open Secret (FBI Joint Task Force)

Thorn (Uncommon Enemies)

Gulf Lynx (Lynx Series)

Year Four

Ours (Kate Hamilton Mysteries)

Cold Red (FBI Joint Task Force)

Even Odds (FBI Joint Task Force)

Survival Instinct (Cerberus Tactical K9 Team Alpha)

Protective Instinct (Cerberus Tactical K9 Team Alpha)

Defender's Instinct (Cerberus Tactical K9 Team Alpha)

Danger Signs (Delta Force Echo)

Hyper Lynx (Lynx Series)

Danger Zone (Delta Force Echo)

Danger Close (Delta Force Echo)

Year Five

Fear the Reaper (Strike Force)

Warrior's Instinct (Cerberus Tactical K9 Team Bravo)

Rescue Instinct (Cerberus Tactical K9 Team Bravo)

Hero's Instinct (Cerberus Tactical K9 Team Bravo)

Striker (Strike Force)

Marriage Lynx (Lynx Series)

Guardian's Instinct (Cerberus Tactical K9 Team Charlie)

Beowolf (Iniquus Certified Cerberus Tactical K9)

Red Line (CIA Color Code)

Sheltering Instinct (Cerberus Tactical K9 Team Charlie)

Shielding Instinct (Cerberus Tactical K9 Team Charlie)

Year Six

Radar (Iniquus Certified Cerberus Tactical K9)

Trusted Instinct (Cerberus Tactical K9 Team Charlie)

Acting on Instinct (Cerberus Tactical K9 Team Delta)

Whiskey (Iniquus Certified Cerberus Tactical K9)

With more Iniquus novels to follow!

For the most up-to-date list, go to FionaQuinnBooks.com

ACKNOWLEDGMENTS
MY GREAT APPRECIATION

To my publicist, **Margaret Daly**
To my cover artist, **Melody Simmons**
To my editor, **Rossana Tarantini**

To Jennie Lopez, who has been such an amazing resource for this novel. She named Rougarou and was my Cajun Bayou regional expert. She helped weave the magic of this book.

To J. Flaherty for answering my physics questions and helping me save my characters' lives. For sure, what I had sketched out would have killed them.

To my Street Force, who support me and my writing with such enthusiasm and kindness.

To all the professionals who shared their knowledge of working K9s, especially the various Virginia search and rescue teams.

Please note: This is a work of fiction, and while I always try my best to get all the details correct, there are times when it serves the story to go slightly to the left or right of perfection. Please understand that any mistakes or discrepancies are my authorial decision-making alone and sit squarely on my shoulders.

Thank you to my family for your love and support.

I send my love to my husband. T. Thank you for all our years in Search and Rescue together. I bet you'll recognize a few of the events in this novel.

And, of course, thank *YOU* for reading my stories. I always smile joyfully as I type this sentence. I so appreciate you!

ABOUT THE AUTHOR

Fiona Quinn is a USA Today bestselling author, a Kindle Scout winner, and an Amazon Top 40 author.

Quinn writes smart suspense with a psychic twist in her Iniquus World of action-adventure stories, including Lynx, Strike Force, Uncommon Enemies, Kate Hamilton Mysteries, FBI Joint Taskforce, Cerberus Tactical K9: Teams Alpha, Bravo, and Charlie, Cerberus Trained, Delta Force Echo Series and now, a cookbook!

She writes urban fantasy as Fiona Angelica Quinn for her Elemental Witches Series.

And, just for fun, she writes the Badge Bunny Booze Mystery Collection with her dear friend, Tina Glasneck, under the name Quinn Glasneck.

While Quinn travels the world to research her books, she is rooted on the Atlantic shore, where she lives with her husband and children. There, she pops chocolates, devours books, and taps continuously on her laptop.

Visit: www.fionaquinnbooks.com

COPYRIGHT